crimes, sins, and misdemeanors

Variations on a Theme by the Bumbershoots
Writers Society and Guests

gordon bonnet   **jc crumpton**

marlon s. hayes   **gil miller**   **david allen**

cly boehs   **r. h. burkett**   **d. t. griffith**

k. d. mccrite   **gary rodgers**

jan k. sikes   **kimberly vernon**

introduction

Crimes, Sins, and Misdemeanors came out of a discussion between myself and a couple of writer friends about how the same overarching theme can result in different writers creating vastly different stories. Going only on the rather thin prompt of the collection title, twelve authors have produced eighteen stories about murder, revenge, and violence—but also humor, pathos, love, and loyalty. The genres include mystery, thriller, noir, dark comedy, and magical realism, and even include one three-scene stage play.

Given the varied nature of the stories in this anthology, there's something in here for every reader. I, and the other authors who contributed, truly hope you will enjoy this excursion into the creative process.

Gordon Bonnet
    Little Bustard Books
    Trumansburg, New York
    April 2024

gunpowder and lead (a rural empires short story)

. . .

Gil Miller

T his time, Caleb was gonna pay.

She stood there in the hot sun, dressed in cut-offs and a white t-shirt, and watched that asshole deputy drive off. He'd dropped her off where the dirt road met the highway.

"I can't go up there," he said, nodding up the hill toward home. "That's private property and I ain't got a warrant."

She stared at him a moment while he grinned back, then got out of the car and slammed the door. One of her eyes was swollen almost shut, her lower lip was split, and her ribs ached. When the car was gone, she turned and started off. There was over two miles to go.

Shoulda thrown a rock, busted out his rear windshield.

The hot sun bounced back at her off the dirt road. She squinted through it to the next patch of shade, where jar flies buzzed in the trees. Narrowing her eyes made the blackened one ache more, but that was life. Just make it to the next stand of trees and out of this broiling sun. Maybe rest there.

But not for long. She had to get home before he did. Had to get there in time to make him pay.

She trudged on up the road. Other than the jar flies and

birds, not a sound came to her. It was like she was the only person left alive. Well, if being the only person left alive meant he was dead, that would have been all right. She knew better than that, though. He was just waiting for one of his family—the same family that owned every inch of land around her—to post bail so he could come after her.

"Don't you marry that boy, Brooke." Mama's voice came to her as clear as if the woman was walking beside her. "He's mean, just like all them Ledbetters. They ain't nothin but drug-runners and outlaws, and he'll treat you bad."

"You were right, Mama. He's nothin but mean, all the way through."

And he was gonna pay. Bank on that.

All them Ledbetters were that way, mean down to the bone. And they made enough money as marijuana moonshiners to put that worthless sheriff, Dennis Masters, on their payroll. That's why she was out here walking this dirt road home. When Caleb went to beating on her and she called the County, they'd hauled both of them into Fayetteville. When they saw what was what, they put him in the slammer and hauled her down to where the dirt road took off from the highway.

But it wouldn't last. That had looked like Dakota Ledbetter's Yukon pulling into the jail parking lot while the deputy pulled out. And you could bet they wouldn't need a bail bondsman to get Caleb out.

And on top of everything else, the deputy had kept glancing sideways at here, trying to get a peek at her boobs. She hadn't been wearing a bra, and he had the air-conditioning turned up, probably colder than usual. Not that she had much to see, small as she was, but still....

Forget it. At least he hadn't tried to rape her, like she'd been half expecting.

She just had to get home before Caleb did. If she could, he'd pay.

Oh, but the shade felt so good. Mama always said walnut trees made the coolest shade. Sure would be nice to just stay here forever, but that couldn't happen.

The sky was so pale a blue it was almost white. A crow flew by, some kind of small bird pestering it. Maybe it was a good sign. Caleb was the crow, and she was the little bird, chasing it off.

But she didn't plan to chase him off. Oh, no. He thought she was made out of sugar and spice, but she was gonna show him different.

Make him pay.

Another deep breath and she started off again. She tried to avoid the gravels, but that was like trying to avoid Razorback fans around here. Or air. Amounted to the same thing.

Not a sign of anyone else. The Ledbetters didn't stir much during the day, and none of them would help her anyway. Didn't matter how long you'd been married into the family, you were still an outsider. If it came down to choosing, spouses of Ledbetters always lost the toss.

Out of the shade, the sun beat down like liquid fire, slowly baking her skin and turning it beet red. All this on top of the beating added insult to injury. But after a while, the misery piled up high enough you got numb to it.

Well, if there was one good thing about being married to one of the youngest Ledbetters, it was that their house was closer to the highway. They all looked out for each other, but once you went to work at the family business, you had to earn all the perks. They'd fronted her and Caleb a small house, and Caleb's job delivering large loads of Mexican pot worked toward paying off that debt. Later, he could work his way up to bigger and better things—new house, new vehicles, cash to flash around, that kind of thing.

So far, though, they were on the bottom rung of the ladder, and that had helped this morning. They were far enough away from the main operation the rest of the family likely didn't know about the fracas. The one he was gonna pay for.

Who knew what had set him off this time? He'd been in for a week so far, in between loads, watching TV and drinking beer during the day, partying and drinking with his cousins even more at night. Smoking pot, maybe even using some meth. There was a small lab up there somewhere, and Caleb had started showing some of the signs. So far, it was just losing weight and being hyper sometimes. But she'd seen enough of it in other people to know what it meant.

Somewhere off in the distance, a small plane buzzed through the hot afternoon. It was hard to hear it over the jar flies. In among trees the insects' song was all but deafening. One started up close by and made her jump. Like she needed anything to make her more jumpy.

She had an idea. A plan. One Caleb wouldn't like much.

For that plan to work, she needed to get to the house, needed to be there waiting for him.

Let him see that not all little girls were made out of sugar and spice.

The gravel bit at her feet, making them feel like tenderized meat. And her skin was taking on that tight, cooked feel that comes from a sunburn. One of the curses of being a redhead. The trees ended abruptly on her right, and she gazed off across the field. Cattle grazed under the hot sun. The grass was deep green in those few places it wasn't brown. Heat and humidity lay on the land like a wet blanket. Sweat rolled down her back and sides, making the t-shirt stick to her.

She could cut across the field and maybe get to the house a little quicker, but that meant crossing a steep, tree-filled hollow. It wasn't all that deep, and she wouldn't even worry about it normally. But normally she hadn't had the shit beat out of her. Sore ribs and tenderized bare feet might complicate things.

One of the cows lifted her head and stared for a moment, jaw working as she chewed a mouthful of grass. Then she must have decided the little human wasn't big enough to be a threat and lowered her head back to graze, tail flicking against the flies.

Brooke pondered her choices for a moment, then decided to chance it. With a grimace, she ducked between barbwire strands. A moment later, she was through. She gave the cow a wide berth, just in case, and moved off across the field. The grass was a welcome relief to her tender feet, even with the heat radiating off it like a griddle, and she picked up the pace.

A few minutes later, she was at the edge of the hollow. She stared down into it, trying to prepare herself for the ordeal. It was fifteen or twenty feet deep, and she'd be across it in two steps. But the sides were steep enough that she'd have to climb in and out on all fours. If she'd had shoes on—even her ugly-assed Crocs—she could have slid down this side. Might have scratched her legs, but so what?

She sighed, then sat at the edge and slid forward, using the saplings to slow her down. Leaves and a few gravels worked their way into her shorts, but it turned out not to be as bad as she'd thought. She made her way from tree to tree, then stood up at the bottom and dusted off her seat.

A minute to rest—getting beat up took a lot out of you— and then she tackled the climb out.

That wasn't as easy. She had to get a grip on a tree and pull herself up, then brace herself and find another within arm's reach. If she tried to stand on the hillside, the flint rocks beneath the leaves slid downhill. One step forward, three steps back. At that rate, she'd be all the way back at the county jail in no time.

By the time she reached the top, her t-shirt had dark spots from sweat, and she was winded. She bent over, hands on her knees, and caught her breath, droplets falling from her forehead and soaking into the dry ground.

Always before, when Caleb got through working her over, she'd just crawled into bed—if he'd let her—and slept some of it off. Maybe taken pain pills, depending on how bad it was. She'd never had to make a cross-country hike afterwards, and she felt like she was recovering from a serious case of the flu, weak and aching all over. Her sunburn was getting worse all the time, and breathing hard made the dull pain in her ribs flare up.

Just another thing he owed her. And he'd pay his debt today.

That Caleb sure was a big man, to beat up on a little girl like her. Calling him an asshole was being too nice. He was a whole-ass. One big walking sphincter.

That brought a smile that hurt her split lip, and she groaned. Still funny, though. You took it where you could find it in a situation like this.

She set off across the field again. She'd saved something like half a mile, maybe more, by cutting across the field. All she needed to do was get home.

Well, back to the house. Hard to call where she lived home anymore. Home meant being comfortable, and living with the World's Number One Whole-Ass didn't make for that.

He was gonna pay, though. Sure as the sun was shining.

He'd seemed so nice back when they met. High school sweethearts and all. Going to movies, sneaking into clubs on Dickson Street, getting older people to buy beer for their parties down on White River or Beaver Lake somewhere. He'd bought her flowers and treated her like she'd never been treated before.

After they got married—against Mama's wishes, but Brooke was eighteen—he turned into a stranger. It was like you took all the bad things you could say about a redneck and poured them into him. He wanted her to bring him beers, cook all the meals, clean the house, all that. She didn't mind doing all that stuff too much, but she had to ask permission to go anywhere, and he was jealous of all her friends, male or female. He didn't want her going out without him. She couldn't even do the grocery shopping alone, and if she so much as spoke to the bag boy, she heard it on the way home.

He wanted to be King Shit. Well, she gave him the title. No argument from her about it.

She had to fight off another laugh. It was good she could still do it, but her ribs and lip didn't like it very much.

He was gonna pay.

There was definitely a change going on inside. Once she'd come up with her plan and decided to go through with it, she felt more... free. Yeah, that was the word. Free. Like the plan took all her binders off, opened up a whole new world of choices.

As long as she could pull it off.

Finally, she was across the field, and there was the house. She stood by the fence bordering the yard for a minute, staring at the building. It looked different somehow. Familiar, and yet new.

Could she go in after what had happened?

Something hardened inside, and a voice said, Yes. She slipped through the fence.

Time to get Caleb's homecoming ready.

Time for that bastard to pay his dues.

<hr>

She stood inside the front door, listening as a car pulled into the yard. A cigarette dangled from one corner of her mouth, the smoke curling up to the ceiling. The car stopped, engine still running, and a door opened.

"Thanks, Dakota." That was Caleb, talking to his cousin.

Dakota Ledbetter was one of the leaders, a man in his thirties who'd worked his way up fast. Hopefully he wasn't staying.

Dakota said something back, but she couldn't make it out over the engine sounds.

"Ah, you know how these bitches lie." Caleb laughed. "I ain't laid a hand on her. She's just pissed I stayed out late last night, that's all."

Lying piece of shit. Well, it would be his last one.

He was about to write her a big, fat paycheck for everything he'd ever done to her.

She took a drag on the cigarette, being careful not to hurt her lip, and exhaled the smoke through her nose. He'd made her quit when they got married. No woman of his was gonna smoke cigarettes like some barroom slut. Of course, he kept smoking, and it was one of his she had. Just to piss him off. She was glad to be shut of the habit and wasn't gonna take it up again.

"See ya after a while." He shut the door on Dakota's truck and the Yukon's tires popped gravel up the road toward home. A few moments later, Caleb crunched dried grass as he crossed the yard.

When he got closer, she could hear him muttering to himself. Couldn't make out the words, but didn't need to. Same ol same ol about how he was gonna show her her place, let her know who was boss, all that. It was like he'd read some manual on how to abuse your wife and used all the standard catch phrases because he wasn't smart enough to make up his own.

"She got a black eye an' split lip cause I had to tell her twice." He laughed. "That's good."

She stepped out from behind the door and shouldered the shotgun.

"If you like that, you'll love this."

It was his favorite, the Remington 870 pump he used for deer hunting. Still loaded with 3-inch magnums from last season. It was gonna kick like a mule, but she wanted to get him first shot. If she didn't, there probably wouldn't be time for a second.

He stopped, eyes going wide. He was close enough she could see they were still bloodshot from the night before. He got over the surprise quick, though. There was no question in his mind that he was still in charge, and little Brooke wouldn't really pull the trigger.

"You stupid bitch, put that thing down before you hurt yourself."

"Only person gettin hurt around here is you." She was scared as hell, but her voice was firm. Kind of surprising, really, but this wasn't the time to think about it. Later, after she'd killed this son of a bitch.

He laughed. "Itty bitty you is gonna shoot me with that big ol gun? It'll knock you over."

"Maybe. But you won't see it."

Something in her voice must have convinced him this time things were different. The arrogant look left his face, dropping off like water falling down a bluff.

"Now, Brooke, you just calm down." He held out a hand, like that was gonna stop the slug. Or her. "You don't wanna go doin somethin stupid. Shoot me and the whole family will come down on you like a ton of bricks. You know that."

"At least I won't have to worry about you beatin on me anymore."

"Well, if you wasn't always pissing me off, I wouldn't have—"

"I'm tired of listenin to you." She pulled the trigger.

She was the only one went backwards. The shotgun kicked her against the wall. If it hadn't been there, she would have fallen over.

Caleb wasn't jerked back like in the movies, though. At such a close range, the slug went through him like he was a wet paper bag. A huge hole opened up on the left side of his chest and a big spray of blood fanned out behind him to settle on the dry grass. He stood for a moment, eyes wide in shock, then slowly crumpled to the ground.

She had another bruise on her shoulder to add to her collection. She'd get over it, though.

Ears ringing, eyes burning from the smoke, she made her way over to one of the chairs on the porch and sat down, still clutching the shotgun. Her heart pounded and there was a queasy feeling in the pit of her stomach, like she was gonna be sick or something.

She'd just killed a man. Her. Brooke Ledbetter. Never thought it would come to this. She stared at the woods across the road, not sure what to think.

The day was unnaturally quiet for a few moments and then the birds and insects went back to their business. Somewhere down the road, a cow bawled, and the sounds of traffic drifted up the hill from Highway 59. Farther up the way, there was a shout, then the sound of an engine firing up.

She laid the shotgun down, leaned back in the chair, and got ready for her in-laws. It didn't take them long.

The first one there was Edna, the matriarch of the clan. She was a widow in her late fifties, and she ran the family by default. Her husband, Ralph, went and got himself killed a couple years back dealing with some backwoods family over in Kentucky. She'd known every part of the business all along, though, and ruled with a firm hand, keeping the menfolk in line. Brooke had heard some of them refer to Edna as a bitch, but never to her face.

Edna stepped out of her Cadillac and gazed down at Caleb for a moment. Her faded strawberry blonde hair was tucked behind her ears and her cheeks were sunken in because she wasn't wearing her dentures. That made her look gaunt instead of skinny. There wasn't no give to her eyes, though.

"What happened here?" she said. More cars and pickups found parking spots in the yard.

"I shot him."

Edna stared at her a minute, then stepped up on the porch. She reached out and took Brooke by the chin, raised her face.

"He do this to you?" She tilted her head in Caleb's direction. There was a good crowd gathered there, Ledbetters and their extended family. Cousins, spouses, even a few hangers-on that weren't related but spent most of their time here.

Brooke nodded as best she could. Edna had a good hold on her chin, so she couldn't say anything. The older woman frowned and turned to the crowd. A couple of the men were muttering and nodding.

She barked out, "Pete!" and a big guy with wide shoulders and a belly that pulled the gut of his tucked-in shirt tight, looked up. "You knowed about this?"

"Sure did, Edna. Hate to say it, but I did." He acted a little like he wanted to crawl under a rock. He wouldn't look at Edna directly.

"Why didn't you say nothin?"

"Figgered it was their business."

Edna spat. "You dumbshit. This kind of thing ain't private business. If this girl run to the law about what we do, us women beatin on her is one thing. But no man ought to lay a hand on any Ledbetter woman, born or married. You hear me?"

"Yes'm."

"How 'bout the rest of you men?"

There was a chorus of yeses and yeahs.

Edna nodded. "All right. This here girl, none of you is to hurt her, you understand? Caleb got what he deserved. She's still a Ledbetter and we'll take good care of her." She looked around, waiting to see if anyone was going to say different.

"All right. Y'all git home. Mary, you come here and look at Brooke."

A plump woman in her thirties walked up on the porch as the rest of the family made their way home. She was a nurse, a born Ledbetter, and she had gentle hands. While she worked on Brooke, Edna sat in one of the other chairs and waited.

"She'll be all right," Mary said. "No permanent damage that I can tell. Might not hurt to have a doctor check her out to be sure, but I think she's fine. Just needs a little time, is all."

"Thankee, Mary. Run along home, now. Me an' this girl need to talk."

Brooke felt like she was in the center of a whirlwind and was glad to see everyone leave. Well, almost everyone. Edna sat in her chair, staring out across the yard to the woods on the other side of the road. Caleb still lay in the grass, staring up at the sky. Were they going to just leave him there?

After a bit, Edna said, "Don't you worry none about goin to jail. I'll take care of it with that limpdick Masters."

"All right."

"Look at me, Brooke."

She turned to the woman.

"Dakota tol' me you had Caleb arrested for that." She nodded at Brooke's wounds. "That true?"

"Yes."

"And they let him out on bail?"

"Um hm."

Edna stared at her for a moment, then went back to gazing across the road. "You got a lot of spunk, girl. More than Caleb had. All he wanted to do was haul our dope out and smoke more than his share of it. I hate it when a man drinks or smokes that much. My Ralph left all of it alone, said it wudn't good to get hooked on none of it."

Brooke didn't know what to say, so she stayed quiet.

"You like to drink or smoke pot? Maybe snort some meth, time to time?"

"No, ma'am. I never got a taste for any of it."

"All right. I think we can find something for you to do, then. If you want."

"Can I think about it?"

"Sure can."

Brooke wasn't sure how to feel. She hadn't expected to still be alive. Or, if she was, she thought she'd be in poor shape. Instead, she was sitting here on the porch, her husband lying dead in the yard and the Ledbetter boss offering her a job. Relief, gratitude, and numbness. It would take a while to sort it all out.

Edna laughed all of a sudden.

"What?" Brooke turned to look at her.

"I just thought," Edna said, a smile on her face. "With Caleb dead, we can get all the bond money back. Guess he ain't out on bail no more."

Now that, friends and neighbors, was funny. Even if it did hurt to laugh about it. Maybe she'd fit in here after all.

Gil Miller had a normal upbringing, which means his parents aren't to blame for him going into crime (fiction). Instead, he blames a steady diet of movies, shows, and books, from Miami Vice and Scarface in the '80s to Breaking Bad and Justified in the '00s. To cap it all off, he discovered authors such as Michael Connelly, Robert Crais, Don Winslow, and the late, great Elmore Leonard.

Gil is a member of the Northwest Arkansas Writers Workshop, whose members sometimes wonder where he gets his inspiration. He makes his home outside Fayetteville, where he is at work on the next of his Rural Empires novels.

Visit Gil at https://gilmillerauthor.com/.

jasmine's dilemma

. . .

Marlon S. Hayes

Mrs. Jasmine Brighton stared down at her splayed left hand. The chatter of the restaurant did not resonate with her, nor did the words of her best friend Lana who sat across from her. Her bright red fingernails were not the center of her attention either. Instead, she was staring at the sparkling three-carat diamond wedding ring on her finger, wondering if it would be all she owned if her husband Colin asked for a divorce.

It was funny because she had always thought that if they ended their marriage, it would be because of something she'd done. In the five years of the marriage, she'd been very discreet in her dalliances with other men, and the only person who knew of her misdeeds was sitting across from her. In all honesty, Lana was the one person in the world she trusted with her innermost secrets, and the feeling was mutual. They'd been best friends since middle-school and were almost sisters as far as Jasmine was concerned. There was nothing they could not share.

"Have you heard anything I've said?" Lana said. "I've been telling you about this amazing sex I had last night and you've been oblivious. What's going on with you?"

Jasmine looked at the concern in her friend's eyes and was thankful for her. She needed some advice and someone willing to listen to her, which was why she'd scheduled this lunch date. She took a sip from her mimosa, and once she'd put the flute back on the table, she looked around the crowded restaurant to see if anyone was paying them any attention. No one was. She exhaled and began.

"I think Colin wants a divorce," she said. "I feel like he's fallen in love with someone and is just waiting for the right time to drop the hammer. I don't know what to do."

"Wait, what? So? Let him divorce you and you can move on to someone who is not as anal as your boring husband. Start over fresh and let it go. How do you know?"

Lana had never liked Colin, so her disdain was not surprising. She thought there was nothing overly appealing about him besides him being wealthy. The funny thing was Jasmine had been bored with her marriage for quite a while, but she couldn't afford life without her husband.

"The other day I was on my way for a massage and realized I'd left my purse inside," she said. "I went in through the garage door and heard him laughing and talking on the phone with someone. His tone was light and I crept to the office door to hear his conversation. He was telling whoever was on the other end that the farce would be over soon and she could start looking for wedding venues. He called her 'baby' and I couldn't stand to hear any more. Now I'm dreading whatever comes next."

"Like I said, it's time to move on. What's the problem?"

"The problem is I signed a prenuptial agreement before we got married. I haven't worked a day since then. I like my lifestyle of Gucci, international vacations, and a beach house in Mexico. I drive a Mercedes and have a maid. If he divorces me, I get to keep my clothes and my jewelry, that's it."

"What do you think went wrong? I didn't like him from

when I first met him, but I thought you were somewhat happy with him."

"I was… for a while. But he wants children and when we were dating, I lied and said I did too. I have never wanted kids, you know that. It would ruin my figure and my time would be spent with runny-nosed brats being my entire existence. It's been five years without a pregnancy, thanks to my IUD, but the spark faded a long time ago. Hell, I told you about the sexual escapade I had with the bartender in Jamaica while Colin was in the room asleep. I'd gladly divorce him, but I need the lifestyle."

Lana gazed at her thoughtfully before sipping her own drink. The menus lie on the table but neither woman had glanced at them. They were however on their third mimosas. Lana leaned forward.

"Then you really only have two choices," she said in a low voice. "You can either accept the divorce and leave with virtually nothing. Or you can keep everything except your husband."

"How? He wouldn't agree to any kind of settlement. That's not how he operates."

"I have a cousin who's in what can be described as the 'waste disposal' business. For fifty grand, he can make the problem go away and you can keep everything. Of course, you'll have to wear black for a while, but it does look good on you."

Jasmine stared at her friend. The thought of having Colin killed had never, ever crossed her mind until this moment. She leaned back in her chair and closed her eyes, trying to imagine not only being free of Colin, but having all of his money and property at her disposal. There was a million-dollar insurance policy as well, which he'd insisted on for both of them. If she went through with this idea, she'd be in clover and Gucci for the rest of her life.

"I can come up with the money," she said slowly. "I have

that and more in my bank account. I'll miss the idea of him, but… I think I can live without him. Make the call."

"I will, and after that, I don't want to hear or know about anything. I hope everything works out."

The two women stared at each other and finally, they picked up their menus and ordered lunch. Jasmine found herself smiling while she imagined her future as a wealthy widow.

She was standing in front of the model train exhibit at the Museum of Science and Industry, where she'd been instructed to go via a two-sentence text on her burner phone. When the meeting was over, she'd throw the damned thing away and wait for everything to be completed. Lana's cousin Dale was someone she'd only met once or twice before when they were much younger and she didn't know much about him except that he was going to expect the $25,000 she carried in a purse within her Gucci shoulder bag. He'd told her to be in position and she was. She watched the trains and tried her best to fight her anxiety.

"Hey, Jasmine," a deep voice said from behind her.

She caught a whiff of a delicious-smelling cologne and turned around slowly. The man facing her was about six-foot-three and he was grinning at her. His clothing was expensive, but very understated and classy. He appeared to be a successful man and he was extremely attractive. She felt a sexual tingle beginning, and hoped she looked good to him as well.

"Hi, Dale. I wouldn't have known you."

"I understand. It's been years. Let's go have a seat."

He motioned to an unoccupied bench twenty feet away and then rested a hand upon her arm. He guided her to their seat and they sat down and faced each other. He was no longer grinning.

"There's a lot I need to know before we move forward," he said. "I need to know the reasons why, the hoped for outcome, and everyone's schedule. I know you have an envelope for me, but I don't want it right now. Come on, we'll go downstairs to the cafeteria. The sounds of infants and children will keep anyone from paying attention to us."

Dale stood up and started walking away. There was a book bag on his shoulder which made him look like a researcher or a teacher. Jasmine stood and followed him; grateful she'd worn gym shoes instead of high heels. He led her to a stairway and she followed him down a flight until they were in the basement of the museum. He held the door for her and she got another whiff of him. She knew she wasn't supposed to feel an attraction, but she could not help herself.

The cafeteria was cavernous and as he'd said, there were too many parents with whining children to pay much attention to them. He found a corner table for four and sat down. Once she was settled across from him, he gazed slowly around the room, appearing to be satisfied with their surroundings. Once again, his face was stoic as he regarded her.

"Pull the envelope from your purse and hand it to me under the table," he said.

Jasmine hurried to follow his instructions and their hands brushed as she passed him the large manila envelope. She felt an electric jolt at their contact and wondered if he'd felt the same thing. He unzipped the book bag on the chair next to him and slid the envelope inside. When he looked at her again, there was a twinkle in his eyes.

"Tell me why you need to take drastic measures in your effort to be single," he said. "I was not told very much about your situation. Are you an abuse victim? Is he a sadistic man? Or is he a philanderer?"

"No, he's not mean or cruel or physically hurtful. I do know he's seeing someone, and that jeopardizes everything else."

Jasmine told Dale about the lifestyle she enjoyed with Colin, their prenuptial agreement, her apathy toward her husband, and her newfound knowledge that he was seeing someone else. When she finished, he leaned back in his chair and stared at her for a long moment, his expression blank. Then he seemed to snap out of his reverie and he nodded at her.

"I guess it's worth it to you. What are the things he likes, such as sports or gambling?"

"He loves sports of all kinds, and when he's not at his company, he's in his office at home watching them while he works. Why?"

"Because college basketball's March Madness starts in three weeks, and any man who loves sports will be glued to the television for about ninety-six consecutive hours. You'll schedule a manicure and pedicure and when you're finished, I'll have performed the service and will meet you. Where do you park when you go to the nail shop and where is it located?"

She gave him the address of the salon, which was in the inner city, and described the parking lot behind the establishment. He made a note in his phone, and then he smiled at her.

"I'll see you when you're finished, and you can give me the remainder. That morning before you leave, tell him you're expecting a package. Make it something huge which will need to be carried in. That concludes our business."

Jasmine started to get up, but Dale put his hand on hers. He was regarding her now in a way that made her squirm from the warmth of his gaze.

"I don't know what will happen after everything is done," he said. "But right now, I can only see you as a very attractive woman. This isn't the time to try and start some sort of relationship. Maybe much later down the line, but I wouldn't mind spending the rest of this afternoon alone with you in an intimate setting where clothes are not a requirement or a necessity? Are you interested in such a thing?"

His fingers were slowly rubbing the back of her hand and she imagined how they might feel on the rest of her body. The tingle was back and much to her surprise, she found herself nodding at his suggestion. It would be quite spontaneous and that added to the sexual allure.

"There's a nice hotel a mile away," he said. "I'll be in room 304 in twenty minutes. I look forward to running into you there."

Dale removed his hand and stood, hoisting the book bag to his shoulder. She watched him walk away and admired his gait. She knew she should just go home, but there was something about the man that was irresistible to her. Jasmine sighed, and then she too exited the cafeteria. Twenty-nine minutes later, she softly knocked on the door of room 304. Before the door was closed behind her, Dale was already using his hands and mouth to stimulate her. It was a memorable afternoon for the both of them.

"What exactly is being delivered?" Colin asked her.

It was the day before what would the last one for him. They'd been cordial to each other and he'd even flirted with her once, but there hadn't been any feeling behind it. There was a distance between them that neither of them wanted to conquer, a further indication to her that they were now married in name only. He'd moved on already with his heart, and she'd acknowledged that he'd really never occupied hers. It had been a financial affair for her, a blessing which had taken her to a far better life than she could have dreamt of. And she would keep it.

"It's a lovely set of bookcases for my sitting room," she explained. "I received an email a little while ago that they would be delivered between eleven and two tomorrow. I have a manicure scheduled for that time, so I'm glad you'll be here."

"That's fine, then. I'll be watching basketball games, but when you get back, there's a discussion we need to have. I'll have dinner delivered."

She nodded at his words, but would not let herself ask what he wanted to talk about. She brushed a kiss on his cheek and retreated to her bedroom to think about how the next day would change her life forever. Jasmine would have the house cleaned immediately, she decided, or as soon as the police had concluded their investigation. She would stay at a hotel and put their home on the market. Once Colin was buried, she would relocate. She didn't know where, but a month at the house in Mexico would relax her and aid in her decision. She wondered if Dale might be interested in visiting her there or was it too soon? She could wait and see, because she would have plenty of time and money to do whatever she liked.

When she was leaving for her manicure appointment the next morning, she had one instant of regret and thought of contacting Dale to cancel the contract. But then she thought about how her new life would be and she left the house without saying goodbye to Colin. In her mind, he was already gone. Jasmine slid into her Mercedes Benz and pulled out of their garage. She drove down the driveway and never looked back.

Two hours later she left the nail salon and walked around to its small parking lot. She was wearing flip-flops so as not to mess up her bright red painted toes. She was humming as she unlocked the car. Before she could close the door, Dale was standing next to her passenger window dressed in black and wearing a hood. He pulled the handle and slid in next to her. He grinned at her and there was that twinkle in his eye.

"It's done, per our agreement," he said. "Let's do this and we'll maybe run into each other later down the road."

She didn't feel a drop of sadness for Colin, she realized. In fact, she couldn't wait until everything was finished, because she knew she would want to have a repeat of the afternoon lovemaking session she'd enjoyed with Dale. She withdrew a manila envelope from her oversized purse, just like the first one she'd given him at the museum. He tucked it into the front of his jacket and much to her surprise, he withdrew a pistol in one graceful move. Her mouth fell open in shock. He grinned at her.

"Sorry it's gotta be like this," he said. "But my cousin and your husband are in love, and you opened the door to this. That's why I never trust anybody."

He fired twice into her chest, not wanting to shoot her in the head because that might shatter the window and he had been a fan of her beautiful face. She slumped against the door with her now blank eyes staring at nothing. Dale grabbed her purse, removed her wedding ring, and let himself out of the car. His gloves probably had not even registered with her, because all she could think of was how rich she would be. Too bad, he thought, as he got into a dirty and rusted Toyota. She'd been really great in bed.

It was treated as a carjacking gone wrong by the police. There were no witnesses and no leads, and it was just another Chicago story of being in the wrong place at the wrong time. Colin was shocked and upset, but Lana was there to comfort him in his grief. He was glad that he'd not needed to go through a divorce, because it might have gotten nasty, especially since he knew all of Jasmine's secrets, thanks to Lana. It had probably worked out better this way, he thought. He hoped the police would somehow find the murderer, because he felt Jasmine deserved some sort of justice. He was ignorant of the fact that she had received exactly what she deserved in Lana's mind.

He married a very pregnant Lana a year later on a beach in Aruba. She didn't want to go to Mexico, and had asked him to sell that house, because there would have been too many reminders of Jasmine. He'd agreed with her and they were starting fresh in a new home. He hadn't even asked her to sign a prenuptial agreement. Love was a bit more important than money this time around.

the deuce 225

· · ·

Marlon S. Hayes

Nobody makes it through life by themselves. There are hills and valleys, highs and lows, some of which would bury us if we didn't have folks to hold us close when needed. We are supported by these folks in all that we do, but even they sometimes don't know our whole story. No matter the closeness of siblings, there are still secrets which aren't shared, dreams that remain unspoken, and hopes about which they have no idea. There are some things which can only be shared with a best friend, and if one is lucky enough, a life-long pal who is close enough to us to be considered more than a brother.

Reggie and I have been best friends since diapers, and that is both a blessing and a curse. On the one hand, there is the fact that we know absolutely everything about each other, from our personality traits to the sometimes-embarrassing events which have occurred over the years. I can mention a name from the past of a former flame and not have to utter another word because we both know the rest of that particular tale. The things we've been through have cemented our relationship as brothers, partners, and friends. From fighting bullies in grade school to our first dates, our initial experiences with girls, being the best man at each other's weddings, godfathers to our kids, brushes with the law, and the death of our parents, me and Reggie had been through it all together.

I woke up this morning feeling as if I had the world on a string. My wife and kids were gone on vacation for a few days and I had the house to myself. I had not been able to go with them because my business needed me to be present. There was plenty of food and adult libations in the house, and I had no plans other than to relax and enjoy the serenity of my solitude. My cell phone was on 'Do Not Disturb' meaning the only phone calls which could come through would either be my wife's or Reggie's. Everyone else wasn't important and whatever issues they were having could wait a while. I fried a mess of bacon, the scent of which can make the soul sing in anticipation, scrambled two eggs with cheese, and toasted two slices of wheat bread. I sat down at the kitchen table and began enjoying what I consider to be the breakfast of champions. I munched my food while listening to the music playing softly from the radio over the sink.

I ate with one hand, and with the other, I pulled my cell phone from the pocket of my robe. I am not, nor will I ever be on social media. I get the premise, but I'd rather keep my personal business to myself. My circle consists of me and Reggie and our families, which is more than enough. I checked my e-mails, deleting the ones which were spam, while marking others to check out later. I am notorious for letting these electronic communications go unanswered and I have vowed to stay on top of them.

My biggest joy about the internet is that I can track flights, plan vacations, shop for clothes, and chase down daydreams I've had my entire life. I am kept aware of the latest deals and trends, and as I chewed my buttered toast, something I'd been following made my mouth go slack. The notification which caught my eye and spiked my heart rate was about my dream car, a Buick Electra 225.

The Buick Electra 225 is known more popularly by it's nickname, a 'Deuce and a Quarter.' I'd seen one as a kid, and marveled at the long, sleek beauty of it, and I told Reggie way back then that one day I would own one. It looked as if someday was growing much closer because I had found two for sale. One was a silver convertible and the other was a black hardtop. They were in immaculate condition and were being sold for less than $15,000. I'd been putting money away for just this daydream, aside from household expenses, business activities, and family saving. I've managed to squirrel away quite a bit just in case. I'd wait for my wife to return from their trip, then I'd inform her I was buying my dream car. I couldn't spend that amount of money without her knowledge, because that's not how our marriage works. I whistled as I washed my few dishes because I was convinced that it would be a great and memorable day.

With nothing on my agenda except relaxation, I meandered through the house, looking around at everything with approval and satisfaction. When a person has achieved many of the things they once dreamed of, it's good to sit back once in a while and smell the roses. It was a beautiful home, filled with family pictures, trinkets, and the things which make our lives very comfortable. I stepped through the sliding doors leading to our deck and smiled as I glanced around. I have two barbecue grills, a wet bar, and I even have a hammock, which is down the steps next to our swimming pool. The sun was shining brightly and I was in such a great mood that I poured myself two fingers of whiskey and sat down in a lounge chair, completely at peace in my surroundings. I placed my phone on the cocktail table and took a sip of my drink. Delicious and decadent, because enjoying a cocktail in the morning is not the norm for me.

There's something wickedly satisfying about drinking in the morning. At least it is for me, a person who rarely gets a chance to sip and relax. My business and family events keep me humping pretty much around the clock and I know I'm in need of a long vacation. The type of getaway I'm envisioning is heavy on sun, sand, alcohol, and relaxation. I think that when my family returns, the wife and I will scoot somewhere tropical for a week or two. Our three children are all teenagers, capable of keeping an eye on each other and doing what they've been taught to do. I have no worries about them, because my wife and I have raised them to be thoughtful and responsible. I picked up my phone and began researching international destinations. Maybe I'll ask Reggie if he and his wife would like to accompany us.

Our business is going pretty well, and when we go away on the vacation I was planning, our laptops will keep us abreast of any developments. We were accountants by trade and based on our friendship and financial acumen, we'd started our own firm a few years ago. It was such a success that we branched into other things which had proven to be quite lucrative. Thinking about the 'Deuces' I'd been tracking had me thinking there might be a niche market for buying and selling classic cars and motorcycles. I made a note to research the idea before talking it over with Reggie.

I was feeling a slight buzz from drinking, and I found myself toasting the nearing culmination of a long-held daydream. The best part about having dreams is having someone to share them with who will help you chase them down. No, I'm not referring to my wife, even though she's integral to my happiness. I'm thinking about my best friend, brother, and business partner, Reggie. We started a business together, scared at first, but with each new success our confidence in the partnership has grown. I think I'll buy the Deuce as a congratulatory gift for myself. I'd take Reggie on a road trip somewhere in the Deuce, with the sun shining down on two kids from a rough neighborhood who found success in a society designed for them to fail.

My cell phone rang and I grinned at the readout. He must

have felt some kind of vibe emanating from the universe. I laughed as I answered Reggie's call.

"What's up bro? You just ran across my mind," I said. "Remind me about classic cars when I see you. There's an idea I want to run by you."

"Classic cars, huh? That's funny," he said. "What are you up to at the moment? I need a favor and I got a surprise you won't believe."

"I'm drinking whiskey on the deck, sitting in my robe, and contemplating vacations, flights, and barbecues."

"Nice. I can see you're enjoying being home alone like that movie. Pour me a whiskey on the rocks and I'll be there in a few. Oh, and put on some damned clothes."

I ended the call, laughing at his words. I dressed in jogging pants, a t-shirt, and an old pair of gym shoes before pouring Reggie a whiskey on the rocks. For good measure, I topped off mine. I took a sip, feeling fortunate enough to be relatively stress-free for a change. I worry a lot, sometimes for no reason. I can't help it because I always have the feeling that this life we've built could be taken away at any moment. It's my biggest fear.

I opened my front door and stepped out onto the porch. I lifted my glass and took a sip before almost choking on it as a blue 1969 Buick Electra 225 glided to a stop in front of the house. Reggie stepped out of the car, and walked up until he was standing next to me. My mouth was hanging open, and he grinned at me mischievously.

"You got my drink ready, bro? My throat is parched, and I'm in need of one," he said. "Man, do I have a story to tell you."

I opened the screen door for my best friend, suddenly wondering if I really wanted to hear his story. His grin had disappeared and he looked grim about something. He followed me into the house and I led him back to the deck where his drink was waiting. I handed it to him and he drained it in one long gulp. He grimaced at the taste when he'd finished, then sat the empty glass down on the table. I didn't like the direction this seemed to be going, as if something heavy was about to be disclosed.

"How much will you give me for the Deuce?" he asked, surprising me. "You've wanted one since we were kids, and I've delivered. Wouldn't you rather buy it from me than one of those internet sharks you don't know?"

"I found a couple on the Internet for about $9,000," I lied, smirking at him, because he knew I was lying. "Is it really yours? Do you have the title to it?"

"Sure do," he said, pulling a folded piece of paper from his pocket, then smoothing it out on the table for me to read. I saw the name of the seller 'Bobby Jo Simms' and wondered who they were. Everything seemed to be legit and in order, and I wondered how much he would really charge me for the car. I hoped whiskey and shared laughter would be enough to get the price discounted. It probably depended on how much Reggie had paid. I didn't think he would hose me, and whatever price we settled on would be considerably less than what I would have spent on the vehicles I'd researched. My dream car was sitting right there in the driveway waiting for me. I couldn't believe it.

Before I could open my mouth to haggle about the price, Reggie tossed the keys in my direction. My eyebrows furrowed as I looked at him, wondering why he'd given them to me.

"It's yours," he said, causing my eyes to bulge in surprise. "When I saw it, I figured you'd get an early birthday, Christmas, and best friend present. I'll sign it over to you today, but first, I need a favor."

"What's the favor?" I asked. I was thrilled that he'd given me the Deuce for nothing, but experience and life have taught me that nothing in this world is truly free.

"I'll explain when I get back, gotta use your washroom right quick."

He walked back into the house and hurried down the hallway toward the washroom. I understood exactly what he was going through. It's that feeling of an impending explosion which can no longer be restrained and I hoped he would make it in time. I chuckled, wondering why people put so much strain on their bladders and kidneys by waiting to the absolute last minute. I jingled my new car keys and went outside to check out the Deuce.

It gleamed in the sunlight, every line of the car exquisite to my eyes. I walked around the car slowly, drinking in the white wall tires, the chrome, pleased as punch that Reggie had procured my dream car and then given it to me. My smile stretched across my face as I looked at the leather interior, imagining the smooth softness of it. My facial expression disintegrated when I saw the body lying across the back seat. I saw the guy's black shoes sticking up from beneath the blanket covering the rest of his body. I couldn't tell how big the person was, but I did take notice that the back seat of the old Buick was huge.

"Yeah, so I need to borrow a shovel and stuff," Reggie said. I hadn't even heard him approaching. I was staring at the body in the backseat, before finally looking my best friend in the eyes.

"How?" I asked. A little grin appeared on his face, as if he'd been doubting my response to having a dead body in my driveway.

"It was the car," he said. "Here we are scouring everywhere for this asshole, and he puts the car up for sale on the Internet and in the paper. Can you believe this idiot? I've been on the lookout for Deuces anyway because of you. When he first disappeared and they gave us the contract, everyone we talked to said how he loved classic cars. It was his undoing.

He's been off the grid for a few years, so maybe his money was running low."

"Did he look different?"

"From when he first testified? Sure. He's grown a beard and let his hair grow pretty long and even wore thick glasses. Gone was the smooth-faced, slick talking guy who got a lot of his friends sent away. I've studied his face for years, adding changes on the computer to see what he might look like now. The car was registered to an old lady he'd come across somewhere. She's living in an assisted care facility in the memory ward with no relatives. I'll clean up his apartment after we get rid of him."

"Do they know yet?" I asked, referring to the syndicate this guy had betrayed, causing them to place a two million dollar price on his head.

"I sent a message about running into an old friend. I'll take a picture with the Polaroid, plus his right hand. That'll do the trick. I'll hand deliver it to their representative, pun intended. The money will be wired next week at the earliest, you know how this goes."

I sure did. About once a year we'd do a "job" on someone, always someone who had it coming to them, no law-abiding citizens or cheating spouses. Our reputation was impeccable, because we always delivered. After we got rid of the late owner of the Deuce, we'd work on our investment portfolios, maybe take a few vacations, then start research on our next contract. We were pretty good at our professions, both of them. Accounting has more than one meaning.

"I have some lime and plastic in the shed and I know the perfect spot," I said. "After we plant this bum, we're going to get the Deuce cleaned and detailed. Then we can go back to the guy's apartment and clean it thoroughly. Let's see what he's hiding. We'll check his computer, the closets, and anywhere else in the place. Any money that we find, we'll donate half to the church. Okay with you?"

"Sure thing," he said. "Let's go to Vegas next weekend after we've collected. We need a getaway. Oh, and after today, don't drive the Deuce for at least a year. Cover it, and be content in knowing you have your dream car in the garage. Also, I'm thinking about opening a hot dog stand. It'll give me something new to focus on. I think it'll make a little money. You in?"

He knew the answer already. It was me and him against the world, as it had always been. I nodded at him, then started walking to the shed to retrieve the things we would need. Reggie fell in beside me, and I thought about how lucky we were to have each other. Another thought struck me just then that I finally had my Deuce, a long cherished daydream. Maybe now I'd start looking for a boat, another thing I'd dreamt of one day owning. I had a pretty good feeling that a boat was in my future. Of course, I'd have to discuss it with my wife first.

An hour later, we were putting our finishing touches on filling in the hole we'd dug for the guy. We wore masks because the Deuce's former owner had been planted in a landfill used for disposing rubbish. It was a fitting place for him. The Deuce would stay parked in my garage for at least a year, covered by a tarp. An idea formed in my head at that moment, surrounded by the garbage and the stench.

I looked over at Reggie and I grinned, because I knew where I would go on the Deuce's first road trip, and I knew who would go with me. Sure, we'd go to Vegas next weekend, then we'd go back to our work for a while, researching our next assignment and continuing to crunch numbers at our firm. Maybe we'd take the wives on a tropical vacation sometime soon. Maybe. But a year from now, I promised myself that on the premiere of rolling out the Deuce, Reggie and me would drive down to the Gulf Coast. I think that's where I'll find that boat I've daydreamed about. Fingers crossed.

Marlon S. Hayes is a writer from Chicago who has been published in multiple genres. Sometimes, he gets an idea that only fits into some specific category, so he goes wherever the story takes him. It might be a romance, a ghost tale, or a suspense novel that leaves readers on the edge of their seats.

Marlon likes to work on multiple projects simultaneously to avoid getting bogged down when a story hits a wall. He's currently working on a suspense thriller, a Western novel, and a coming-of-age story.

His latest two releases are a Western novel, <u>A Man Named Purse</u>, and a short story collection, <u>Gauntlets and Conches Volume One</u>, with fellow author Gordon Bonnet.

In addition to writing and recording, Marlon's other passions are traveling, baseball, and barbecuing. Every year he tries to combine his loves by taking a trip to see a game, while investigating local barbecue joints. He's also best friends with his passport and uses it at least four times a year in his quest to visit at least fifty countries to match his domestic feat of visiting every state. His count is currently at twenty-two. He collects quirky salt and pepper shakers, and has completely filled a curio cabinet with them.

Marlon's mantra is "Life is a banquet," and he does his best to follow it. He's also a willing mentor and soundboard for other creatives, no matter what they're artistic passion might be. His belief is that giving support and encouragement is necessary to the psyche of every artist.

Family is important to him, and he attends a family reunion every year, accompanied by his wife, their two daughters, and their only grandson so far.

Marlon is putting the finishing touches on the audiobook for his novel 11:59 and performing and producing audiobooks for other authors. He can be followed on social media at Marlon's Writings and contacted at <u>marlonshayes@gmail.com.</u>

billy

. . .

David M. Allen

Martin Steadman moved along Wallace Avenue like a hunted man. He'd been thinking too much again, turning circles in the sweltering silence of his apartment. Chewing his lip and drumming his fingers while his wife, Nancy, read some novel on the sofa across the room. When he couldn't stand it any longer, he'd risen and said he was going out. She hadn't even looked up from her book. An amazing woman, his blonde-haired darling, enduring his remoteness, his disquiet, all this time. If she suspected anything of him or his nighttime wanderings, she had never hinted so. He had helped her to build a good life and he always came home, and so maybe she had simply made her peace with it. Steadman kept his eyes and ears busy as he walked, soaking in the catcalls and laughter, the horns, headlights and neon that surrounded him. On warm nights like this, people swarmed the sidewalks thick as ants and he craved their cathartic energy. He dug into the breast pocket of his denim jacket, feeling around behind the small New Testament some Gideon had given him. He touched the stack of folded bills he had been squirreling away, enough for plenty of alcohol or—what? *Yeah, a good dousing of beer*, he thought.

He searched the street, hoping to find a club that offered deafening music and a party girl to scream in his ear for an hour or two. He found the club. But he also found a boy who looked just like—*Billy!*—standing beside the front steps. Steadman froze. The shock registered in his heart, which seemed to seize and then began drumming furiously. But no, it couldn't be the same boy he'd seen leaning against a back-stop in the park a year and a half ago. Not the same boy he'd watched for so long before finding the nerve to approach him.

He stood still for a long moment, trying to decide what to do. He really needed to breathe, and took a long, uneven pull of air. He fell in among the sidewalk crowd and drew closer to the young man by the steps. Keeping some distance between them, Steadman strained to get a better look. The boy relaxed against the bricks of the building, smoking a cigarette, one finger hooked in a belt loop at his waist. He had tugged his jeans down a bit, exposing the tops of his hips. His shirt hung open and Steadman could see the gleam of a silver ring at his navel. The glow from a lighted sign above him revealed delicate features beneath closely-cropped hair. He wore a practiced smile. So much like Billy. Steadman felt the ice rising in his veins.

The crowd swept him along, suddenly oblivious to the din around him. A cancerous weight had bloomed behind his eyes. He stopped. Made up his mind, turned, took another deep breath and broke open the fists at his sides. He made his way back toward the bar, trying to figure out what he would say. Steadman composed himself as best he could as he drew near. He had time to think, didn't have to say a word yet. As he walked past, he leveled his gaze directly into the young man's eyes, arching his eyebrows to make his intentions as silently clear as he could. He got a thin smile in return. Steadman had seen eyes like those before. They betrayed the toughness hidden in the soft lines around them. The man did not look back until he had moved far beyond the apron of light in front of the club. He saw the boy following him, a silhouette with billowing shirt tails and red cigarette eye.

By the time they had reached the hotel two blocks down, his pursuer was close enough behind that he held the door for him. The desk clerk barely acknowledged their presence when they entered, his only reaction a slight tugging in at the corner of his mouth as he reached for a room key. Cash for key exchange completed, they turned down a hallway to the right of the desk and took some stairs to the second floor. The boy joked as they climbed. "You can spoil me if you want to, baby, but an alley would've done just fine."

"No alleys!" Steadman insisted, his reply fired like a bullet. His mind's eye opened on a brick-walled corridor, empty but for a few scattered bottles and an industrial trash bin. A boy standing before him, half his face softly lit, half in shadow. Steadman paused, turning slightly, as he reached the top step. He ground the points of the room key into his palm, focusing on the pain. His voice softened as he said, "Not a very safe place to conduct business, my friend."

They reached number 206 and he unlocked the door. It opened into a sparsely furnished room. One double bed, a small nightstand and lamp. A scarred Windsor chair with a broken rail. Steadman felt uncomfortably warm, so he moved toward the window, asking for his companion's name as he reached for the locks.

The young man moved to the bed and removed his shirt, wasting no time. "Call me anything you like, big guy," he said. "I'm whoever you want me to be. Got a favorite choir boy?"

Billy! The word formed like a cold knot in Steadman's brain. *What the hell am I doing here?* he wondered. *Idiot!* He fought with the window for a moment, but it was jammed shut.

"Nothing comes to mind?" the boy asked. "Um, how about Steven?"

"Steven is fine." Steadman answered. He repeated it several times in his mind like a mantra, willing the other name away. Steven began to recite his list of terms, but Steadman interrupted him. "I don't want sex."

"No?" the boy asked, frowning. "Well, what do you want, then?"

"I don't know. Say, listen—tell me about yourself. I just wanna talk. What d'you charge for a little chat?"

"Huh?" Steven replied. "Oh, are you a talker? Gonna tell me your fantasies. Or maybe your life story? I hope you don't want mine, 'cause it's just not that interesting." He reached slowly for the button on his jeans, smiling at the way Steadman's eyes followed his hand. "You look like you'd rather..."

"No!" Steadman exclaimed, his eyes darting toward the door. "I... look, let me ask you...Why do you do this? Are you a runaway? Got a habit or something?"

The boy laughed, obviously enjoying himself. "Hey, these are my life skills, baby." he said, sweeping his hand along his body as he would a fine leather sofa. "My résumé don't float in the personnel offices, ya know? And besides—I like it!" More laughter, and then his smile faded. "Wow." He groaned. "You're not here to save my soul, are you? 'Cause I really don't..."

"Can't say I speak for God," Steadman said, his frustration increasing. He felt the weight of the little pocket Bible he'd gotten from the Gideon. The man had promised he would find whatever he needed inside. He'd found that he could never quite bring himself to open it. "How old are you, kid?" he pressed. "Sixteen? Seventeen? Can't you see what this does to people?"

Steven rose from the bed and stepped toward him, clearly tired of the conversation. "I see what this does to *you*," he said. "C'mon man. I know what you want. Get outta my head and let's just..."

"No, kid!" Steadman said, fighting to control his anger.

"You just don't get it. I'm tryin' to tell you where you're headed. Just listen!" He placed a hand on the boy's shoulder to command his attention, and to keep him at a distance. His fingers rested on smooth skin covering lean muscle. The touch of it cemented his desire, and infuriated him. He shook his head. "Stupid kid." He sneered, seizing Steven's shoulder tightly. "Stupid faggot. You're gonna end up just like Billy! Don't you see it?"

Billy! It wasn't his real name. Steadman knew that, but he'd said it was Billy and God, he was so... He did business in the alleys too, down there on his knees like some dog, hawking himself to any half-witted drunk for a little drug money and just—taking you like that, and reaching for your wallet when he thought he had you really gone...

Steven swatted Steadman's hand away and backed off, reaching behind him for his shirt. "I don't need this, man!" he spat. "This little party is over. Hey, and you are a freakin' nut case, so just fuck off!" He moved quickly toward the door, cursing and struggling with his shirt. Steadman lunged after him, grabbing his shoulder again. Steven spun on his heels and swung hard, his fist striking the man's chin dead-on and snapping his head against the wall beside him. He threw open the door and bolted for the stairs, leaving Steadman reeling in a daze behind him. Steadman fell heavily against the wall and sank to the floor, his vision buzzing black in the storm that ignited in his nerves. He struggled on the edge of consciousness. It seemed to him as he tried to stand, that he felt the rough edges of bricks at his back.

His head hurt badly and he recalled that he'd been in a fight or something. He looked around him, trying to find something he had dropped, or lost? There on the pavement a few feet away. The dim light from the alley's entrance revealed a dark lump. He retrieved his wallet and it was open so he could see the little photo of his wife, and he saw the accusation in her smile. He looked away and his eyes came to rest on a young man lying face down beside a dumpster. He'd struck his head hard on the edge, on the corner of it, and there was so much blood on the cement. Panic began to well up in him. He couldn't let anybody find him here with Billy, not like this. It would kill Nancy for sure. He had to run, get out of there, if he could just get his feet under him again.

blue tuesday

. . .

David M. Allen

The day dawns blue. Blue Tuesday. Freedom Tuesday and today Tomas will be free, free to step out under the sun and leave this city behind, to fly away on four wheels, to take me in his brown embrace above the sapphire Mexican sea, to love me, cooling engine at my back, his wild-boy heart above, beyond the reach of jealous fools and lawmen. Lucky is the day. I rise early (9 A.M.) with my mission clear. Deck myself from head to toe in the color of freedom, kiss my kiss-off mom goodbye, my cornflower crystal earring tangling hers. She croaks her daily interrogation like she could really give a shit, and the front door stubs out her ramble-on words like they're one of her stinky cigarettes. Hip hop, trip hop, lucky day. A swig for the nerves and I'm on my way. Steady girl, got lots to do. Skip down these stairs toward the urban zoo. Gotta find some money, beg, borrow, steal. Got a man to set loose and nobody– not lying friends, kiss-off moms, or the bigot law–gonna stand in the way of love. Out the big street door, beneath that Olympic-blue sky I go, morning air whispering a promise.

But I see what I see every morning when I leave, every night when I come back home. A sad little girl, lonely eyes beneath her natural curls, sitting by herself on the steps. There's just something in her face. She's a sista in spirit. I think she lives in that first floor apartment, just inside the street door on the left. I hear a little girl crying sometimes through the window, or hear somebody yelling and I'll bet it's her dad. Now she's playing with a ratty old doll, telling her in a serious "grown-up" voice what a beautiful princess she is, and isn't she excited about the "ball at the Fahmily von Trapps's mansion tonight?" "Oh, yes, she's sure that handsome Prince Elmo will be looking for a princess to marry." That makes me giggle—can't help it—and the little girl looks up at me and kinda frowns. She's got a nasty bruise on her cheek, just below her right eye. She's always hurting herself. Clumsy, I guess, or just unlucky. It's probably that red dress she wears with the white polka dots and the kinda tattered little white sash. I never see her in anything else and red is just about the unluckiest color I know. That little girl needs something in robin's egg or aquamarine. I gotta ask her what's her name and where's her momma when I come home. For now the day's callin', Freedom Tuesday, and my Tomas, no matter what they say.

Margaret told me what happened to Tomas. Good ol' Mags. Lorrrd, what she been smokin'? Either that or she's tryin' to break us up. Wouldn't surprise me. She swore off boys herself and went dyke. Says boys are too rough. They like to hurt her and now she wants a sista 'cause they know how to treat each other right. She was even jonesin' for me and I tried it once, but I don't go for that, not when I got Tomas. He's so beautiful and all the girls want him, but he loves me. I know he does. Mags can keep on talkin'.

Anyway, what she told me was Tomas got roped because he almost killed a girl. Mags said he was with this little princess–I dunno–fifteen or something. They were with some people, smokin' at Jules's place. Mags said Tomas took this girl in Jules' bedroom and he was doin' her in there–no I don't believe that– and the girl was letting Tomas sorta choke her, 'cause oxygen deprivation is supposed to make it better. Then, Mags said, Tomas got carried away when the girl started struggling 'cause she got scared, and Tomas was getting off on it. Mags says T would'a killed her if Jules's brother Miguel hadn't heard her gaggin' and screeching and busted in on them. They had to take "Princess" to the hospital and they arrested Tomas for assault, and it's a good thing he's not eighteen for another eight months.

"An' you love dis guy, 'vette?" she says to me, like I'm an idiot.

I don't buy that shit for a second. That's not my T. He would never hurt anybody on purpose, unless Jules told him to. You know how these things go, though. Little bitch probably smoked some bad stuff and got sick or fell in the bathroom or something, then laid it on him. Didn't want to blame whatever tool really did it to her–something like that. Whatever the truth is Tomas went down 'cause he's Latino. In this town that's a GUILTY sign hangin' from your neck. The only chance Tomas has is if I spring him on bail. Nobody else is gonna help him. Not his mama or his sister. They think he's a pendejo. He's got me. That's it. We're gonna blow this town and take that trip he always talks about, him and me. He wants to see Mexico and he's got a car you wouldn't believe. As soon as I put enough cash together that ride is gonna take us all the way to Zihuatanejo. The mighty blue Pacific is waiting. Now about the money…

I'm not even sure how much I need for Tomas's bail. Guessin' $1,000, $1,500 maybe? I dunno. I could've nicked a good amount of it from Mom if her checks had come through yesterday, and it's not like she would've missed the money much. Half the time she loses the damned checks and has to go begging one of her boyfriends to get her through the month. Then she's gone for weeks 'cause you know the guy ain't gonna give it for free. And my dad? Believe me I wouldn't call that cabrón even if I knew where he was. So here I am, bitches, out on the gray streets doin' what a girl gotta do.

I'm ready though—ready Freddy—steady on and on my way, around the corner, down along Ocean Ave. where Mags lives. I'm heading there because it's Ocean Ave. (even though it runs along-side a river?) and what's the color of the ocean? Lucky Luuuckyy. I figure Mags owes me one too, after telling me that lie about Tomas. I'll go easy on her though, 'cause I can't blame her for wantin' to dis my boy. Tomas doesn't really like her and he always calls her "Maggots", instead of Mags. She gives it right back to him, but I can see the look in her eyes when he walks away. Margaret should have some money. She cons it from her dad whenever he's got a little extra, and buys Molly from Jules. If she's out of funds I'll use her phone to call some of our friends. They better give it up for my T. Don't have a phone myself. Mom wouldn't allow it even if we had the cash to pay for it. She says having a phone just makes it easier for the social workers to mess in our business.

I climb the stairs of Mags's low-rent palace to find her apartment on the third floor. Door number 306, on the right beneath a broken light bulb that's never been replaced in thirteen years. There's this little plastic butterfly sun-catcher hanging from the doorknob, which means her mom's at work and she's slappin' donuts with somebody. I wonder who the lucky girl is and whether I can get Mags to come to the door. I picture her in this big wrinkled T-shirt she threw on, with no pants and her red hair all wild from rollin' with that girl, all bitchy-faced from bein' interrupted, and I giggle nervously. This is so uncool, but it's already 10:15 and I gotta make some progress here. I knock quietly, then I rap-rap-rap-rap-rap a couple times, even pound and give her my sweetest "Maaaagsayy?" Nothing, not even a muffled "Piss off!" from the other side. And of course it's locked. She's in there, I know (bitch!) but I can't be mad at my sista. Just can't.

That leaves me haulin' it back up Ocean Ave., weighing my options. Think, girl…think think think. I reach the corner of Ocean and DuBois (that's my street) scanning for a sign and–ahhh, what I need is a drink Ha! A drink to help me think. I fish out this really cool silver flask that Mags and I found one Friday night on the steps at the library. It was sooo shiny, even in the dark, but when I unscrewed the cap and took a whiff it wasn't Dewar's I smelled. It was god-awful, kinda like a fine, vintage pee. Mags said to throw it away, but I said "No way, not this girl. I'll bet it's worth quite a bit and the wizz, or whatever, is nothing a bit of hot water won't take care of." Right now I'm thinkin' Hmm, maybe this flask would bring a nice bit of cash for Tomas's bail, but I hate to part with it. It's such a beautiful container for my fortitude. Omigod, Mom calls it that. Fortitude!

So I take a pull to grease my wheels and I'm looking back down my street from the corner and there's the little girl again. She's being hauled up our front steps and inside by some guy. He's yankin' her by the arm, and I can hear her bawling from here. I'm thinkin' Friggin'-A, kiddies! Some-body's pretty unhappy with her. I don't like it at all. It's making my stomach pretty unhappy, to be honest. Not knowing really what to do, I keep my mind on my quest and, casting around, I find the sign I've been looking for. Down along DuBois, in the opposite direction, I see the Nash building all tarted up in high-polish glass and steel, reflecting the azure sky. It's calling me to the retail stores downtown. No friends are gonna give me my boy's freedom today, so I'll go and get it myself.

Mags taught me some tricks for nicking cheap bling and stuff and I've done it a few times when I was short on cash and I figured I'd die if I didn't get my hands on some really sick shoes or a jacket Tomas liked. No big deal, and wouldn't you know down the street and around the corner there's a couple guys who have a little business specializing in "no hassle returns." A few minutes later I'm borrow-browsing at Feinstein's, nervous as heck, but cool on the outside. The girly behind the counter cares as much as I do about her boss losing the merch, so I nab some pieces easily. On the way past the register I hold my breath, flash Brenda Slacker my sunny day smile and sssslide out the door. Well those goods net me a whoppin' twenty-four bucks and I'm thinking this is gonna take some work. I've got to find a better way to bring in some funds. Turns out I have to anyway, 'cause I walk into another store and it's like the clerk has been waiting all his life for me. He gives me the look and asks for my messenger bag and hat (What, no wine and candles first?). I won't get past Super Cop without a strip search. Fun's over and this sista is done shoppin'.

Well here I am, draggin' it up the street, slightly pissed now, 'cause it's 11:30 and it's getting hot and I've got $24 for the judge. I'm hungry, but I can't spend Tomas's bail money on corn chips. I take a drink to make my tummy warm and happy for a while. What next, girl? Thinkin', thinkin', thinkin' and drinkin'. There's this musician a ways up the street, out in front of Talley's restaurant. He's playing guitar and I can hear the music. I don't have any better ideas at the moment, so I decide to wander up there and listen. I'm getting closer and I think maybe the guy is blind! He's got dark sunglasses on which lends the usual cool, but he's moving his head back and forth that funny way that makes it seem he's not really looking at anything. There's one of those skinny white canes leaning on the wall behind him.

Nobody is out here listening to him now, but it looks like somebody was, 'cause he's got a nice little pile of bills and change in his guitar case. Can he spare it? I know he probably needs that cash to feed himself every day and maybe have a bed for the night, but suddenly I'm thinkin' "this is an emergency, this is love bein' stolen and lost". This is my heart breaking if I lose my T and this guy would understand that because he sings about this stuff all day in his lonesome bluesy voice. He's so good and once lunchtime hits and the business folks are on the street he'll get that money back in no time.

Blues Man keeps picking and singing about "the last words she said" while I look up and down the street. Nobody close or really looking this way. I decide, move in like a cat, my heart pounding like crazy, eyes everywhere, trying not to breathe. I crouch down, he's less than four feet away, looking opposite direction, moving about. My mouth is so dry, heart thundering in my head (this is nuts!). Reach out with a thumb and pointer (don't rustle them leaves, now). One (heart's gonna burst!)--he's still lookin' away--two (you're evil, girl!)--three (Hell is HOT and you know what your hair looks like when things get sweaty).

I straighten as quickly, quietly as I can and scurry off like a rat, head throbbing like mad from the heart pounding and the not breathing. *Please forgive me Blues Man*, I think as I suck in some air, and just as I'm about to step out of earshot he sings "….and she lifted all my green. Now I'm sleepin' in-between…the devil and the deep, unyieldin' bluuuue." I look over my shoulder and Blues Man is looking in my direction, sad smile on his face, and then turns to strum and stroll away from me. I want to go back and drop the bills in his guitar case. They suddenly feel awfully heavy in the hand I've got tucked in my bag. What to do? I kinda feel like this hermano gets it, like he understands about love and struggle and all. If I walked right back there and explained he'd be like "Aw, mija, It's okay. You keep the money. Go get that man o' yours." I should go back and apologize but I feel so awkward now and time is tickin' and I gotta move on. I'll find him again and do something really nice for him some day. Thank you, sweet Blues Man.

Eighteen ones and a five is what I fished out of his case. It's 12:08 and I have $47. Five more hours and the courthouse closes. I gotta get him out today or my luck will run out. I can feel it. I don't exactly have time to hold a bake sale or telethon. I need a major donor right now or it's gonna be game over! The thought of that makes my breath hitch and my eyes tear-up a little. What to do? What to do? The sick little part of my brain says "Ask to see the judge and do him an under-desk favor!" and then I want to hurl. NOT FUNNY! That's beyond disgusting, girl, and no more floozy juice for you today! Now I'm standin', still clueless, at the corner of Guilford Ave., staring up at the bright blue street sign. Not my favorite shade, really, but the blue comes through! There's really only one person who can save the day and he lives on Guilford. Jules. He's the only one I know with that kind of green, but I gotta be crazy! Crazy in love, right?

Jules's mom rings me in. She lives in the apartment next door to his and Jules takes care of whatever she needs. She had a kinda stroke about three years ago and she can't do much these days, but she is the sweetest lady and she loves me. She loves all of Jules's friends and she's like everybody's second mom. I'd trade my mom for her any day. Theresa lets me into Jules's apartment and asks me how's Tomas 'cause she hasn't seen him in a few days. Nobody told her 'cause it would break her heart. We keep a lot from her because she's fragile. I tell her T is staying with his cousin across town for a while. Theresa tells me she don't know when Jules will be home but I can chill while I wait. Just lock up if I gotta leave. We all know that to leave Jules's apartment open means death. He's got stuff in there that could get him in a world of trouble if the wrong people found out about it. Of course nobody who knows him would dare mess with that and he flies so far under the radar the cops don't have a clue how he makes his money. But he makes a lot of it dealing and he takes good care of everybody, his customers and his friends. He's not flashy but he doesn't live like no pauper either.

Jules teases me so bad. He knows I got a big, weird birthmark just above my butt, from throwing me over his shoulder once so my shirt tugged up along my back. He calls that mark my tag and tells everybody he's my pimp. T hates that but he always laughs just the same. Really, Jules is like a big brother to me, and I feel safe here and I just flop down on his big, poofy couch and wait. But the waiting gets kinda long and that couch is so dang comfy when I stretch out to rest my tired feet. Next thing I know my brown eyes fly open like Tom the cat when that mouse smashes his foot with a hammer. It's 2:30! Court is in an hour and half, so I'm freakin'. "Jules, where the fuck are you?" I shoot a look at his entry door and will that man to show -- focusing all my feminine power—but he doesn't. I can't think. I'm doin' like the potty dance and hoppin' around, pace into the kitchen and back, down the hall to the bathroom, back to the living room, twirl and back down that hall.

I stop at the room on the left, twist the handle and push. Jules's room. I've been in here before but only by invitation. Jules sometimes lets me hang and listen to his work-out tunes while he lifts and I trash-talk him to make him bench and curl more. He eats it up and we both laugh, dude and his "Li'l Sistah". Other girls, they come in here and they got bragging rights forever. Guys step in and they come out untouchable unless they screw up and piss him off. But you don't open this door and go through unless the man calls you in. Not if you're sane. Guess I'm not 'cause I hold my breath and I do it. I'm so scared it's hard to breathe. My brain gets paralyzed for a few seconds. Why am I here? And then I'm in a frenzy. He's gotta have a stash in here somewhere and I gotta find it and get the hell out, and then pray Jules doesn't figure out who took it. I'm feeling under his mattress thinking "Do I just take it all and run, or count out what I need?" Take it all and I'm beyond dead. Take just what I need and maybe I'm just regular dead? Nothing in his bed so I start rifling through his dresser, as careful as I can, then shove my hands in under the carved swoops in the base. No money. I check his closet, his gym bag, underside of his lifting bench, trying hard not to leave anything looking disturbed. I'm trying hard not to cry 'cause my luck is running out fast.

My last chance is sitting in the corner, right side of the bed: Jules's congas, his djembe, his cajon. The man is a freak about drumming. Working out and drumming are how he de-stresses and when you hear the boom boom whatever business you got with him, you wait until the boom boom stops. I drop to my knees and fish up through the bottoms of the congas but there's nothing up there to hold the goods, nothing stuffed up inside the djembe. I pull the cajon away from the wall and turn it. It's so beautiful, with a mahogany tapa and adjustable snare, padded seat and a big ol' sound hole in back. I reach my skinny-girl arm in and down, my fingers dancin' in there and I strike gold! A squishy bag of Kush and a big, fat, folded stack of bills. I yank the money out and damn!, my knuckles bang with a wooden thud on the cabinet walls. It's not big bills but there's a lot of 'em. I count out what I think I'll need as fast as my fingers can separate the paper, fold and rubber band it again. I was gonna ask you for it, Jules, but I can't wait. It's almost Three! Maybe leave a little note? I hear a soft little noise behind me and it turns out I don't have to.

"Find what you were lookin' for?" he asks, and my heart stops.

The thing about Jules is he can be your best friend in the World, or your worst enemy, and that means your worst nightmare. He's got guns like you wouldn't believe and his reflexes are sick! Nobody messes with Jules. I saw two guys with knives walk away once rather than take a chance with him and he had nothin' but his fists and his feet. He's got beautiful eyes and smile, make any girl fall in love with him instantly, but you don't want to see Jules angry, not ever. He just destroys stuff, obliterates it, and drops people easy as crackin' open a beer. The water pumps switch on and I turn around, shaking like crazy. "Jules," I say, "I wanted to ask you for help. I waited and waited, but I…"

"Shut it!" he barks at me.

He just stares at me and his face is like a storm brewing, not quite ready to unleash. The way his jaw is shifting it looks like he's chewing on whether to end me or let me crawl out alive. His eyes are lit up. You wouldn't expect to see that kinda fire in brown eyes but it's there, sure enough. There's something else, too, and it makes me all the more sorry. I go to apologize again and I see his jaw set even harder so I keep my mouth closed. .

"Take it," Jules says. He knows what I'm up to. I pocket what I counted and set the rest down softly on the bed. I'm suffocating and my head is pounding, feels like I'm about to pass out, but then Jules jerks his head hard toward the doorway and I gasp! My legs won't work at first, so I'm like *Come on legs…* and then I'm moving! I rush past him, but his hand closes on my collar.

"You, out of everybody, never owed me a thing, baby girl," he says quietly. "Now you owe me. You should carefully consider whether that fool is really worth it." I run out of Jules's apartment, into the corridor and I'm practically jumping down the stairs. Theresa is shuffling down the hall toward Jules's place and I hear her call my name behind me. Sorry, Mama. I'm gonna miss you so much.

Out on the sidewalk I start bawling, because man, did I just screw up, and Jules's voice keeps repeating in my head, "Consider whether that fool is worth it." And all of a sudden, I'm not sure. Tomas is so beautiful and he's always been pretty good to me. Never hurt me, really. But nobody's sayin' anything good about T these days. Not Jules, not anybody except for me. Why would he do what they say he did? Why would he do this to me? I gotta look him in the eyes and hear it straight from him. And anyway he's my ticket out of here, out of that dump of a place I live in, away from pathetic, drunk-ass Mom, away from liars and bigot cops–all of it. I spent all day on this crazy little mission and practically got myself killed for it, so I'm bringin' the man his money and he'll see who's got his back.

I'm standing by this gate across an alley between two buildings with my eye shadow running, wiping tears and dribble-snot on my sleeve and this old man steps up to me. "Hey, Sweetie," he says, "What's a'matta?" and I start to get creeped out 'cuz he called me "Sweetie" and I hate when old guys do that, but one look in his eyes, you can tell he's practically blind and the dude was walking about as slow as a frozen turd rolling uphill. He's harmless.

"Whatever it is, little girl, it'll get better. It always does. Here," he says, "fresh from the wash" and he pulls a dark-blue hanky out of his pocket, that kind with the curly designs on it. I don't wanna take it ("Little girl? Seriously?"), but it's neatly folded and looks brand-new, and it's really kinda sweet of him. He's like somebody's granddad. I wipe my face and ask if he knows the time. It takes forever for him to flip his arm up and then he's having trouble reading his watch, which has a scratched, cloudy dial, and he can't see anyway, but he finally says "It's abooooouuuuut–threeeee–fifteen, little girl." (again with that!). Omigod!--3:15, and the courthouse is like twelve blocks from here. I start to panic again and I'm looking every-which-way, when I see a bus-stop half a block up the street and I run for it. "Thank you, Mr. Hanky Guy!"

One good thing about this city is we got a lot of buses and they run pretty good for the most part. I make it to my desti-nation with about twelve minutes to spare. I hop out at the corner by the courthouse and make a dash for the steps up to the big entrance, but I see something that stops me dead in my tracks. Tomas's mother and his sister are walking down and they both look real angry. In fact, T's mom looks like she's been crying. They see me coming and both of them just stop. Tomas's mom turns her head and she won't look at me. I climb up to them and ask "What's up? What's happening?"

I see Pam grit her teeth and she says "He did it." That's all she says. Tomas's sister looks beyond disgusted, and she tells me "Tomas did what that girl says he did. He admitted it to Mom. Ese pedazo de mierda! Messed her up pretty bad, too, from what they say." I feel my jaw pop open and my mind freezes, the words "He did it" and "Messed her up pretty bad" spinning around in there. My fingers just sort of open up on their own and my handbag slips out and hits the steps with a "FWUP!" sound. Angela's speaking about "garbage!" and "animal" and "--all that Mom's done for him–humiliate her like this!" and I'm breathing heavy, like I can't get enough air and "FFFFFFFUUUUUCK!!", I scream, because it's all I can think of. Everybody on the street turns to look at me and now my face gets hot and I'm embarrassed and I feel like a fool and dammit, Mags was right! I pull that blue hanky out of my bag and bury my wet face in it. I must look like a horror show by now. It's all for nothing, all that I did for him and Tomas and I are goin' nowhere. I feel a hand on my shoulder.

"Yvette, honey," Pam says, "I don't like saying this because Tomas is my son, but he's a complete idiot and he's just thrown his life down a shit-hole. He's done some stupid things and this one–he's goin' in and he's not coming out for a long time. When he does, if he does, you're not gonna want to be around him. You shouldn't want to now, not ever. Forget about him, Sweetheart."

Pam has never been too fond of T's friends and she always figured Jules was going to get him in major trouble some day, but she never really had anything against me. She's never unkind to me, but there's always been something in her eyes whenever she looks at me. I look up and I see in her eyes what I never recognized before. Pity. This time I look away, but she touches my shoulder again. I look up and she's holding out her hand, fingers closed around something. I reach up and she drops a set of keys in my hand. "The car is yours," she says, then continues down the steps, Angela's arm around her.

Next Tuesday I park my new chariot a bit down the street from my apartment and start filling it up with my stuff. Tomas's buddy, Richie, was out on business for Jules, like he is most mornings, so I drove it out of the lot behind his building without anybody chasin' after me and filled up the tank. I guess the best thing Tomas ever did for me was teaching me to drive. It's only ten-thirty and I've had a busy day already, delivering some envelopes. One's got fifty bills for that musician, who isn't out in front of Talley's where I found him but the waitress I talk to knows him and she'll see to it he gets my loan payment plus interest. Never stop minting joy from sorrow, Blues Man. The other envelope I give to Mags to deliver to Jules for me. I wrote to tell him I'm sorry and "thank you" for not killing me, and for looking out for me even when I was being an idiot. I tell him I'll start paying him back as soon as I get on my feet 'cuz a debt is a debt and I take that seriously. Not just a money debt, a debt of kindness and mercy. And I hope he can find in his heart to still call me "Li'l Sis" even though I screwed up so bad. XOXO.

I tell Mags the deal with Tomas and that I'm goin' to visit a cousin to try and get over it and no, she can't come with 'cuz they don't have space for anyone else in their little place. The only cousins I really have are on my long-gone, shitty dad's side and I wouldn't hide out at their place if everybody else in the world had a bullet with my name on it. Mags would be no use to me where I'm going. The girl's just lazy, truth be told, and I don't need to be haulin' that dead weight all the way to the Pacific. Yeah, I'm goin' and I guess I'll miss her some, but she's headed nowhere whether she leaves here or not.

So I packed up as best I could, clothes and stuff I can't live without, tossed the teddy bears T gave me straight into the dumpster–except for the nicest one–and grabbed what few non-perishables we had in the cupboards. I left a note on the counter:

Hey Momz,

T and me are done. He blew it big time and he's going to jail. I'm going away for a while. Not sure when I'll be back. Please take care of yourself and try to get it together.

— Yvey

Wasted words, but I can't just leave without saying anything. Never havin' anybody to come home to is probably the worst feeling in the world.

I lock up and head downstairs to vacate, teddy bear in hand. No little angel on the front steps this morning. I got a feeling I'll regret it, but I stop at her apartment, hesitate, and then knock on number 1-A. Nobody answers, so I knock again. I start to leave, but then I hear a little voice, kinda scared sounding.

"Who is it?"

"It's Yvette, your upstairs neighbor. Can I just say hi?" (well, "bye"). Maybe her dad is out or sleeping, and she can't open up. But I hear the bolt slide and the door opens a crack. I see a little blue eye with a lock of dirty brown hair hanging over it. The door opens a little more and I see that awful bruise still healing on her cheek.

"Are you okay, bunny?" I ask. She just shrugs a little.

"My daddy's not home."

"Did he go out for work or somethin'?" As if he ever does that.

"Don't know."

"Has he been gone a while?"

She holds up two fingers.

"Two hours?"

"Days," she says, barely loud enough to hear.

She's four, maybe five years old and left by herself for two freakin' days, and beat up on top of that. Jesus and Mother Mercy, how can somebody treat a kid like that? As if I didn't know. And then, crazy as I gotta be, I decide I'm takin' her. Mom's outta the picture I guess and I'm not gonna let that piece o' shit hurt her anymore!

"Hey, lonely girl," I say, "I'll bet you're hungry, huh? Prob'ly didn't have any breakfast this mornin', did ya?"

She shakes her head slowly.

"I'm hungry too! You wanna go get some yummy eats, you 'n' me?" She looks a little nervous, but I see her eyes light up. I kneel down and look her square in the eyes. "Hey sista, I got a guy that hurt me pretty bad, too. I'm really sad right now and I don't wanna be anymore, and I don't want you to be. I'm gonna go some place where I think I'll be happy. Do you think you might like to go there too?" She thinks for a minute and then a little smile creeps in and she nods her head "yes."

"Can Lilly come, too?" That sad lookin' doll.

"She sure can!" We gotta fly 'cuz her creep father could come back. She doesn't have much for clothes besides that dirty old red dress, but I get an idea so I run up to Mom's place and sure enough, there's still a box of my old stuff on the shelf in her closet. I rifle through, toss aside a little blue gown—no luck in that—and find a bright green dress with ruffles and a white sash. I smile, remembering how much I loved this dress when I was her age. Green is her lucky color today, the new color of freedom.

Five minutes later I pull the car up—not many people on the sidewalks this morning—and hold the door for my new li'l sis. Emma's her name, and she tells me Princess Lilly likes pancakes with peanut butter and bananas. She likes her new teddy bear boyfriend, too. We cruise on down the street, I'm hopin' in the general direction of the interstate and points south. I don't know if we'll end up dancin' on that beach in Mexico. I don't know how far we'll get, really. All I know is that someplace won't be here and that's all that matters.

David Allen has been bringing his dreams, fantasies and observations on the human condition to life since his childhood years in Upstate New York, via short fiction, poetry and the occasional passionate essay. He first caught the writing "bug" when a first-grade writing challenge spurred him to pen (or crayon) the harrowing account of a doomed summer hayride. From that day on he delighted in authoring original tales of the supernatural, or life on other worlds, mostly for his own entertainment, eventually completing two unpublished novels by age sixteen.

Throughout high school, college and beyond he was encouraged by instructors who were impressed by his imagination and descriptive talents, while the canvas for his visions expanded. Poetry will always be the most immediate, versatile outlet for his emotions, experiences and the existential challenges we face among a chaotic, imperfect humanity.

When not scribbling, David can often be found tramping through local forests of the Finger Lakes region of New York, indulging in amateur photography, delighting captive audiences with his vast knowledge of global politics and gratefully serving as his beloved cat's favorite piece of lounge furniture.

her choice (from the cassidys series)

. . .

K. D. McCrite

J ess Cassidy trudged up the lane and across the back yard to the house. His weak muscles and clouded perceptions of immediate surroundings forced him to focus on putting one foot in front of the other.

Can't let Carol see me like this.

The thought trembled in his brain like a butterfly's broken wing. In the thirty years they had been married, he'd been strong and steady for her, faithful in all ways. But today....

He opened the back door and stepped inside. The scent and sound of sizzling bacon in the cast iron skillet greeted him like a slap in the face. Maybe he'd caught the flu or was coming down with a late season cold.

"Hey, lover," he said as he came into the kitchen.

"Mornin', sweetie." Carol glanced over her shoulder at him. Her going-gray blond hair strayed from its loose knot on the back of her head and curled around her face. In pink flannel pajamas and favorite robe, she looked dearer than ever. "You took off early this morning. I didn't even hear you get up."

He reached for his favorite coffee cup, dark green, plain

and large. "Woke up feeling a little restless, thought I'd take a walk."

His words weren't entirely a lie. He'd woken feeling completely unlike himself and wanted to shake off this troubling unease.

"Wish you'd get me up to go with you when you take early walks." Carol lifted a couple of eggs from the carton. "Scrambled or fried?"

He shook his head as he filled his cup and the fragrance rose. "Just coffee."

Carol put down the eggs and crossed to him.

"You feel all right, hon?" She touched his forehead. "Your face is sweaty and cold."

He sipped the coffee as casually as he could and hoped she didn't see how his hand trembled. "It's a cool spring morning, and I was walking."

She narrowed her eyes. "Sure you're okay?"

"I'm fine." He dropped a kiss on top of her head and set the cup aside. "I'm going to go over to the ten-spot and check the berries."

"Gordon checked them yesterday. He said they looked good. Full of blooms."

"I know, but I'm gonna have a look, anyway."

"Don't you trust your son?"

He laughed a little at that. Headstrong and opinionated, Gordon liked making changes without letting Jess know, and in the fruit growing business, changes could mean failure if done improperly or at the wrong time.

"Back soon, lover." He smiled at her and slipped outside before she could say more. He'd almost reached the pickup when the back screen door squeaked open and banged shut. Carol trotted toward him in her slippers, tying the belt of her robe.

"The girls can finish making breakfast," she said. "I'm going with you."

They drove down the narrow paved road to the ten-spot – ten acres that lay between Cassidy Orchards and Duncan Farms, and the ride seemed to take longer than the usual three minutes.

Jess leaned forward, squinting hard through the wind-shield most of the way, struggling to keep the truck in the lane.

"You're scaring me," Carol said. "There's something wrong."

He sat back and pulled the pickup onto the gravel parking area near the berry field.

"Nothing's wrong." Then, "Who's that? What's he doing?"

Carol followed his gaze. "Long black ponytail and scruffy jeans. I'd say it's Kirby Harris. But I don't know what he's doing."

Jess strained his eyes, then thumped his fists on the steering wheel.

"He's spraying the plants with something, that's what he's doing!" He leaped out of the truck and staggered slightly, gasping for air. Jess wasn't a man to let discomfort stop him. He forced his way forward. His heartbeat thundered, and he staggered.

"Jess!" Carol screamed.

She was clambering out of the truck, coming after him, but he pressed on.

"What are you doing to those berries?" he shouted at Kirby.

The young man swayed and bounced from side-to-side, head down, moving forward, ignoring Jess as he approached. He jumped like a startled rabbit when Jess grabbed his arm. The odor of gasoline nearly made him retch.

"What are you doing?" Jess asked again.

Kirby gaped at him, then yanked the earphone from his

left ear and reached into his breast pocket to turn off his transistor radio. He reeked of pot.

"Man!" His dark eyes widened. "Don't creep up on me like that. I was in the service, man. The army, man."

Kirby never left the shores of the United States during the war, but he liked to use his brief service record as an excuse for everything from veterans benefits to getting out of work.

"Why are you spraying gasoline on my strawberries?" Jess yelled.

Kirby blinked at him. "Huh? Oh, this?" He shrugged. "I need the bread, man. Buck pays good."

"Buck? Buckhart Duncan hired you to spray my strawberries with gasoline?"

"Yeah, man." He turned to start spraying again, but Jess grabbed his arm and yanked the sprayer and canister from his grip.

"Get out of here," Jess said.

Kirby gawked at him like a half-wit.

"Get!" he shouted, gesturing toward the far side of the field. "Now. And don't step foot on this property again."

"Relax, man. I'm going." Kirby slouched away as if his joints, like his brain, were made of pudding.

From far off a high-pitched hum began to fill his brain. It grew louder as Jess tried to catch his breath. The crisp newness of dawn blurred and faded. He heard Carol call out his name, saw her peering into his face from somewhere high above him, then he surrendered to an enveloping darkness.

Carol Cassidy watched as light faded from her husband's eyes.

"No!" She clawed at the collar of his shirt, felt for the pulse in his neck.

She shouted for help, straddled his chest, and pumped his

heart with her hands. She sobbed, pumped, screamed without awareness. Her total focus was on his eyes, bringing light back into them.

"I'm here," a voice said above her. "Carol, what's happened?"

She ignored the voice and kept shoving into Jess's sternum. Then she was hauled backward and sprawled like a toddler amidst the strawberries. The smell of gasoline made her dizzy.

She clawed, flailed, screamed. "No. I have to save him!"

"Carol. Carol, honey, it's Tina. Let Buckhart work on Jess. An ambulance is on the way."

The words seeped into her consciousness, and she turned her head, bit by bit, until she faced Tina Duncan.

"Is Jess going to die?" she asked. Some part of her reminded Carol that Buck and Tina could not care less if Jess died.

"I don't know." She slipped her arm around Carol and clung to her while Buck kept Jess's heart pumping blood until the sound of sirens finally chased away early morning birdsong.

Tina went home, and Buck drove Carol to the hospital. He said very little but shot an appraising look at her often as his midnight blue Cadillac tailed the wailing ambulance over the hills and around sharp curves.

"You okay?" he asked a few times. She nodded, said nothing. How strange it was that this man who was their enemy had become their savior.

"Will he die?" she asked as they neared the hospital. The words had hung between them, unspoken on the drive between the farm and town.

"Jess Cassidy is too stubborn to die. A weaker, less determined fella would already be dead."

Hospital paperwork. Why did it seem so necessary when one's very soul was in a small room with doctors and nurses and a loved one suspended between life and death. She tried to write, but her cold fingers shook too hard. Buck gently took the form from her and filled it out. That was fine. He knew the information as well as she did.

"You sign right there," he said when he finished, and stood close as she scrawled her name.

She gripped Buck's hand and leaned on him as they followed the nurse to the room where Jess lay attached to wires and tubes. A machine beeped rhythm. Her knees folded, and Buck caught her. He and the nurse settled her in the chair near Jess's bed.

"Calm. Quiet," the nurse cautioned. "No sudden noises or movements."

Buck stepped back and waited near the door, as if those few steps afforded the privacy this moment needed.

Carol took Jess's hand in both of hers and pinned her gaze on his face. His eyelids fluttered and opened. For a minute, he stared up at the ceiling, then slowly, he turned his head until his gaze rested on her.

"Lover," he whispered.

"Shh," she said. "Rest."

"You okay?"

She nodded, knowing she must look a fright, still in her pajamas and robe, her hair pinned in that scrappy, careless knot.

"Buck's here." She felt something quiver through his body as he gripped her hand. "If it hadn't been for him…. He saved your life, baby."

An expression she failed to interpret shot across his face. Jess sought the man with his eyes. Stared at him hard.

He asked one simple question. "Why?"

Buck took a single step forward, his face impassive. He met Jess's gaze.

"You know why." He transferred his look to Carol, held it

there a moment then pivoted and walked to the door. "You both know."

He stepped out into the corridor, leaving them alone. He was right. They both knew.

Carol took his hand in both of hers and gripped it tightly.

"I'm so glad you chose me all those years ago," Jess whispered as a tear slipped from her eye and he slipped into sleep.

grover and melly go for it

. . .

K. D. McCrite

"Quick, toss me that other shoe," he said. Before she could find it, the lights went out.

"Never mind that now," she told him. "Get in bed before Tammy comes around for bed check."

"Drat and tarnation," he muttered. "Eighty-seven years old and have to be put to bed like a kid. Melly, when we get out of this place…."

"Never mind! Get in bed, Grover, before she gets here."

Melly crawled into the small, hard bed and pulled the blanket up to her chin. She heard the rustling noises of Grover getting into his own bed a few feet away. They couldn't even sleep together anymore.

"I hear her," Grover whispered. "Squeak, squeak, squeak. Shoes on the tile."

Melly strained to listen but her hearing had faded, just like the blue in her eyes and the rosy bloom on her cheeks. Grover, good old Grover, had the hearing of a teenager, but he depended on Melly's keener eyesight.

The door to their room opened and both lay motionless, eyes closed, faces impassive, even when the flashlight beam danced dimly against closed eyelids. A blink, a twitch, and

Tammy would know. Then she'd make them sleep, whether they wanted to or not. Like Carter, they might get sick and never wake up.

When the door thumped closed, Melly cracked open one eye the tiniest bit. Although the light in their room was controlled from the office, the security lamps outside provided enough illumination through the curtains for her to see Tammy had not lingered to catch them in their deception.

"Okay," she whispered, shoving back her blanket at the same time he did. "There's your shoe, under the edge of the bed."

It took him a minute to put it on and tie it snugly enough to suit him. He always had been persnickety about things like that.

"Forget your perfect bow, Grover. Time's a-wasting."

He grumbled something at her but she couldn't hear it. She didn't care, either. He straightened and brushed his hands down the front of his black jacket.

"You look fine!" she told him, forgetting for a moment to whisper. "We need to beat the pavement."

"See if she's out there."

Melly went to the door and gingerly opened it a crack. Tammy stood at the far end of the corridor, peering into Helen's room. As if Helen would be anywhere but in her bed, where she'd been for the last two years whenever her wasted body wasn't tied in the wheelchair. Melly closed the door silently as Tammy came back down the hallway.

With her ear pressed to the door, she could hear the screaking of the woman's sneakers against the shining white tile as Tammy passed their door. Melly counted slowly to twenty then turned to Grover.

"Let's roll."

• • •

He nodded. Grover went to the window and pulled the curtains wide open so unfiltered light came into their room. He unlocked the sliding window, slid it open and as quietly as possible popped out the screen.

"If they'd ever thought we could do this," he told her in an undertone, "they'd've nailed the windows shut."

Together they removed the three drawers from the small chest and carried the chest to window.

"I'll go first and help you out," Grover said.

"Be careful, hon. Don't fall."

Grover made an impatient gesture with his hand. He settled the black fedora on his head at its typical rakish angle. "I won't fall. Hush, now."

As easily as a man twenty years younger, Grover slipped through the opening and onto the ground.

"You got the pills and the Depends?" he asked her.

She lifted the bag she'd packed earlier that evening.

"Right here." She handed it to him, then tied a black scarf over her head. With both of them dressed all in black, their white hair would shine like beacons in the darkness.

Grover held out one hand. She crawled up on the chest, then edged her way half-way through the window, astraddle the sill. She wasn't as hefty as Tammy, but she wasn't whip slim as her husband, either. Melly knew a moment of panic.

"I don't think my bosoms are going to go through," she whispered loudly.

The light glinted off Grover's teeth as he grinned.

"You always were a fine looking woman, Melvina."

She slapped away his groping fingers.

"You just hang onto my hands!" she said. With considerable wriggling and nearly toppling to the ground, Melly got through the space and stood a moment on trembling legs.

"You okay, honey?" Grover asked.

She took a deep breath. "Fine. Let's go."

Eyeing each window on the side that faced them, she saw

every curtain closed tightly. Lucky for them the office was on the other side of the building. They stole quietly along the edge of the home, staying in the shadow of the Bradford pear trees, and nearly jumped out of their skins when the entry door opened.

"Get down!" Grover whispered. They squatted, pulling their headcoverings closer to their faces. One of the nurses stood a moment, then lit a cigarette and took her time smoking it.

By the time the woman went back inside, Melly figured she'd never be able to stand, but with a heave and a grunt and a tight grip on Grover's bony hand she pulled herself up.

They got past the home but stopped at the edge of the parking lot.

"We'll have to hurry some," he said, "'cause it's bright as daylight out there."

Together they scuttled across the blacktop and reached the sidewalk beyond.

Two blocks from the nursing home, Melly began to relax. It wasn't very late, about nine-thirty, and no one would think it suspicious to see an old couple taking a stroll. Of course, the bag Grover carried might look a bit odd. Well, if anyone asked, they could say it was her knitting. Didn't most people think all old ladies carried their knitting everywhere?

After five more blocks, she was winded. Grover strode along as if he could walk all night. She'd keep up; they were on a mission to stop murder, and she'd not let a little heart palpitation slow them down.

"Up there," he said at last. "There's Doc Kerber's house."

"Then let's hurry, before he goes to bed."

Doctor Kerber opened the door right away and stared at them in considerable surprise.

"What are you two doing here?"

Grover held up the bag.

"We got something for you to look at."

The doctor invited them inside, had them sit down, offered each a glass of water then took the bag. He pulled out two medication bottles and a used Depends, wrapped in a plastic Wal-Mart bag."We think Carter was poisoned, and we think they're trying it on some of the rest of us," Grover said.

"I snuck that Depends out of Carter's trash can. Maybe you can test his pee. And I swiped some of his pills, too. Those other pills belong to Grover and me. We've been cheeking them for a while, because we've been suspicious they might try something like this."

Doctor Kerber gazed at the items and sighed, then he looked at the two of them.

"Well, folks, we've known each other a long time. If you have your suspicions, I'm sure you have good reasons. I'll take these to the lab at the hospital and see what we can find out."

Grover and Melly smiled at each other.

 "Suppose we could spend the night, doc?" Grover asked. "I don't think they'll want us back at the home."

The next morning, as soon as they were up, bathed, dressed and downstairs, Doctor Kerber sat down at the breakfast table with them.

"Grover and Melly," he said, "it won't surprise you to know the lab found Valium in lethal amounts in these capsules." He held up one of the medication bottles, put it down and picked up the other. "They found arsenic in these, and guess what? Arsenic was in Carter's urine. Thanks to you, an investigation is underway as we speak." He looked from one to the other. "So...looks like you two won't be living at Peaceful Manor anymore."

They smiled. Grover held out his hand, and Melly put hers in it.

"That suits us just fine," she said.

Multi-genre author K.D. McCrite has written everything from chapter books and middle-grade fiction for kids to cozy mysteries to paranormal novels to domestic thrillers.

She was the recipient for the 2021 Laura Ingalls Wilder Children's Literature Award. Her book, <u>In Front of God and Everybody</u>, placed in the top twelve for Mark Twain Readers Award, and another of her middle grade novels, <u>Charlotte & Mr. Abernathy</u>, has been nominated for this year's Mark Twain Readers Award.

K.D. was reared on a dairy farm in southern Missouri, and most of her books are set in the Ozark Mountains of Missouri and Arkansas. Readers will find the characters who populate K.D.'s stories are ordinary, everyday people. As the author of more than thirty novels, K.D. feels there is no better life than the life of a writer.

a clockwork mouse

. . .

Gordon Bonnet

J acob Clay was already in a black mood when he got sent to his room by his grandmother early one Saturday morning.

It had been raining for four days straight. Under other circumstances, this wouldn't have been a problem. Had it been summer, rain was just an invitation to run around in the back yard wearing nothing but a pair of shorts, pretending to be stranded on a jungle island, fighting off wild animals, dragons, or cannibals, or possibly all three. But the windy chill of October had settled in, and getting soaking wet when it was forty degrees outside wasn't appealing. Inside, there was only so much time you could spend reading and playing with toys, many of which had outlasted his interest in them. So he had amused himself for a while messing with his grandmother's stuff.

This was always dangerous ground. Grandma Connie was a stern woman with slim patience for children. She could tell a mean ghost story when she was in the mood, but she was not someone who simply enjoyed kids being kids. So when she found Jacob in the living room, playing Jungle Adventure with her collectable porcelain animal statues, and discovered that he had already chipped the unicorn's horn, she promptly sent him to his room with an adjuration to "Stay there until you learn how to respect others' property."

Jacob stomped up the stairs, his face set in a twist of irritation, and plunked himself down on his bed and looked around. There was even less to do here. If he was at loose ends in the whole house, what did Grandma Connie expect him to do when he was confined to his room?

He tried, for about five minutes, to look through one of his books on dinosaurs. Then he dropped that on the floor, and pulled out a box with a jigsaw puzzle with a picture of a puppy on the front. He knew that that one had a piece missing—one of the puppy's ears—and he shoved the box under his bed with his foot. Then he sighed, listening to the rain slashing against the window.

After a moment, he stood up, went to his door, and opened it, and listened carefully. Grandma Connie was down in the kitchen, it sounded like, probably baking. Whatever else you could say about Grandma Connie, her cookies, pies, and cakes were first-class. He heard the clink of measuring cups, and then a drawer opened, and then closed.

Jacob eyed the stairs at the end of the hall. One set led down, back into the living room, where he was certain to get caught if he was heard.

The other set led up to the attic.

It had been a while since he'd been in the attic. It wasn't off-limits, not explicitly, but the one time he'd gone up there alone, his grandmother had said, "What were you doing up there? Cobwebs and old books and spiders and god-alone-knows-what up there. Nothing to interest a ten-year-old boy."

She was sorely misjudging what would be of interest to a ten-year-old boy, of course. Just the fact that it was mysterious, dimly lit, and smelled like dust and antiquity made it attractive. So did the fact that Grandma Connie obviously didn't want him to go up there. What, exactly, was she hiding?

Jacob peered down the hallway. There was no reason he'd get caught, if he was careful. He knew from experience that once he was banished to his room, he was effectively forgotten, at least until lunchtime or dinnertime came. He tiptoed down the hall, and then looked up the stairs to the landing.

The stairs were wooden, and creaked, and he hadn't been up them enough to know which ones were the noisiest. But at that moment, Grandma Connie turned on a blender in the kitchen, and Jacob seized the moment and sprinted up the stairs to the landing, then turned and went up the last set to the closed attic door.

He reached out and turned the doorknob handle, and pulled the door open at the same moment that the noise of the blender ceased. The door hinges made an alarming groaning noise, and he froze, listening for the noise of footsteps. When, after a moment, there was no sound of pursuit, he walked into the attic.

The floorboards squeaked softly under his light tread, as he walked around looking at the bookshelves. There were hundreds, maybe thousands, of books up here—a twenty-volume set called *History of the World*, a set of gardening encyclopedias that looked like they might be antiques, some books written in French and Spanish and Dutch and Swedish. Jacob had heard Grandma Connie talking about her husband, Jacob's grandfather, whom he had never met—Grandpa Charles had been a language professor, "fluent in everything," his mother had once told him, but had died of a heart attack twelve years ago in his classroom. Jacob wished he'd known him. He sounded interesting.

Further along were rows and stacks of boxes. Some of them sounded boring. "Linens." "Christmas Decorations." "China." But then he happened upon one that said, "Toys—Jamie."

Jamie? Who was Jamie? The box was taped shut with strapping tape that was peeling and yellow with age, and the adhesive was mostly crumbly, and bits of it clung to the fingertips like damp flour. He moved some other boxes aside, and pulled it out into the center of the floor, and then pulled the remains of the tape away and opened the flap.

The items inside were old. Jacob knew that immediately. There were stuffed animals, but not the shiny plush of the ones he'd only recently outgrown. These were made of cloth, with button eyes and noses of felt, and when he picked one up, it was heavy and a little stiff, like it was stuffed with sawdust. There was a game called "Bagatelle," which had steel balls in a glass-topped wooden maze; the aim, it seemed, was to move the balls around and drop them down holes. There was a Lionel metal train that looked like it had seen hard service. Its paint was chipped and worn, and the one of the cars was missing the hook to connect it to the next one. Jacob set all of these aside.

In the bottom of the box was a mouse. At first, Jacob thought it was a real mouse, and he felt a little flutter of fear, but very quickly realized his mistake. The mouse wasn't very lifelike. It was small, and white, but made of smooth metal, with painted-on eyes and whiskers. It had wheels instead of feet, and a hole in its back for a key. It, too, was well-worn. There were dings in the enamel, and one of the wheels was a little crooked.

He picked it up, and all of a sudden, all of the angry feelings that had been building in the last weeks coalesced into one furious, needle-sharp thought; here he was, stuck with his grandmother because his parents Needed Time To Talk About Their Relationship, and anyway they had to work during the day, and Grandma Connie didn't even want him around, and now he was stuck with rummaging around in some old junk in the attic to entertain himself.

Bitterly, he tipped the box, and heard a low *thunk*. He

looked in, and saw what it was—the clockwork mouse's key. He took it out, fit the key into the hole, and wound it up, then set the mouse on the floor. It began to scoot around in circles, making rhythmic squeaking noises that actually did sound fairly mouse-like. Something about the way it moved made all the frustrated rage in him bubble to the surface. The mouse seemed to be carving a circular hole in the wood plank floor, a hole in which to pour all of his anger. He felt its creaky little voice say, a voice only he could hear, *Give me your fury, and I will make something of it.*

"I hate this," Jacob said, watching the mouse scurrying in its pointless loops. "I hate everyone. I hate them all, and I especially hate Grandma Connie. I wish she'd fall down and break her leg."

There was a sudden shout and a crash from downstairs, and Jacob looked up, his heart thudding in his chest, as the mouse wound down and stopped moving.

<hr>

Jacob's mom came home from work just as the paramedics were lifting Grandma Connie into the back of the ambulance. One of the paramedics asked Jacob's mom if they wanted to ride in the back of the ambulance to the hospital, which sounded to Jacob like it would be fun, but Grandma Connie said, her voice thin with pain, "No, Eva, can you just clean up the kitchen? I don't want..." She glanced at Jacob, and Jacob knew she meant, "I don't want him bothering me when I have a broken leg." Then Grandma Connie looked at Jacob's mom and said, "You can come down later."

So Jacob's mom brought him back inside, and gave him a big hug through her tears and told him what a brave, smart boy he was, that he remembered how to call 911 and kept his head and took care of Grandma Connie. Then she looked around her at the kitchen, wiped her eyes with the back of her hand, and said, "Well. We better get this cleaned up, and then we'll go down to the hospital and see how Grandma is doing."

The little step-stool that Grandma Connie used to reach high shelves lay on its side, and a glass mixing bowl was in sharp, multicolored fragments all over the linoleum. Another bowl, with eggs and milk and cream and molasses, sat forlornly on the counter. Jacob's mom got a broom, and told Jacob to go put on shoes so his feet wouldn't get cut. Then they cleaned up the kitchen. Jacob had a momentary hope that his mom would finish making whatever it was that Grandma Connie had been working on, but she upturned the mixing bowl with the eggs and everything over the sink, and ran some water into it, and then said, "I need to call your aunt and uncle and let them know what happened."

Jacob went back upstairs, and heard just the beginning of the conversation, "Hi, Susan? It's Eva. I'm calling to let you know there's been an accident. Mom fell in her kitchen... yes, she's going to be fine, but she broke her leg. She's been taken to St. Stephen's. We'll be going down soon... Jacob was home, he called 911... yes, he is..."

The voices faded as he walked back up to the attic. The door was still standing open. He saw his footprints on the dusty floor, the barefoot impression of toes, sole, heel, leading along the bookshelves and then to the box of toys, which still lay scattered on the floor. He looked down at the clockwork mouse, still now, its painted eyes staring up at him.

He looked at it for a long time, without moving. The key still protruded from its back, and he could just see beneath it the misaligned wheels that had sent it in wild circles earlier. He reached down, and picked it up, held it in his hand.

"What else can you do?" he asked it solemnly.

It didn't answer.

"Jacob!" he heard his mom's voice calling from downstairs. "Let's go. We need to go to the hospital, and see how Grandma is doing."

"Coming!" he shouted, but never took his eyes off the mouse.

Then he thought of the way the weekend was being eaten up. His grandmother ruining the morning by sending him to his room, and now he was going to have to spend the afternoon at the hospital. He'd been to the hospital before, when his Great-Aunt Judith had been dying of liver cancer, and mostly what he remembered was the smell of antiseptic and the color white and the boredom, great crashing hours of boredom, sitting still and waiting for it all to be over so he could go home. And now, his precious weekend was being taken again, and looming on the horizon of Monday morning was the bulky frame of Mrs. Marshall, his fourth grade teacher, whom he and his classmates couldn't stand. Mrs. Marshall seemed to leer at him, waiting, waiting for him to leave the attic so she could confine him to his seat and make him multiply and add and read stupid stories about the Pilgrims and write down answers on stupid worksheets.

"Jacob!" his mother called again.

Jacob quickly wound up the mouse, and said, "I hope Mrs. Marshall gets really sick." Then he set down the mouse on the floor, and let it run its squeaky circles by itself. He ran downstairs to his bedroom, and was just putting on his jacket when his mother came up to see what was keeping him.

***

Mrs. Marshall did not show up to school Monday. The sub, Miss McLaughlin, let them have free read for as long as they wanted to, brought her guitar and sang songs with them, and art class ran a half-hour over into math before she realized what had happened.

When Mrs. Marshall still hadn't returned by Thursday, the

principal, Mrs. Stefanovic, came into the class with a grave expression and said that Mrs. Marshall was in the hospital with pneumonia, and probably wouldn't be back for a while, but not to worry because she was already improving. The children, Mrs. Stefanovic said, could help her get better by spending art class designing a big card to send to Mrs. Marshall in the hospital. Miss McLaughlin said they'd be happy to.

Jacob walked home that day, thinking about how he would destroy the clockwork mouse when he got home.

Maybe he could bury it in the back yard. It'd rust and the wheels would stick and even if someone found it, it wouldn't run. Then he thought about taking a hammer to it, watching the frame dent, the eyes skew, as the springs and gear wheels that drove its axles came flying out. Then it'd never run again. It'd never hurt anyone again.

Then, another thought came to him: *What if the mouse won't let you destroy it? What if it tries to kill you?*

But this was such an awful idea that he started to repeat to himself the mantra he always used when he'd been scared at night when he was little—*not real, not real, none of that scary stuff is real.* And by the time he got home, he *had* convinced himself. None of it was real. He hadn't caused Grandma Connie's accident; he hadn't caused Mrs. Marshall's pneumonia. There was no need to break the mouse, any more than destroying his book *Ten Terrifying Ghost Stories* would have made any difference to what he dreamed at night, alone in the dark.

Grandma Connie came home from the hospital three days after her fall. She'd had surgery to pin her leg bone where it was broken, and Jacob's mom had said, "Falls at that age are never easy to heal from." Grandma Connie was sterner and crankier than ever, and Jacob seemed to spend most of the time he wasn't at school getting her tea, glasses of water, toast with butter, and turning the television off or on, turning the volume up or down. When Jacob's mom came over to have dinner with them, which she did every three evenings or so, she never stayed long.

Jacob didn't mention about Mrs. Marshall being sick.

Friday night, Jacob's mom came for dinner, and after cleaning up the dinner dishes and helping Grandma Connie to her recliner, she took Jacob aside.

"Jacob, honey," she began, and then stopped.

Jacob tensed. His mother never called him "honey" unless it was bad news. She'd called him that when his other grandmother, Grandma Abigail, had died. She'd called him that when she'd told him he was going to live with his grandmother while she and Jacob's dad Worked On Their Relationship.

"What, mom?" Jacob said, his voice shaking a little.

"Your dad and I... we've decided it's for the best for everyone if, well, if we live apart. Your dad... he's been seeing someone. Her name is Cecile, and he's going away to live with her. He's moving to Baltimore."

"He just *left* me?" Jacob's voice came out a squeak, like the wheels of the clockwork mouse. "Will I... will I get to see him?"

"Yes, of course. When he's moved in and settled. He left this morning, and we'll... you'll... go and visit him soon." She tried to smile, and failed. "But it means that you will come back to live with me again. I know you'll miss your Grandma Connie, but..."

Jacob jumped up, ran out of the room, ignored his mother's cry of, "Jacob, honey, wait...", ignored his grandmother's annoyed exclamation as he ran through the living room, passed the cabinet with the porcelain animal statues, and up the stairs. He didn't pause by his bedroom door, but continued up to the attic, slamming the door behind him, pulling the chain that turned on the single light bulb hanging by a cord from the ceiling, setting it swinging, making crazy rocking shadows move across the walls and floor.

The clockwork mouse was still where it had run down from the last time; no one had been up here since. Breathing hard, his face pinched with anger, Jacob grabbed the mouse, and wound it up. He hadn't even set it down before he snarled, "I hope my dad gets in a car crash on his way to Baltimore and has to stay in the hospital for five years."

The mouse's wheels had only begun squeaking before Jacob's mom appeared in the attic door, and she said, gently, "Jacob, honey, come downstairs. We need to talk. It's going to be okay."

Jacob stood, hearing the clockwork mouse skittering over the floorboards behind him, and went to her, thinking bleakly, *She's lying to me, and she knows she's lying. It will never be okay.*

When the call came the next morning, Jacob wasn't really surprised.

He was up in his room, still in his pajamas, playing with his old GameBoy. He tensed when the phone rang, and listened – and he heard his mom say, "Oh, God, oh, no," and start crying.

Her appearance at his door ten minutes later, with a tremulous, "Jacob, honey, there's been an accident," was met with a blank stare. He already knew what she was going to say.

After that, it took hours before he had time to escape, unnoticed, to the attic. Family and friends came over, everyone wanted to talk to him and comfort him and reassure him. Even Grandma Connie tried to be nice to him, offering to read him a story. But eventually he was able to get away, and he walked barefoot up to the attic, crossed the floor to where the toy box was.

The clockwork mouse still sat there, its emotionless eyes looking up at him.

"You did all this," he said to the mouse.

The mouse said nothing, just kept staring at him.

He picked up the key, and wound it three times, feeling the springs tense as they coiled inside the metal body. Jacob looked at the mouse, and said, "I wish everything bad that has happened would be gone. Grandma Connie's broken leg, Mrs. Marshall's pneumonia, and my dad… being in a coma." His voice broke a little on the last one, but he was able to finish the sentence, and he set the mouse down, and listened to its little squeaks as the mechanism inside it propelled it around on the floor.

He watched it until it stopped moving, and he stood completely still for a while. Surely, soon there would be some kind of shout from Grandma Connie that her leg was miraculously healed, the phone ringing that his father was awake and was going to be okay?

Nothing happened.

It hadn't worked. Alarm shuddered its way through his body. Maybe it could only do bad things.

"You did all this," he said again, anger rising in his voice. He picked the mouse up, held it close to his face, and a thought came, seeming to come from outside him: *No. You did. You did all this. Your anger. Your rage. You. Not me. And once done, things cannot be undone. You chose, and that is all.*

"No," Jacob said. "It was you. Why? Why did you do it?"

He looked into the mouse's eyes, searching for some sign of life, some sign of recognition that he existed, but its expression was as lifeless as ever.

I am only guilty as a knife used to slay a man is guilty. I was only the tool that you used. The fury that accomplished it came from you.

"Who was Jamie? Did he turn you evil?"

I do not remember him. If I was simply a child's toy once, that is done now.

"I'll destroy you," he whispered to it.

It won't change anything. You will still have done what you have done, even if the tool you used is broken.

Jacob fell to his knees. A pair of tears slid down his cheeks, unnoticed. He said to the mouse, "What can I do?"

Nothing. It is too late.

Jacob inserted the key into the mouse's back. As he wound it up, he heard his mother call to him, "Jacob, honey, where are you?"

He shouted, automatically, "Coming, mom," and continued to wind.

Too late. I have done what I have done, and it is too late. Too late for Grandma Connie, too late for Mrs. Marshall, too late for my dad. And too late for me.

The springs reached full tension. He set the mouse down, and said, "I wish I was dead."

The mouse started its chittering run, and Jacob felt a sensation of being lifted. He was on his feet, turning toward the stairs. And he thought, *It was lying. The mouse was lying. It's not just a tool; it's evil.*

He felt his legs being forced to move. A part of his brain shouted, *Stop! Stop!* but his body wouldn't obey. It was a monumental effort to resist it, but he was able to turn and snatch the clockwork mouse up from the floor. He felt its wheels turning frantically, their vibrations tickling his palm, and that was all his conscious will could do. His feet began to move, walking, then running, toward the top of the stairs, not pausing as the precipice approached.

He saw the open door, and outside it the narrow staircase,

rush toward him, and with a last desperate shout he hurled the clockwork mouse against the wall. He heard it strike the metal hinge of the door frame, and saw it explode, wheels, cogs, and springs flying into the air about him. The desperate force pushing him stopped suddenly. His frame relaxed, and a smile crossed Jacob's face, but his momentum shot him forward like an arrow from a bow. His body, as graceful as a high diver, flung forward into the air, and he fell headlong down the stairs.

the pool of ink

. . .

Gordon Bonnet

It wasn't until the ninth lash that Fernán Sorel cried out, and he didn't weep until the eighteenth. He had told himself, when they said he was to be flogged, that he would not beg them for mercy, not scream at them to stop. And he made it to the thirtieth lash with at least that much of his dignity intact.

After the flogging was finished they left him strung up by his wrists for several minutes, then a man came with a knife and cut the cords. Sorel looked over at him through eyes still blurred with tears, and it was a moment before he recognized him.

"Joanet," Sorel said. "What the hell are you doing here?"

Gaston Joanet did not answer, but took Sorel by the upper arm and propelled him from the room, down a long hallway paved with stone flags, and then down some deeply-shadowed stairs.

"You are helping these bastards?" Sorel asked, and still Joanet did not answer. "You and I went to school together. You knew the rebel songs better than I did!"

Joanet looked over at him—just a brief glance, and their eyes met. He looked away almost instantly, and still didn't say anything, but in that moment Sorel knew. Joanet had sided with the militia, with the men who had raped Sorel's sister, struck his father in the face as he was leaving church, and taken Sorel himself from his home and given him thirty lashes simply for having been at the university, and he had done so out of nothing but fear. Joanet, for all of his size and muscle and bluster, was a coward at heart.

"You must get a message to my father, tell him I am alive."

Joanet opened a wooden door with a ring set in the middle, and shoved Sorel through it. He stumbled down two more steps, then his feet touched earth and he fell forward onto damp ground.

The door closed behind him, shutting out every trace of light. But in the moment the hinges creaked as the massive wooden plank slammed shut, he heard Joanet utter three words, whispered as if he didn't even want that much overheard.

"I am sorry."

Sorel lay for a time on the cool earth of the cell. He was still shirtless, and his shoulders and back were lacerated and aching. He finally stood, and went to the door. He knew it was fruitless, but hope being what it is, he had to test it.

The door did not budge, and in fact seemed to have no handle on the inside. It was made as a prison, to hold a man until his captors decided otherwise.

Sorel placed his ear against the wood, but either it was too thick to hear through, or else there was no one nearby. Possibly both. He then took a slow circuit of the room, clockwise, and found nothing but what he'd encountered at first—a dirt floor, stone walls, and complete and utter darkness.

He reached the door after a few minutes, and realized that he was exhausted. He had no energy left in his young body after being seized the previous night, awakened from a sound sleep, followed by the drumhead court that morning during which he'd been found guilty of collaboration and sentenced to be whipped. The worst was the waiting, from the time the sentence was pronounced until they took him into the court-yard, stripped him to the waist, and tied his wrists. He had almost fainted several times from the sheer terror of what was to be done to him. The actual flogging, when it came, was almost a relief, when after a dozen strokes he thought, *This is horrible, but I can survive it. I will not beg them to stop.*

Sorel lay down on his belly, folded his arms beneath his cheek—his cut shoulders burning as he brought his arms up —and was asleep within minutes.

He awoke, who knew how many hours later in that unchanging night, with a full bladder. He stood, feeling the scabbed-over welts crack as he moved, and looked for a basin or bucket in which to relieve himself. Finding none, he peed in a corner, kicked some dirt over the wet patch, and went back to his spot near the door, still warm from his body's heat, and sat down.

He squinted into the darkness until he had a headache, and finally closed his eyes, but phantom lights and shapes still floated in his vision. The silence, too, was unnerving. He had never been in a place so completely silent before, without even the rustle of the wind or a distant bird's song to remind him that he was still in the world of men. Here, he might have been blind and deaf, and there would have been no way to tell.

After a time, he stood, and decided to take another walk around his prison, trailing his fingers on the rough stone. When he reached the door again, he found that someone had slid a platter with a cup of water and a large piece of bread through a hatch in the base of the door. The hatch was low and rectangular, and like the door only to be opened from the outside Sorel pressed his eye to the edge, trying to find even a flicker of light, but it was too well sealed. He saw only the ghosts of his own memory of vision, and finally gave up.

A day later fever set in, and Sorel spent hours hugging his knees, moaning and shivering in the cool darkness. He raved for a time, imagining himself still hanging by the wrists, the whip still cutting lines into his skin, but had periods of sense when he knew that the pain was infection and swelling as his cuts tried to heal. Eventually the fever broke. One morning he woke, ravenously thirsty, and the throbbing ache in his back had finally subsided. He was weak, and drenched with sweat, but knew that he was not going to die, at least not from the flogging.

He cleared his throat, and crawled his way to the door, feeling for the water and bread that his captors put there every day, always while he was asleep. He downed the lukewarm water at a gulp, and said—it may have been the first words he uttered since he'd been thrown into the cell—"It's so good."

And an answering voice from the darkness said, "It's so good."

Sorel whirled around, dropping the bread into the dirt, not that it mattered much. "Who is there?" he said, in a choked whisper.

"Who is there?" the voice said. It repeated what he said, but its tone was not mocking. It could have meant anything.

"I am Sorel. When did you come here? I thought... I thought I was alone."

"Alone," the voice said.

"What is your name?"

"My name..." it said, and then paused.

"Yes. I am Fernán Sorel. I have been here for..." He stopped. "I do not know. Days. Weeks, perhaps."

"Weeks," the voice said. "I do not know. Weeks. More."

"But," Sorel said, hesitating, "I have been alone. Were you in another cell?"

The voice did not respond for a moment. "They hurt you," it finally said.

"Yes. I was flogged. But I am healing. I thought I might die, down here. I took sick with a fever from the whipping, but I seem to be healing."

"Others have died," the voice said. It sounded sad.

"Yes. Pernal and his brothers were hanged. They were imprisoned and finally hanged."

"Hanged," the voice said. "Terrible."

"I am afraid that they might have the same in mind for me. Seeing how their first attempt to kill me failed."

"You will not be hanged." The voice sounded more confident than it had.

"How do you know? And your name… you never told me your name."

"Give me some of your bread, and I will tell you my name."

Sorel stooped and picked up the fallen loaf, and tore it in half. "Here." He felt an unseen hand take the offered piece. "I would give you all of it, in exchange for the company. I have been here in this pool of ink, alone, for far too long."

"Pool of ink?" the voice said, a bit indistinct because its mouth was full.

"I have come to call it that. Do you not feel it? The darkness… it is not like the ordinary darkness of night, where darkness is an absence, something that can be changed by lighting a candle. Here, it is a positive substance, like ink. Do you not have the feeling that if a candle was lit here, the darkness would snuff it, like trying to light a candle under water?"

"Yes," the voice said. "It is so."

Sorel shuddered, hearing his companion agree so flatly. While at the university, Sorel and his friends had enjoyed intellectual arguments, comparing one thing to the other, topping each other's metaphors and similes to see who could construct the most absurd one. He had only meant, when he was alone—or thought he was?—in this prison cell, to create a way to think about the darkness around him, but he had been playing a game, until now. Now his companion's simple acquiescence had made the metaphor a reality. He had the sudden unshakeable conviction that if he left his cell his skin would be stained black from his weeks of being submerged.

"What is your name?"

The voice replied, softly, "I am called Guilhemet."

"And why are you here in prison, Guilhemet?"

"Why are you?"

Sorel shrugged. Even that motion would have been painful a few days ago, but his skin was knitting back together. "Because I think wrongly, I guess."

"Thinking wrongly," Guilhemet said, "is no sin."

"It was enough to earn me a beating from my captors."

"Then the more fools they."

"I suppose. But fools or no, they are in power." He swallowed. "If they tie a rope around my neck," Sorel said, and he felt a nauseating clench of fear at the thought, "and swing me from a tree, I don't think it will matter much whether they are fools or not."

"Maybe," Guilhemet said. "But you are wrong about why they whipped you."

"Oh? Why did they do it, then?"

"They did it for the same reason that all men do what they do. Because they can." Guilhemet paused. "And in this case, because they do not know what else to do. You are one man, and have opinions they don't like. Because you are one man, they could flog you and no one could stop them. So they did it."

"But surely they know that torturing me won't change my mind."

Guilhemet gave a dry laugh. "You think they care about that? This is not the university. They are not teachers or philosophers; they are fools who have guns and swords and whips. Ideas are only ideas, but whips can hurt you, and guns and swords can kill you. Learned men say an idea is more powerful than a weapon, but I think that is because few learned men have ever received a whipping."

The days passed, then weeks, trackless and smooth and unmarked. Sorel slept and waked, ate and drank, and finally felt well enough to keep his strength up by running laps around the perimeter of his cell. Guilhemet shared Sorel's meager meals, and talked to him sometimes. Sometimes he spoke wisely, and his words kept Sorel's spirits up. Other times, he seemed to babble foolishness, singing snatches of songs that Sorel could remember from his childhood, telling tales of talking animals and wise foresters and lost princes, beginning them in the middle and then trailing off before the end. Sometimes he seemed angry or maudlin, and wanted nothing to do with Sorel at all.

One time, Sorel heard Guilhemet weeping softly, and came to him in the center of the cell.

"What is it, Guilhemet? Why do you weep?"

He did not answer, but continued to sob softly.

Sorel went to him, knelt next to him, and reached out and found the man's shoulders. Like Sorel's own, they were bare, and as he put an arm around them, he felt raised scars—he had been flogged once, too, it seemed.

"Don't be sad, Guilhemet," Sorel said. "We will be free one day. Like you said once—free one way, or free the other. We will leave this cell and walk back to our homes, or we will walk to the gallows and be freed by death to what waits beyond. Either way, they cannot hold us forever."

"Afraid." Guilhemet rocked back and forth. "I am so afraid."

"I am as well. Or, I was. I don't feel afraid right now, but I have been. I surely will be again. Do not let your fear unman you. We can face it, whatever it is they have in store for us."

"They have hanged others, many others, while we have been in here. Tortured men, raped women. It is evil here, it is evil out there. All is evil."

"Not all," Sorel said. "I am not. You are not. There is much that is bad, but there is much that is good; and the evil cannot triumph, not forever."

But Guilhemet's sobs became louder, and he would not speak again, for a long time. Finally he lay down, and Sorel lay next to him, one arm still encircling him, and they slept curled up together like two stray dogs, needing only warmth and a kind touch.

"Sorel," Guilhemet said one morning. There was no way to know what time of day it was. Sorel had weeks ago become convinced that after he woke up it was morning, and decided that it didn't matter one way or the other if he was wrong.

"Yes?" Sorel yawned. He went over to the door, but the day's food wasn't there yet.

"You will get out soon."

"How do you know that?"

"Things are changing outside, out there."

Sorel snorted. "How do you know that, being that you are in here with me, here in the dark?"

"The pool of ink. But I can see out."

Sorel sighed. It was going to be one of Guilhemet's less lucid days, he could tell that. "How can you see out? How can you see anything? And through stone walls? You have powerful magic, Guilhemet. You should use some of it to get us the hell out of here."

"It does not work that way. But do not forget me. Promise me that you will not forget me."

"I promise." Sorel shook his head in confusion. "Why would I forget you? You saved my mind, you made this bearable." He laughed at himself. "Listen to me, talking like it's over. You know, Guilhemet, when we get out you should become a lawyer; you have a way of making the most absurd statements sound absolutely convincing."

Guilhemet did not respond.

"Guilhemet?" Sorel said, and felt his way forward.

At that moment, there was a searing light, like a lightning bolt across his eyes, and he cried out and fell to his knees, thinking that he had been struck down by God. But it was only the door opening, and a line of gentle light from outside appearing as it swung open. And as he knelt, unable to open his eyes, strong hands pulled him to his feet and dragged him up out of his cell and into the flagstone hallway and out into the courtyard, where the full light of the summer sun struck his face. He was propelled out through doorways and finally into the streets of the city, where he was left, shirtless and filthy and barefoot, and his captors fled back the way they had come before he could even see who they were.

He started back toward the fort where he had been imprisoned, but he saw people coming toward him—crowds of men and women and children, rich and poor alike, and there was gunfire. A man caught Sorel by the arm and said, "You! Beggar man! You'd better clear out of here, the rebels are about to take the fortress! You'll be killed!"

Sorel turned to look, but there was the explosion of a cannon shot, and the doorway through which he had just come was blasted to rubble. Terrified, he turned and ran.

The rebels smashed the remnants of the militia that had held the town, and the men who had tortured and imprisoned Sorel were one by one rounded up and made to suffer the same way he had. Such is the way of the world, Guilhemet had once said, that sometimes it is hard to tell who is the hero and who is the villain, they look so much alike. Sorel went back to the fortress as soon as it was safe, and asked about other prisoners, asked if there had been a man named Guilhemet who had shared his cell. No one had heard of him. The cell itself was destroyed in the sack of the fort—if he had been there when it fell, his bones now lay mouldering under tons of stone.

But I will not forget, Sorel thought, not so long as I live. I will not forget what you did for me.

Sorel found what remained of his family. His father had survived, as had his sister and older brother. They had come off better than many, and still had a house and land to farm. Three years after his release, he fell in love with a girl from a neighboring town. As he was making love to her for the first time, she ran her fingers across the ridged scars on his back, and his skin quivered a little, like a horse's skin when a fly lands on it.

"Does it hurt you?" she asked, as they moved together in the dark.

"No," Sorel said. "There is no pain. In all the world right now, there is nothing but sweetness and pleasure."

And the pleasure was very great, so they married the following year, that they might have more of it whenever they desired. Sorel moved to his wife's town, where her father had need of a foreman for his vineyard. And Sorel became the vintner after him, and did not return to his home town for many years.

Sorel came back the year after his wife died, in his own seventy-seventh year. He was still healthy and strong, his only concessions to age a cane and a pair of eyeglasses that he needed in order to read. He felt drawn to the town where he was born, now that his wife was gone. He saw his sons and grandchildren often, but without her there was time to think, time to remember, although the scars she had caressed had healed to fine white lines, like a spiderweb on the tanned skin of his back.

So he had come home. The central square was quiet now, with families and merchants and pairs of young lovers; there was a fountain in the center, and a small garden with benches. The old fortress wall had been rebuilt, but now housed shop fronts. There was no trace of the building where he had been flogged and imprisoned.

All for the best. Would that all evil could be so quickly, and completely, buried.

But also buried there, somewhere, were his friend Guilhemet's bones. Perhaps they were beneath this very garden, nourishing the flowers, as Sorel's own bones soon would as well. It was good that things take such paths, that the world turns and light comes and goes, and all comes around once again.

"Sorel?" a creaking voice said, a little incredulously. "Is that you? Fernán Sorel?"

Sorel squinted up against the light at a man who stood, leaning on a cane, next to him. "I am Fernán Sorel."

"Can you not recognize me?" the man said. "It is Gaston. Gaston Joanet."

Sorel's heart pounded in his chest. "Joanet."

Joanet moved stiffly toward the edge of the bench. "May I sit?"

"Of course."

Joanet sat down heavily, and then looked over toward Sorel. "When I saw you, I could not believe it. But you have not changed that much, you know."

"Nor you, now that I see you properly."

The two old men looked out over the city square without speaking for a moment.

"I am sorry," Joanet said. "For what happened to you. When I saw you, I knew I had to say at least that. Now, if you want to tell me to go to hell, I will not argue with you."

"Why would I do that? You could not have stopped what happened. You simply would have shared my fate."

"It would have been better. I could have endured the whip. I know that now. It would have been better than spending the last fifty years knowing that I am a coward."

Sorel shrugged. "It is in the past, my friend. We will have a glass of wine together, and it will be over. Who is the coward, you or I? I would have gone mad had it not been for Guilhemet, you know. I was terrified that I would be hanged, or worse still, left in that cell to starve."

"Guilhemet?" Joanet said. "Who is that?"

"The man who was in the cell with me. He was imprisoned shortly after I was, and died during the siege of the fort. At least I presume he did, as the fort was destroyed hours after I was freed."

"Sorel," Joanet said, "there was no man there with you in the cell."

Sorel looked at Joanet as if he were mad. "Have you lost your memory, Joanet? He was there. I spoke with him, I gave him comfort when he despaired, as he did to me. I shared my food with him. He spoke with me every day, until the day I was released."

Joanet looked at Sorel, his face a study in astonishment. "I swear, Sorel. I swear by the holy blood of Jesus. You were alone in that cell. I brought you the food and water—as much as I was allowed. I was commanded not to speak to you, on pain of flogging, and I did not. I was so afraid to suffer your fate, I dreamed of your ordeal sometimes, I thought I would go mad if they did that to me." He shook his head. "Sorel, you were alone. The whole time. Four months, and there never was another man there."

Sorel looked at Joanet, staring into his wide, amazed eyes, eyes that looked more than a little frightened. "I speak the truth; nothing less than the simple, honest truth. There was someone in the cell with me."

Joanet crossed himself twice, and kissed his fingertips. "Sorel," he said in a hushed voice. "I think you were visited by God."

Sorel looked up at the clear, blue sky, filled with the warm light of day. "I tell you, Joanet," he said finally, "if you are right, then part of what the priests have said is true—that God is good. However, what they have never told us is that God is also mad—and the world is as well."

Gordon Bonnet got his start telling stories when he was six years old and hasn't stopped since. He is the author of over twenty novels, including tales of magical realism, murder mysteries, and historical fiction. His most recent publications, a sweeping trilogy called <u>The Arc of the Oracles</u> that spans almost fourteen hundred years, left one reader saying, "It's somewhere beyond gripping—absolutely impossible to put down."

When he's not writing, he can be found involved in his other passions, which are music, gardening, running, and making pottery. He lives in rural upstate New York with his wife and three completely spoiled dogs. You can find out more about him at gordonbonnet.com.

be your best

. . .

D. T. Griffith

Todd's asshole boss deducted from his bonus for an IT issue that occurred during an internal CEO webcast. Why? Todd wasn't in IT. He couldn't wrap his head around it.

"Because corporate didn't like your presentation deck and someone has to take the hit," Gavin said softly while staring beyond Todd's shoulder at the portrait of the company's founder during his annual review. It's not like Todd didn't do everything right, he was only responsible for supplying the deck, but Gavin obviously didn't care. So, the five-thousand-dollar bonus he was counting on to take his fiancée to the Bahamas in April for her birthday became three thousand eight hundred dollars before taxes.

"Thanks for screwing up my life," Todd said, standing up.

Gavin smirked. "It is what it is. And one word of advice – pay more attention to *our* corporate reality if you want to get ahead."

"Sure," Todd said as he exited the conference room.

"Be glad you're not on the IT team," Gavin called out after

Todd. "Someone's head is about to roll for that town hall fuck up."

At home, Todd broke the bonus news to Jenna. "But this is how it always is in corporate America," Todd said justifying the cut. "Yesterday we received a memo that said no one would get their bonuses on time either."

Jenna looked up from her patience management self-help book. "Wait … what?"

Todd shrugged. "I won't have the money until April fifteenth at the earliest. Maybe mid-May."

"We are supposed to leave on April tenth," Jenna said. "Do you even have room on a credit card to cover this?" Todd sensed the venom pooling in her saliva, dripping with menace, malice, and malaise. He knew that scowl that made the left corner of her mouth drop, that joyless full-bodied tone in her voice; it was time to disappear into the loft with the sixty-inch flat screen and the new Call of Duty for the next six hours. At least till she drank herself to sleep.

"Um, yeah, I suppose I could make something work with my cards, but that's what HR said."

"Those assholes!" She paused to drain half her glass of wine in one mouthful. "How're we supposed to pay for this trip, Todd?"

"I thought you had money, too."

She glared at him.

"Dammit, I'll put it on my cards!" Todd put his head down and both hands in the front pockets of his khakis. His wispy blond hair dropped over his eyes. According to one of Jenna's many rants, delivering and handling bad news was not and never will be his forte.

"You're gonna make this right, Todd?" Jenna sat up and threw the book past Todd's head. It landed with a loud flop in the stairway leading down to their condo's front door on the other side of the living room. "Tomorrow, you march right into your HR office and fix this."

"I'll try."

"You better more than try," Jenna said, clenching her teeth, "if you want this relationship to work." All Todd needed for the relationship to work was her hot body and her good side, which rarely showed itself anymore since moving in together, but he never dared mention it.

The next morning, Todd wiped his mouth with the back of his hand after kissing Jenna on her sweaty forehead. She laid in bed nursing a headache and sick stomach following a nightlong bout with food poisoning. And a hangover judging from the empty wine bottles he found next to her on the chaise at four AM when he escorted her to bed.

"You should really have thrown out that sushi from Saturday," he said as he readied himself for work. Jenna admitted to indulging in the leftover bag she found in the fridge. She said she was too pissed off at him about the bonus and too caught up in her second bottle of cabernet to care about the sushi's weird odor.

Todd decided it was a good morning to take solace in her misery. He showered in the guest bathroom, as Jenna had previously declared the master bathroom was off-limits to him in case she had an emergency.

He arrived at work to the rumblings and whispers of coworkers complaining to each other over cubicle walls as he walked to his desk. He opened his email to find a new urgent memo from HR. It had been sent out around midnight.

Dearest Corporate Family,

We hope your week is going well and look forward to another positive and productive day!

It is with mixed feelings of pride and a sense of obligation that we inform you that we received the direction to redact your annual reviews and eliminate your annual bonuses for this fiscal year. That said, as we can empathize with a heavy heart the disappointment you must sense in the pits of your stomachs, you are hereby invited by request to attend developmental meetings with our new HR Leader of Talent & Emotional Development, who (whom?) we just hired away from our competitor at a steep, but somewhat reasonable price.

Please welcome Erin Winslow to our family. She will occupy the corner office that overlooks the park and riverfront in the HR Suite. A Meet & Greet is scheduled for 12:00PM today. All employees are required to skip lunch and attend of course, otherwise, well, you don't really want to know now, do you? LOL! That said, please enjoy your business day here in the BYB office where we do every-thing right!!!

Be Your Best,
  HR Management
  BYB Technology

"Those assholes!" Todd shouted at his computer screen.

"Todd, shut up," whispered Christabel, his teammate and cubicle neighbor to the left, "they'll hear you."

"Sorry Christabel, but I've had it." He wiped both hands across his eye sockets and brow. "Had it!"

"What do you expect? They don't care about us."

"What's the problem over here, Todd, hmmm?" asked Gavin.

Todd spun around; he felt the challenge. "Oh, you really wanna know?"

"Todd, watch it," Christabel said.

Gavin smirked that stupid smirk he always smirked when he knew he had the upper hand. "Christabel's right, Todd, watch the *'tude*, dude."

"Huh?" Todd blinked hard and turned to completely face his boss. "*Tude*, dude?"

"Todd, let me explain something about working here at BYB – this is a battle zone, you dig? And things are never easy here. Hell, I can't remember the last time my job was easy or enjoyable. But you know what? *Disubordination* is not tolerated among any employees below manager status, particularly on my team." Gavin peered slowly to his left and then to his right, his eyes focused on Christabel's silk blouse throughout the full movement.

Christabel crossed her arms high, middle finger raised on the hand closest to her neck. "Fuck off, man. I will go to HR."

Todd was stupefied. "*Disubordination?* Is that even a word?"

"Whether it is or isn't, it is in the eye of the beholder," Gavin said with his hand outstretched, palm facing up, "but who are we as humans to say what is or isn't language, what words are supposed to mean, you know?" He snatched at the air with confidence to accentuate the "you know" and turned away from Todd. With a final glance at Christabel, Gavin crept backwards and disappeared into the nearby conference room doorway.

"What the hell was that?"

"Fuckin' creep," Christabel said. "He was leering at me the whole time."

"Better tell HR," Todd said, "even though I doubt they'll care. I'll go with you to corroborate your story if you want."

"Could he be more obvious? I mean, his eyes were trained on my chest."

"Really? I thought he was admiring your manicure."

Christabel laughed. "Screw you, Todd." Her mood hardened. "This is serious, though, it keeps happening."

An hour later, amidst an unproductive morning of employees fuming over their lost bonuses and Christabel's frustration in finding anyone in HR who would listen, another emailed memo landed in everyone's inbox.

Good morning team BYB!

Are we being our best?!?!?! And ... wait for it ... are we winning??? (LOL)

We here in management hope you are having a great day. Again, we empathize with you, all our lower-tier staff members, for your sudden and unexpected redaction of unsecured bonus compensation. Alas, it is not for us to judge, as the universe dictates our fate and our destinies and leads us through the shadow of the valley of death in these tough economic times. Who are we to define the unexplainable? That is unless you are upper management, for which then you don't need to continue reading the wonderful message that follows.

P.S. Upper Management: Enjoy your new perks! We're tickled!

As part of our sorrowful heavy-weighted souls filled with concrete, anguish, and lost opportunities, our new Talent & Emotional Development Leader, Erin Winslow, has agreed with Mr. Edwards (our corporate CEO if you're new to BYB, in that case, Welcome!) to have a sit-down with each and every one of you to determine whether you are cut from the right cloth to make a difference.

So, ask yourself, our new favorite question of the month this month: Are we winning?

If your answer is YES, then you just might be from the right fabric to excel a few steps beyond where you find yourself now. Not just any nylon fabric, mind you, but a fine polyester-silk blend. However, if it is a resounding YES, and not just a meager whispered yes with shrugged shoulders, then get ready for a half-level promotion! Look out, upper management! (LOL!) But there is a catch — like a catch 22 with a .22, you could say — we need to reduce your pay by 5.7%. However, only by 5.2% if one of you is willing to take one for the team and accept a 5-month severance today, but only before 5:00 tonight.

The choice is yours, team, who will it be?

Gratefully yours,
   Stan
   Business Unit President, HR Management & Senior Team Liaison
   P.S. As we all like to say here at BYB Tech – Be Your Best!!!

As Todd finished reading the last sentence, he heard glass shatter. He looked up to see Jeremy Wright, the quiet guy in Program Management who sat on the other side of the office space, shouting and throwing a stapler and other unidentifiable implements from his desk at an inner-office window. Gavin and another senior level manager, Bradley, whose last name and title were a mystery to most everyone in the cubicle farm, quickly escorted Jeremy, each holding an arm, to the elevator. Todd wasn't sure, but he thought he saw Gavin holding a small gun to Jeremy's back.

"Unbelievable," Todd muttered.

"This is bullshit," Christabel added, watching the same scene.

"Can this day get any worse? Guess I should call Jenna and give her an update." Todd sat down and picked up his mobile phone. Jenna answered on the fourth ring.

"What," she said followed by a muffled groan.

"How're you feeling, hon?"

"Ugh."

"I have some bad news." Todd waited for a response; he could hear her breathing speed up.

"What now?"

"Why is your voice echoing?"

"Huh? Must be the connection," Jenna said. "What's the … uhhhhhhh … bad news?"

He could hear her groan some more with the phone muffled, as he was about to speak.

"They're taking away our–" A toilet flush interrupted his thought. "What was that?"

Jenna's voice perked up. "What was what?"

"Jenna, please tell me you're not doing what I think you're doing. At least mute the phone."

"What?" She said with a sigh as he could hear her hand cover the phone again.

"They're completely taking away our bonuses. We're screwed out of our trip."

"Assholes!" Jenna screamed through the phone.

Christabel peered over the cubicle wall. "Tell her to keep it down, they'll hear," she whispered.

"I know," Todd said softly into the phone. "It sucks. Just keep the volume down."

"The volume? Are you fucking serious? Don't these assholes you work for understand we're supposed to be in Nassau for my thirty-seventh birthday?"

"Uh, gotta go, hon, someone's coming." Todd ended the call as he could hear Jenna scream what sounded like *truckers*. "Food poisoning," he told Christabel. "She has a sick stomach and stuff."

"Sounds like she's having more fun than us today," she said.

An unfamiliar woman approached their cubicle cluster. Todd studied her. She wore tight black pants with a coordinated black top and dark red blazer. Far more professional than anyone else at the office outside of HR. Her blonde-dyed hair was cropped chin length, and her face layered in a powdery foundation with dark eye shadow which gave her a corpse-like appearance.

"Hello, hello!" She exclaimed cheerfully as she extended her right hand towards Christabel. Christabel greeted her with a questionable shake. The woman turned to shake

Todd's hand. "Hello, hello! Erin Winslow, so nice to meet you both!"

"Nice to meet you, Erin. I'm Todd Williams, this is Christabel Van Heusen, we're part of the creative department."

"Awww, I love creative," Erin said with a huge gum-revealing smile that Todd felt the urge to stretch out further by inserting his forefingers into either side of her plastic mouth. "Christabel. Such a unique and lovely name."

Christabel stepped back toward her chair. "Yeah, thanks."

"So, tell me Toby and Christabel, are we winning?" She giggled.

"Huh, yeah," Christabel said. She looked at Todd and rolled her eyes. "Hell yeah, we're winning," she said flatly.

Todd held up his pointer finger. "My name's Todd, not Toby."

Erin looked at Todd. "Yeah, okay, so I figured I would jumpstart the meet and greet process and get to know the team. I hope you both don't mind?" They nodded in agreement. "So, tell me, what do we do here in creative?"

"*We* create graphics for the website and design internal communications materials … presentations, mostly. We have an offshore team that handles all the packaging production Christabel and I manage." Todd rattled off.

"No, I mean, *what do YOU do?*" Erin said.

"I'm not sure I follow," said Christabel. "We are the Creative Services team. We do creative."

"Oh Christabel, I just love that top," Erin reached out and delicately grabbed the blue Japanese floral silk shirt just above Christabel's waist. She rolled a shirt button between her thumb and forefinger. "It's so soft, can I feel?"

Christabel shook her head in exasperation, "sure, you're already this far you might as well cop a feel." She gestured toward the HR suite. "Not like anyone over there would care."

Erin looked up with her blank ghostlike face, and then laughed five seconds later. "Oh Christabel, you're so funny! I can tell we're gonna be great friends."

"Dream come true," Christabel muttered.

"Well, I have to skedaddle. It was a pleasure meeting you, Christabel. I look forward to us getting to know each other." She turned to look at Todd. "Oh, and you too, Toby."

"It's Todd."

"Yeah, so don't forget to come to the meet and greet in a little while. *T-T-F-N.*" Erin whisked herself away leaving behind a waft of eye-watering lilac perfume and fresh scent fabric softener.

"Can today get any weirder, Christabel? I mean, this has been the worst day!" Todd dropped into his chair and shook his head.

"The hell if I know," she called back from behind the cubicle wall. "Fuck this place. I'm sending out my résumé tonight."

Another hour later, Todd received another email from HR, this time, an *Org Announcement.*

Dearest BYB Family,

We are pleased to announce with mixed emotions and a heavy heart that our beloved friend and colleague, Jeremy Wright, has resigned today, to spend more time with his family. We wish him good luck and fortune.

Also, FYI, your decrease will only be 5.2% now that Jeremy was terminated … isn't that great news? No sad pandas over here. ☺

Yours truly,

Team HR

P.S. Be your best!!!!!!

P.P.S. By family we meant his cats. He lives alone.

. . .

"Is this for real?" Todd said aloud. "Can I go home now?"

Christabel peeked over the separator. "How about we go postal on this place. I think it's time."

Todd shrugged. "We should do something."

"Do what, gang?"

Todd spun his chair around to see Gavin propped against the cubicle wall with a coffee mug dangling from his outstretched soft and slender fingers.

"Do something about this pay cut, Gavin," Todd said. "This is lunacy."

"Ahhh, Todd, Christabel, just how the cookie crumbles … you know?" Gavin shrugged his shoulders.

"But why?" Christabel asked, "Why are we being punished?"

"Because someone always has to take the hit, in this case, all lower tier staff like you two."

"Take a hit for what? It's not right, Gavin." Todd said.

"Who are we as a company to say what is right or wrong, Todd, are we gods?" he looked around with his hands raised so everyone knew he was posing a serious question.

"This is a private company, gods have nothing to do with it," Todd said.

"Oh, if you only understood the secrets of the universe as we all have in upper management. Rule number one: suck it up and walk it off." He held up two fingers in front of his face. "Rule number two, don't forget you're gainfully employed." Gavin glanced at Christabel's chest for a few seconds, accentuating the awkward silence by tapping the coffee mug on the top of the cubicle wall. "We're not finished putting out this fire. I'll circle back with you two after the meet and greet," he said and slithered backwards through the same conference room doorway.

"Why does he do that?" Christabel's face contorted. "Fuckin' creep was staring at me again. I'm resigning – today."

"Attention staff," interrupted a woman's fuzzy voice over the office PA system, "please join us in the HR suite now for the meet and greet with your new Talent and Emotional Development Leader, Erin Winslow."

Todd looked at his watch. "It's only eleven-thirty," he said loud enough for other staff to hear his frustration.

The fuzzy voice continued, "and remember staff, this is mandatory. Signing off … ha! I've always wanted to say that." The speakers emitted a screech followed by a static pop.

"Signing off? Goddammit!" Christabel sighed and waved her middle finger high over her head in the general direction of the HR suite.

"Come on, let's get this over with." Todd felt defeated. "I really want to go home. Oh wait, not while Jenna is still sick and gross." Christabel exhaled slowly with emphasis as they walked together to the HR suite in the far corner of the office space. Other employees joined their walk and arrived together in a mob of repressed anger.

Christabel leaned closer to Todd. "When this bullshit meeting is done, I'm giving them my verbal resignation. Can I use you as a reference?"

The business unit president, Mr. Stanowich, whom everyone called Stan, stood in front of the HR staff gathered proudly behind him. He held up a wine glass filled with what Todd assumed must be white grape juice during business hours and tapped it three times with a large pinky ring.

"Good morning team BYB!" he shouted with pep rally exuberance.

"Good morning," the staff droned in sloppy unison.

"We here at BYB strive for corporate excellence. Last year, we scored in the ninety-sixth percentile for employee satisfaction in the country. But that's not good enough – we deserve a one hundred!"

Stan paused as the HR team applauded. His shifting eyes

scanned the quiet staffers directly in front of him and then continued.

"Therefore, in our efforts to achieve a perfect score, I want to introduce you all to Erin Winslow, your new talent and emotional development leader." He panned the crowd of the hundred or so employees gathered around him, his eyes meeting each person's before continuing. "Let's give her a big BYB Tech welcome!"

Everyone clapped like they heard a heartfelt speech at a funeral. Todd noticed HR looked and sounded far more enthusiastic, though. Erin stood up from her throne – a high-backed ergonomic office chair only reserved for senior management positioned in the center of the HR team standing around her. She clenched hands in front of her chest, bowing to the applause with her gummy smile.

"All hail pervy Queen Erin," Christabel whispered to Todd.

"Pervy?"

"Yeah, she was totally hitting on me, you were there too."

A loud pop cut through the applause.

"What the hell?" Todd looked around frantically. Everyone was doing the same.

"Oh my god!" Christabel pointed at Stan laying on the floor. "He's bleeding! Call nine-one-one!"

Another loud pop, the crowd attempted to disperse from the HR corner. They shoved past each other like rats racing for food scraps on a restaurant floor, knocking into cubicle walls, bouncing off the large HR printer-copier. Gavin fell into a large potted plant. Jane from Accounts Payable screamed from the floor as other staff trampled her.

Five more pops, closer than before, broke through the cacophony of screams and shoving. Todd realized he was hearing gunfire. He dove under a nearby meeting table pulling Christabel by the arm with him and scanned the room. They watched as Erin Winslow took a bullet to her forehead; blood poured over her pale face and red blazer as she flopped into the high-backed chair she had risen from just minutes before. Todd's line of sight between chairs, tables, and large plants enabled him to watch as employees who had not ducked for cover ran screaming and tripping over Jane and office chairs as they scrambled to reception for the elevator and stairwell. Another loud pop dropped a man wearing a white sweater from a shot to his mid back. Todd saw his face as he slammed into the floor and recognized him as Ned the internal comms director.

"You're all free," shouted Jeremy Wright waving a hunting rifle with a rather large magazine over his head. "Hey, you in the back behind the cubicle in accounting – you're free! You can leave now." Jeremy turned and walked over to Stan and nudged his lifeless head with the toe of his shiny leather shoe. Members of the HR team lay slumped over around him. Maria, the benefits manager, was still alive and groaning. Jeremy held his rifle to her head.

"Oh my god," Christabel whispered, "I can't believe this is happening. I don't want to see this." Todd wrapped his arm tight around her torso to comfort her, the feeling of her closeness temporarily removed him from the situation as he recalled the last time he held Jenna that tight – five months ago on the first night after she moved in with him.

"Get out!" Jeremy shouted at Todd and Christabel. "You *don't* need to see this. I'm doing this for you." He fanned out his arms pointing the rifle above the table where Todd and Christabel took cover. "For all of you!"

Todd noticed how empty the rest of the office appeared, except for Jane who was crawling toward the exit despite the injuries she sustained.

"Hey Jeremy," Todd felt he needed to call out, maybe it would save their lives, even Maria's life. "Why are you doing this? Why are you shooting everyone?"

"I'm not shooting everyone, just HR and management. I'm

saving your sorry asses from these corporate clowns," he returned to pressing the muzzle against Maria's cheek and she yelped.

"That's really kind of you," Christabel said, her voice wavered with each syllable. "You're a good guy, Jer. You won't hurt us, okay?"

Jeremy smiled and dropped the gun. He shoved Erin's corpse off the chair and took it for himself. "I knew you guys in creative were cool." He took off his glasses and wiped away some red specs with his plain black tie. "What do you think?"

"About what?" Todd said.

"Can we get back to normal now?" He put his glasses back on and stood up. "And you think I should just put Maria here out of her misery? I mean, she's bleeding from her chest and she's –"

As he was about to finish his question a softer pop was followed by a window cracking behind Jeremy from a bullet hole. He turned to look for the source and a second shot was fired, dropping Jeremy on top of Erin's body. Blood sprayed from just above his ear.

"Oh my god!" screamed Christabel.

"Sure, we'll get back to normal," Gavin said, stepping out from behind a cubicle wall, a pistol in his hand. "And for the record, you creatives aren't as cool as your friend Jer thinks – or thought."

"Yeah, normal," Todd whispered.

"Thanks Gavin," said Christabel as she propped herself up against the table they had been hiding under. "And fuck off."

Todd followed Christabel out from under the table. "Yeah Gavin. That was crazy, thanks for saving us."

"Police," a woman's voice shouted from the stairwell at reception. "Drop your weapons and show us your hands!"

Gavin placed the pistol on a desk and turned toward the

voice as a team of police officers entered the office space and rushed toward him.

Todd stood up slowly with arms raised to show he was a victim, however that worked in these situations he had no clue. He carefully studied Jeremy's limp body as he put his arm around Christabel and pulled her tight, thinking about how Jenna wouldn't allow him to do this in public.

"Is anyone on the floor alive?" An officer asked as she approached the HR area with two paramedics right behind her. Todd noticed her name badge read STARLING.

"Yeah, over here," Todd pointed to Maria.

"And no one's helping her?" asked Officer Starling as she approached. "She's bleeding from her chest!"

The two medics that followed strapped Maria into a stretcher and rushed her out past the flurry of emergency personnel still entering the office space.

After taking statements, Officer Starling escorted Christabel and Todd toward reception. "I'll never understand the lack of human decency in these office cultures," she said as they navigated tossed office furniture and paramedics caring for injured employees. "That poor woman was bleeding out and none of you helped her?"

No one answered as they passed Gavin in handcuffs, who stated that his gun was a gift from the CEO for such matters, and he therefore didn't require a permit.

They walked around a paramedic dressing Jane's right leg in bandages. Todd figured it was convenient she had chosen to wear a skirt that morning. They exited down the elevator with no other spoken words and stopped at the gathering area outside the building's front entrance.

"Please stay here until I get back," said Starling. She turned and reentered the building through a revolving door.

Todd assessed their surroundings. Police cars and ambulances enclosed much of the front plaza and street a few steps below. Everyone from BYB who was still alive and without life-threatening injuries was crowded into what Todd used to think was a large open space.

"Oh good, we're all here," a woman wearing a gray tweed pants suit announced, holding a megaphone in front of her face. She stepped up on the low wall encircling the plaza's fountain. "I am your new temporary HR leader, Tabitha Sloe. I was just sent over from corporate down the street to appease your minds and relax your souls."

Todd perked up. "What the hell is this?" He asked Christabel as they watched from in front of the revolving doors.

"It is with a heavy heart that I must confirm the alleged demise of your illustrious HR team and incredible business unit president, Mr. Stanowich. Stan was a great man, he will be forever remembered as the last savior of this bleeder, I mean troubled business unit." Her voice drifted. "Stan the man. I always love how he used L-O-L in his emails." She paused to lower the megaphone and wipe her eyes with her wrist and then looked up at the sky.

After what seemed to be a moment of silence, Tabitha cleared her throat and continued. "He will be forever missed. Now ... you're all deeply important to us, which is why rather than prolong your misery for fear of uncertainty our CEO has decided to let you all go with a generous six-month severance effective immediately, as long as you sign a nondisclosure about what has transpired here today." She paused and took a playful tone. "And a little agreement promising not to sue us. But," her tone hardened, "you must sign today or you will forfeit this more than generous offer."

The crowd let out a collective groan mixed with shouts of "screw you" and "go to hell."

"This *heart-rendering* activity has upset us deeply at BYB Holdings and the entire BYB portfolio of companies, and we are empathetic for each and every one of your situations," she continued slowly gesturing a hand across the crowd. "You matter."

"This is bullshit!" Shouted a weak-voiced man in a camel brown sport jacket with gray elbow pads Todd only knew as Jeffers.

"Oh, you're such a darling," Tabitha said, smiling in Jeffers' direction. "You'll receive a two-month severance. What's your name?"

"Why you…." Jeffers rushed at Tabitha and shoved her off the fountain wall. It was hard for Todd to make out, but he could see flailing brown-clad arms smacking at Tabitha's upper body. The entire crowd swarmed her, arms swinging, sounds of the impact met with groans, screams, cries, and yelps. Moments later the tweed blazer Tabitha had been wearing emerged over the crowd's heads torn and flung about, a trophy of the mob's take-down.

"Stop it!" An approaching police officer yelled waving his pistol in the air. "Stop this immediately!"

Hands in the crowd lifted Tabitha overhead and tossed her around until she dropped out of Todd's sight. If she was still alive, he hoped, maybe the mob would tear off more of her clothes. He pulled Christabel further back from the crowd as it edged toward them.

The officer fired his gun into the air. "Stop this immediately!" a voice screamed through a patrol car's speaker. By then several more officers had surrounded and infiltrated the crowd. "Stay where you are!"

"Look, Christabel," Todd pointed to a spot in the crowd. Bradley, whom he last saw escorting Jeremy from the office earlier in the morning, was shielding Tabitha, his arm hooked around her midsection as others pushed and pulled at her.

"She needs a medic!" he screamed.

Jeffers appeared from behind and hit Bradley in the side of the face with a high heel shoe. The impact was followed by a gunshot as Bradley spun around and Jeffers stumbled backwards landing on top of a small woman. Bradley recovered his stance to reveal the heel of the shoe had entered his eye socket.

"That's it!" Todd threw his arms up. "I've had it with this place! Had it!"

"Todd, this isn't about you!" Christabel grabbed his wrist.

"You people suck! You're fuckin' monsters!" Todd let out a long scream. "I'm going home to my fiancée who hates me so we can fight about a fuckin' vacation!"

Christabel clasped his hand between both of hers. "You can't, dumbass, this is a fuckin' crime scene. We were told to stay here. Remember? Call her, tell her what's happening."

Bradley yanked the shoe off his face, acting as if he wasn't injured, and approached the area where Todd and Christabel were standing, one arm wrapped around Tabitha's mid-section dragging her along.

"What the hell, Bradley, your eye," Christabel said. "You're like a zombie."

"Hold it right there, sir, let us help you," an approaching police officer commanded.

"It's okay, I'm senior management," Bradley said releasing his hold on Tabitha. "And I'm not hurt, much," he pointed to his bloody eye. "I can still see some shadows."

Tabitha wobbled a bit as the police officer caught her and sat her down on the plaza's red brick floor. Bradley turned to Todd. "Some days in the battle zone just suck, dude. Can't cry over spilt milk, you know?"

"Battle zone and spilt milk? You sound like Gavin. Are you for real?"

"Now let the cops take care of the low-hanging fruit, like Jeffers over there lying on top of poor Audrey from accounting, he's probably dead from that gunshot someone put in his chest, and keep your mouth shut about this and we'll take care of you." He opened his jacket to reveal the hilt of a pistol poking out of the interior pocket. "I know what you saw.

Capiche?" Bradley then blotted his bloodied eye with his pocket square.

"Poor Audrey, I can only imagine what she must be feeling right now," Bradley quipped to no one in particular. He glanced at Christabel's chest for a long moment, trying to use his bloodied eye, before a paramedic stepped in front of him to clean and cover his wound. The medic took him away while another medic and an officer assisted the half-conscious Tabitha.

"Fucking creep," Christabel muttered. She pulled her right arm around Todd's back and shoulders tighter. The crowd was moving closer to them as police were pulling Audrey free from underneath Jeffers' limp body.

Todd's phone rang, he answered with his free hand. "Jenna, oh my god! You won't believe what's going on."

"Did you straighten out this mess with those assholes?" Jenna's voice was audible to everyone standing nearby.

"No," Todd whispered, a tear trickled down his cheek. "Something really bad just happened."

"What could be as bad as *those assholes* taking away *my vacation?"*

"There was a shooting. Lots of shooting. A bunch of people are all dead. Someone else just died right in front of us. It's horrible!"

"Serves those assholes right," Jenna shouted through the phone. "Work is closed for the day, right?"

"Yeah and I was fired. We were all fired."

"What?"

"They're closing our business unit. The office is a wreck.... I might have an opportun–"

She cut him off. "I agreed to marry you, and this is how you repay me?" Todd recognized her heavy breathing. That seething malice he became all too familiar with since living together.

"Screw it. I'm going to Nassau alone and maybe I'll meet someone else there. Don't come home tonight."

The call ended. Todd looked around. He realized Christabel and some other employees were in earshot, their faces told him so. He couldn't take anymore of being dumped on. Dumped on by his employer, dumped on by the woman he thought he loved, dumped on by this world.

"Excuse me, I need to do something," Todd said to Christabel. He removed her arm from his shoulder and speed walked to the back of an ambulance where Bradley was seated with new bandages over his eye.

"You're the problem, Bradley," Todd said as he reached for the pistol in Bradley's jacket. "You, Gavin, Stan, Erin … all those fucks in corporate. You're the reason this all happened."

"You're not as smart as you think you are," said Bradley as he slipped the small pistol from his left hip pocket. "Look at that?"

Todd froze as Bradley pointed the gun at him.

"You don't pay attention to what's right in front of you, do you? After this moment is over, I'll continue to have a superb life."

Tears streamed down Todd's cheeks.

"You could have had a good thing, Todd. You could – you should – have been your best."

Bradley pressed the gun into Todd's abdomen and pulled the trigger.

David T. Griffith (D.T. Griffith) loves to write psychological horror and dark fiction. He draws inspiration from classic and modern works, spanning a full range of literary masters of varying genres, visual artists, comedians, and punk rock musicians. In the horror and dark fiction realm, David has published several short stories and a novella with small publishers and serves as an editor for other horror writers. One of his biggest projects to date was conceiving and editing a dystopian horror anthology for Demain Publishing. When not working in fiction, David is a contributor for an ecommerce blog and writes and edits in other business capacities.

David holds an MFA in Creative and Professional Writing and a BFA in Fine Arts. He is a member of the Horror Writers Association and co-chairs the Connecticut chapter. He lives in his home state of Connecticut with his wife Melissa and their pug. You can find him on social media platforms as @dtgriffith and learn more about his work on dtgriffith.com.

insatiable hunger

. . .

Jan K. Sikes

When was the last time primal hunger consumed you? A hunger so raw and powerful that you'd sell your soul and sacrifice everything to satisfy it?

A few short months ago, I would have answered that question with "Never." But that was before Levi.

I stare into the almost empty coffee cup, growing cold in my hands along with my heart. Closing my eyes, I'm transported back to where my story begins— the first time I saw Levi Jackson.

My co-worker, Kelly, dropped into the empty chair across from my desk. "Emily, a few of us are going for happy hour drinks after work today. Come with us."

"I don't know. I'm not much for going to bars."

"Seriously, Em. When was the last time you gave yourself a night out?"

If I answered truthfully, it had been so long I couldn't remember. Instead, I smiled and said what any dutiful wife would. "I'll have to check with Malcolm to see if we have anything going on tonight." I knew damn well we had nothing, but it seemed like the right thing to say.

"Have him meet us there. It'll be fun, and you never go. Plus, I heard there's live music tonight. You do like music, don't you?"

Do I? Somewhere in the recesses of my mind, I vaguely remember enjoying music and a lively dance floor. But Malcolm and I had grown resigned to a dull, safe life, set in our routines like hardened concrete. "Of course, I enjoy music. I'll give him a call and let you know."

After she returned to her office, I stared at the phone for a long minute before dialing his cell.

Malcolm released a loud breath. "Hi, hun. What's up?"

"Some of my coworkers are going for happy hour drinks after work. Would you like to meet me there? It's a new place, the Thirsty Tortoise."

"You know that's not my thing, Em, and I'm dog-tired. But you go ahead. I'll order in or pick up something on the way home. Go have fun."

"Okay. Just wanted to check with you. There are some leftovers in the fridge."

"Don't worry about me. I'll grab something." Someone called his name in the background. "Gotta run."

"Bye."

But he'd already hung up. I sighed and texted Kelly.

As I walked into the Thirsty Tortoise with Kelly, Paul, Julie, and Dave, I'd never felt more out of place in my Anne Taylor work suit and Sam Edelman heels. A part of me longed to be in jeans, kicking back on the sofa with my feet up. But I'd promised, and I never reneged on promises. Plus, it was a teensy bit exciting to do something completely out of the ordinary.

A life-size neon green sea turtle perched on a shelf above the bar, his neck weaving back and forth, red eyes blinking. What a clever disguise for security cameras.

Rock music blared from giant speakers mounted on the wall, and a lively crowd was already gathering.

"Here." Kelly shoved a glass of wine in my hands. "First one's on me."

With drink in hand, I followed the crew to a table near a corner stage where microphones and guitars stood like silent sentinels waiting to be used.

"Cheers." I raised my voice, then my glass.

A chorus of cheers resounded around the table.

"Here's to the weekend," Paul from accounting added.

I've always been a people-watcher. From my vantage point, I observed patrons laughing and talking. There were a handful, obviously alone and looking for a bit of relaxation before going home to resume life.

It was easy to spot the ones who worked together. It was as if they shared a private secret. I could relate. I felt the same with my group. People who worked together for any length of time developed a sense of family, an unspoken sense of loyalty. We had each other's backs.

Conversation floated around me. A sharp elbow jab to the ribs from Kelly jarred me out of my reverie. "Wake up, Emily. Julie asked you a question."

"Sorry." I blinked and took a sip of wine. "It's so loud in here."

Julie laughed. "This is nothing. Just wait. My question was about the new girl they hired to man the front. What do you think of her?"

"She's young. But seems capable. We should have invited her."

Dave leaned forward. "She's a hottie."

"Dave! Don't ever say that in the workplace. HR will be all over you."

He laughed. "Think I don't know that? What happens at the Thirsty Tortoise stays at the Thirsty Tortoise." He stumbled over his words. "Damn. Many more drinks, and I won't even be able to say Thirsty Tortoise."

Everyone laughed and took turns trying to say Thirsty Tortoise three times in a row.

I finished my drink as the knots in my shoulders unwound for the first time in forever. Yes, it had been too long since I'd done anything remotely related to fun. When had I gotten so old? Surely, life wasn't over at forty-five.

After an hour and another glass of wine, I stood. "Think it's time for me to get home. This has been fun."

Kelly tugged on my arm and whined. "No. Don't leave, Em. The music is going to start soon, and besides, it's not even dark outside yet. Stay."

Others around the table chimed in. "Stay, Emily. You can't be a party pooper."

"Okay, fine. I need food if I am going to have another drink. Someone order a pizza and put it on my tab. In the meantime, I need to visit the little girls' room."

I wound my way through the growing crowd toward a neon sign that flashed *Restrooms*.

Just as I raised my hand to push open the door, I found myself pushing against a hard-planed chest instead. I jerked back. "So sorry. I wasn't watching where I was going."

When I looked up at the handsome face and striking blue eyes that accompanied that rock-hard chest, my breath hitched. I swallowed hard. *Damn!*

"No problem, pretty lady." His deep, rumbling voice awakened my previously thought-to-be-dead lady parts. *Shit!*

My heels were glued to the floor by some magnetic force.

He reached past me and opened the door. "There you go."

"Um. Thanks." I ducked inside, face flushing and my heart pounding. *What in the holy hell just happened? Who is that? He must be a model or a movie star.*

The feeling gradually returned to my legs, and I darted into a stall. My panties were moist when I pulled them down. Something was horribly wrong with me. I've never been the kind of girl to let a handsome man affect me like that. I groaned. *It had been too long…for everything.*

For two cents, I'd sneak out of the bar and go home—only one problem. I'd left my purse hanging on the back of my chair. I couldn't leave without it or without paying my tab. If nothing else, I was responsible.

I finished my business, regained my composure, and hurried back to my coworkers. I grabbed my purse, poised to flee when he walked onto the stage and picked up a guitar.

There it was again. I swear my lady parts twitched.

As if I were a puppet manipulated by unseen strings, I dropped back into my chair and openly stared.

Kelly chortled. "You oughta see your face, Em. He is a gorgeous hunk, isn't he?"

I nodded, afraid my voice would be nothing more than a squeak. He looked my way, flashed a grin, and an almost imperceptible salute. He then turned his back to the crowd and tuned the guitar. His backside almost looked more appealing than the front—almost.

Stunned at my reaction to this lean, hard, sexy-as-hell man, I forced myself to look away and cleared my throat. "I do hope pizza is on the way."

"Ordered, but you aren't paying for the whole thing. We all pitch in. That's the way we do it." Paul leaned back, and the others nodded.

"And I ordered you another drink," Julie offered.

"Good." The way I was reacting to this man, I wasn't sure if I needed tons more alcohol or if I'd already had too much.

Something told me I needed more. More alcohol and much more of him.

Four months later, I sit staring into my cold coffee, wondering if I should make more. I almost laugh out loud. That's my big decision of the moment—to make more coffee or keep staring at my cup. My nerves are shot to hell.

A mere six hours ago, I drained my bank account, packed one lone bag, left Malcolm a note, and drove to the remote cabin on Lake Serenity. What an appropriate name.

My face now flushes with embarrassment when I remember how I'd skipped and twirled across the front porch like a giddy schoolgirl only a few hours ago.

The truth is, I've been here many times over the past few months.

Our last conversation replays like a movie reel.

"Em, run away with me." Levi's sexy drawl vibrated in my ear as my head lay on his chest.

I met his blue-eyed, intense gaze. "You can't mean that."

"Never meant anything more in my life."

"I'm fifteen years older than you."

"I don't give a shit about age. We could start fresh somewhere, just you and me." He tucked my hair behind my ear, and I shivered. That's how deeply he affected me. Just a touch, the sound of his voice, his warm breath on my skin left me craving more. He was like a drug. No, worse than a drug. I had an insatiable hunger for all of him. He consumed my thoughts every minute of every day. If I could've crawled inside his skin, it wouldn't have been close enough to satisfy me.

"Where would we go?" I hated myself for even considering it.

"I don't know. Anywhere but here." He caressed my back,

leaving butterfly touches and goosebumps chasing each other down both arms.

"Let me think about it."

"Don't think too long, baby."

When his mouth found my pebbled nipple, all logical thought fled. It was in that instant, I knew I'd give up everything I'd ever valued to be with him.

I sigh long and loud, dragging myself back to the present. Where is Levi now?

Perhaps he's been involved in an accident. Yes, that has to be it. He said he would be here, and he's never let me down.

My mind is a mess of jumbled thoughts and emotions.

A sharp pang of guilt crawls up my spine. It was a cowardly act to leave Malcolm a short note. By any stretch of the imagination, it was a piss-poor way of saying goodbye to a twenty-plus-year marriage. Yet, strangely enough, it had been one of the most natural things I'd ever done.

The thought of another confrontation was more than I could handle.

Seems all we'd done lately was disagree. My dissatisfaction with our marriage had become more and more apparent. It could no longer be fixed. Was it really Levi's fault, or was it me?

The naked truth is that I disconnected from my husband years before Levi. I never had a reason or motivation to acknowledge it.

Before I turned out the lights and locked the door for the last time to the home I'd shared with Malcolm, I gave one last backward glance at what had been my life, then tossed my suitcase into the backseat of the Mercedes and drove away.

My gaze lingers on the king-sized bed where I've spent blissful hours having mind-blowing sex with Levi. No one had ever made me feel like he did. Lying in the circle of his toned, tattooed arms, I found my center. He made me feel like a beautiful goddess. And when he wrapped my legs around his waist and took what I freely gave, the earth tilted on its axis.

He made walking away from my safe, stable, dull life with Malcolm easy.

I finally decide to pour water into the coffee pot and set it to brew. Levi will want fresh coffee when he finally gets here. "Where are you, Levi?" My voice echoes off the knotty pine walls, giving no answer.

Minutes tick by and turn into hours. I dial Levi's number for the umpteenth time, and it goes straight to voicemail.

Malcolm should be home from work by now. How will he react to the note? I picture him sinking into his favorite chair and dropping his head in his hands. He will eventually come to realize I've set us both free, and thank me.

My cell phone rings, and I jerk it out of my pocket, my heart ratcheting. Tears fill my eyes when I see it is Malcolm. The last thing I want to do is talk to him. I hit the disconnect button and drop it onto the kitchen counter. The walls are closing in on me.

I tug my cashmere sweater closer. Despite the warmth it provides, I shiver uncontrollably. I'm having trouble defining or controlling my emotions. Fear, excitement, and anticipation are intermingled like glass in a kaleidoscope I'd once seen in a shop in Arizona.

Unable to sit still, I pour a cup of coffee and grab my phone. I am in desperate need of fresh air.

Outside, I pace the length of the wooden dock that stretches out over the cerulean blue water of Lake Serenity. "Levi will be here," I say to the emptiness. "He just got hung up somewhere." My gut clenches at the thought that something horrible has happened to him.

The sun's rays cast a fiery red-orange glow across the

water, almost as if the lake itself is catching on fire. But it cannot compare to the inferno that is building inside. Stark terror grips me.

As the sun begins a slow descent below the horizon. I toss the remainder of my coffee into the water and trudge toward the cabin.

"He'll be here soon. He promised." A cardinal chirps nearby as if to answer or perhaps to mock me.

Time slows to a crawl.

My heart is hollow. The lonely hooting of a nearby owl only adds to the gripping despair that squeezes the very breath out of me.

Back inside, I wrap a soft blanket around my shoulders and lay on the sofa. I take in every detail of my lover's lair as tears trickle down my cheeks. I've spent the best hours of my entire life here.

A sense of foreboding snakes up my spine. Something is terribly wrong.

Maybe Levi got cold feet. Or perhaps he met someone younger and prettier. Did he sleep with me only for what my money could do for him? All the doubts, insecurities, and mistrusts I can conjure up rear their ugly heads, bringing with it a pounding ache in my temples.

I'd invested in this cabin and bought him a new Taylor guitar. He'd shown his gratitude by bringing me to earth-shattering orgasms—the kind I never imagined possible.

I retrieve my phone then dial his number again. After leaving yet another message, I close my eyes and attempt to slow my breath and my thoughts.

Reliving our conversations, I search for clues…for anything I might have missed in my blind acceptance.

Darkness descends, and the silence is deafening. What to do now?

Bitter bile rises in my throat as the stark reality of my situation sets in. A situation I created out of lust.

My cell phone buzzes, and I grab it with both hands, my breath hitching.

Levi's name pops up, followed by a text that lights up the screen. —*Sorry.*

That's it. That's all he's going to give? I threw my entire life away for this man, and all I get is one word. I honestly believed in my deepest heart that I'd found my lifetime soulmate. I thought I mattered to him, that all his words were honest and genuine.

Fool isn't a strong enough word for me.

I sit forward on the sofa and toss off the wrap. Admonishing myself isn't going to solve anything.

Tears flow down my cheeks, and I clench my teeth so hard I'm afraid they'll crack.

I jump to my feet and dash out the back door. I don't stop running until I reach the end of the dock.

My life is crumbling around me. I've sacrificed everything.

Now, there is nothing to go back to. No job, no husband, I've even forsaken my children for this man.

I lift my head and let out a primal scream that leaves my throat raw and aching.

One plunge into the deep water could end it all.

I curse the day I walked into the Thirsty Tortoise.

How did I let this happen? I'm an intelligent, mature woman who should have known better. He charmed me, put me under a hypnotic trance with his magic tongue and gorgeous body.

My mind races with jumbled thoughts. The wind picks up, and I sway slightly.

An unearthly calm settles over me as I lean over the edge of the dock and stare into the water.

Yet, I can't make myself take the plunge. Perhaps it is my upbringing or the religious teachings that suicide is an unforgivable sin. Or perhaps it's from some inner strength I didn't know I had, but I raise upright and square my shoulders.

Swiping angrily at my tears, I hurry to the cabin with one thing in mind.

I will leave this place and never look back.

Inside, I grab my suitcase from where it still sits by the door, and without bothering to turn out the lights or even close the door behind me, I race to my car.

I sit staring for a long minute at the place that brought me untold pleasures when a red gasoline can next to the porch catches my eye.

Without giving myself a second to back out, I lunge from the car and don't stop until the can is in my hand.

Through a mixture of tears and maniacal laughter, I douse the entire front of the wooden structure. What does it matter? I'll never see Levi again, and this assures he'll never bring another woman to our cabin.

The pungent odor of gasoline assaults my nostrils as I step back inside to search for matches.

My heart is frozen. I no longer care.

Moving back a safe distance, I strike one match, then another and another, until flames leap high into the air, fueled by the dry wood of the structure. My hands tremble uncontrollably, and still, I toss matches onto the gasoline-soaked wood until the box is empty, then toss it into the flames.

By the time firefighters arrive at this remote location, it will be too late.

There will be nothing left but smoldering ash, exactly like my life.

When I'm sure it will continue to burn, I return to my car and drive away with angry orange flames reflecting in my rearview mirror.

And while a tiny spark of satisfaction settles in the center of my chest, it doesn't make up for the crushing pain.

The weight of guilt presses on my shoulders.

Tears continue to flow until I'm sure there can't possibly be any more.

I've lost it all.

What to do now? Where to go? I can see my lovely home in my mind's eye, knowing I can never return. Malcolm deserves better.

When I reach the blacktop, I hesitate for a brief second, then make a righthand turn and increase my speed.

It doesn't matter where I'm going.

I will drive until I can no longer see the road.

Then, piece by piece, I will find a way to rebuild a life somewhere new. And maybe I can have a relationship with my children again through forgiveness. After all, love is stronger than our sins.

Levi's handsome face appears in my thoughts, and my heart shatters into a million tiny pieces.

I roll down the windows and let the cool night breeze dry the moisture on my face.

Never again will I give in to anything remotely close to insatiable hunger.

While this story is purely fictional, it was inspired by an actual event. I do hope Emily's plight inspires someone to make the right choice when faced with an insatiable hunger that requires the ultimate sacrifice.

Jan Sikes writes compelling and creative stories from the heart.

She openly admits that she never set out in life to be an author, although she's been an avid reader all her life. But she had a story to tell. Not just any story, but a true story that rivals any fiction creation. She brought the entertaining true story to life through fictitious characters in an intricately woven tale that encompasses four books, accompanying music CDs, and a book of poetry and art.

And now, this author can't put down the pen. She continues to write fiction in a variety of genres, and has published many award-winning short stories and novels.

Jan is an active blogger, a member of Story Empire, a devoted fan of Texas music, and a grandmother of five. She resides in North Texas.

For more visit jansikes.com.

synthia

· · ·

JC Crumpton

Alister kept his head down as he shuffled across the lobby. Thirty consecutive weeks of mandatory brownouts meant he and the other residents agreed to an eighty-percent reduction in power consumption. That meant more shadows than illumination covered his route to the stairs.

He always took the stairs. Taking the lift meant he might have to explain to someone why he was out past curfew. At least on the stairs, he could feign a hurried excuse. *I've left the kettle on. Sorry.*

His pack weighed down on his shoulders, the straps swinging against his elbows with each step. A burn started in his thighs and calves by the time he reached the third story. Only four more to go. He feared the darkness in the stairwell. Not for the same reasons he did as a child, but more because he didn't want to take a misstep and damage anything.

When he stepped out onto the landing on the seventh floor, he glanced to the right. The ResMan rarely wandered the halls at night, but he still didn't want to run into her.

He turned left down the corridor that was just as empty. The lights on the walls cast a sickly yellow pall and only one every ten meters even burned. As he rounded the last corner to the right, he nearly ran over his next door neighbor Lukas.

"Whoah." He threw himself to the side, twisting so his shoulder rather than his pack hit the wall beneath the light. "Sorry. I didn't realize anyone would be out."

"Not a problem." The larger man looked down with his brown eyes, almost black in the dim light. "But you shouldn't really be ranging around either should you?"

Alister shook his head. "Just needed to clear my mind."

"Everything all right? Home or work?"

"Both?" He looked up and shrugged. "Neither."

"Heard." Lukas sniffed and looked over his shoulder down the hall. "Sometimes I just need a moment to myself."

"Yep. I'm heading back now. Long day planned tomorrow."

He pulled off the wall and took a step down the hall.

"Hold on a minute."

Heat flushed up the back of his neck. He felt the warmth spreading onto his ears and cheeks, hoping the dim lights hid it from the man.

"Yeah." He turned back around and smiled. "What is it?"

"I hear you try to sneak out during the night."

Alister swallowed, but Lukas just smiled.

"You need to be more careful."

"What do you mean?"

His neighbor motioned his head over his shoulder behind him. "The ResMan is out to get someone in trouble. I heard a rumor that the Housing Authority wasn't pleased she hadn't found any contraband or violations. They don't believe our floor is that well behaved."

"Why not?"

Lukas shrugged. "Statistics don't bear it out."

"I guess."

"Besides. I can't stand her incessant questioning. What we do with our lives is none of her damn business."

"Moira's just doing her job, mate. I'd hate to have the responsibilities of a Residence Manager. She still has a regular job to keep her off UBI. She doesn't want to move to the subBlocks. I wouldn't either."

"Am I really your mate?"

The question came out of nowhere, and Alister wrinkled his brow. "Sure. What do you mean?"

"Why then have you never had Roger and I over for dinner or just to chat it up?"

"It's not me." Alister winced and cast a quick glance over his shoulder. He looked back at the other man. "Synthia suffers from severe social anxiety. You know that. On top of her agoraphobia, it's really getting to me."

He held his hands up and waved them around. "As you can see. I've had to change everything about my life."

Lukas chuckled quietly, but his broad shoulders and chest shook slightly. "The things we do for love."

"You've got that right." Alister nodded at him.

The smile on his neighbor's face widened. He winked and waggled a meaty finger.

"I think that is great that you guys are still so in love."

"What do you mean?"

The big man nodded past Alister. "You and the wife were really going at it last night. And at your age. Good for you guys."

He smiled and shook his head. "Good night, Lukas. Be careful tonight."

"Will do." He lifted two fingers to his brow and saluted. "You too."

Alister twisted around and started back down the hall. He let a long sigh escape through puffed cheeks. Glancing over his shoulder to make sure Lukas had continued down the hall, he shuddered.

The adrenaline that had coursed through his body moments earlier dumped out of his system, and he started shaking. His fingers trembled as he tried to punch his code into the security pad on his door.

It took the code on the second try, and he sighed again. Screwing up three times would have locked him out, and he would have had to ring Moira and try to explain to her why he was outside his apartment at three in the morning.

He pushed the door open and walked through. After closing it behind him and leaning back against it, he closed his eyes and cleared his throat. His heart raced in his chest, pounding against his ribs and pushing blood through him hard enough that he heard it rushing through his ears.

"I'm home, Synthia," he said as he pushed himself off the door.

The numbers from the clock on the fridge cast enough light for him to see his way across the kitchen. Letting the pack slip from his shoulders, he set it on the kitchen table. A tiny unit that folded down into the side of the counter, but that they never stored away. It had become a catchall for anything that had yet to find a place. An aluminum oxynitride tumbler tipped over against a pile of three books he bought six months ago but hadn't read or even opened.

Across the narrow living area, a light flickered on beneath the edge of the bedroom door. The handle twisted down, and it opened. Synthia stepped into the doorway. She stopped and reclined back against the frame.

Just enough light let Alister see her. His breath caught in his throat just as it did the first time he found her. Her alabaster skin, smooth and unblemished, seemed to glow with a power of its own. Her blue eyes shone, and her flittering eyelids couldn't even hold them back.

Her lithe frame resembled a marble statue he once saw in an art book. And every time he knew how lucky he was. Her right arm stretched up above her head, but her left one remained motionless at her side.

He frowned. "I found a new servomotor for that shoulder."

Her smile warmed every corner of his body. He took a deep breath through his nose and felt like he would float away as his chest expanded.

"That's great."

Her voice melted all the stresses he felt burdened with. His fears drifted away to the point she filled his focus and pushed everything else out as trivial.

"Can it wait? We can fix it after, right?"

He felt himself flush. "Again?"

Her right shoulder shrugged. "Why not?"

Alister spread the fingers on both hands as wide as they could and held them barely above the desk surface. The little fingers trembled. Moments later, his whole hand quivered.

He swallowed, frowning until he felt the tension across his forehead. Clenching into fists did not stop the shaking, and he set them down on the table. As he pressed down harder, the backs of his arms started to tighten. The muscles across his chest grew taut, and he felt like he had just stepped out of the gym.

Mr. Covington from Human Resources told him the interview had gone well, but he could think of nothing that went smoothly during the entire process. He feared they would notice his shaking the entire time. Surely, they saw it? Maybe it would help if he bit the back of his hand like he would when he was little.

Several questions had proved too difficult for him, and he had fumbled through the answers. No department head in all of Lonford Enterprises would pull him from the cubicle farm as a resource, lifting him out of the daily grind and granting him a view from higher floors.

"Are you ignoring me, mate?"

After setting his hands onto his lap, he spun his chair around and looked at his cube mate. "Sorry. I was thinking about how I really screwed that up earlier."

Edwin shrugged. "Don't get it twisted. I'm sure you impressed the shit out of them."

He took a deep breath in through his nose, shaking his head. "I wouldn't be so sure of that. Even with all my study and preparation, they gave me a couple of questions out of nowhere that I couldn't answer."

"As daft as you are, it's a wonder you even got the chance at that kind of promotion." Edwin shook his head and rolled his eyes.

"What do you mean?"

The other man shrugged and scratched the three days of orangish stubble on his chin. "They always give you questions like that just to trip you up. Can you think on your feet?"

"I'd like to think so."

"Did you?"

Alister looked up at the ceiling, thinking back to the interview. Did he hesitate? Did he just blather about like an imbecile? He pushed his bottom lip out and arched his brows.

"I gave them what I thought was the best answer I could given the limited amount of information they gave me."

"Did you fumble about or stutter?"

"I don't believe so. I may have taken some pauses as I tried to gather my thoughts."

"Sounds promising." Edwin shrugged. "And soon you'll be leaving us and forgetting about all of the little people you knew back when you were slumming it."

A quick snort escaped his mouth. "Not bloody likely you'd ever let me forget."

Edwin shook his head. "You do know you could have had an easier way to the top, don't you?"

"What do you mean?"

"What do I mean?" He lowered his head and looked at Alister from under his brow. "You only missed the party of the year last night."

Alister held his hands to the side. "You know Synthia has social anxiety. She can't handle all the people crushing in on her at events like that."

"Then why didn't you at least stop by?"

"I spend too much time away from her as it is."

"That's not going to fly much more." Edwin scratched at his neck above his collar. "Especially when directors from the upper floors are in attendance. Besides...we all know the truth."

A knot gripped his stomach just beneath his ribs. "What's that?"

"We know you think you're smarter and better than all of us peasants."

"That's not true."

"Isn't it?" His cube mate leaned back in his chair. "Didn't you compare this department to life in the subBlocks and our incomes—and I quote—almost as paltry as UBI?"

The left corner of his mouth clenched, and Alister lifted his brows. "I guess I did. But I'm just tired of only scanning physical documents and collating them in e-files."

"Aren't we all?"

Alister lowered his eyes. He never meant that he felt his department or work was beneath him. He just felt like he could do something more with his life. Besides, he needed more income. Repetitive use eventually caused Synthia's parts to break down. It happened more and more often lately. Not to mention that as she continuously learned, she needed upgrades to her processing units.

"Are you still there?"

He jerked up. "What?"

"Where do you go?"

"Sorry." He frowned and gripped the tops of his legs. "I was just thinking about something else."

"Obviously. Maybe it's best if you move on and leave us peasants down here in the mud."

"Hey." Alister grimaced. "That's no way to talk. Anyone can move up if they try hard."

Edwin shrugged and looked past him out into the walkway. "At least this keeps people like me that aren't as gifted as you out of the subBlocks or the Barrens."

"Don't let anything hold you back."

"Sure. Which local area were you born into?"

He took a deep breath, filling his lungs and holding it for a long second. Edwin didn't know. None of them did. He never talked about it. His chest relaxed as he sighed.

"My parents still live in the Bethany Green subBlocks."

"What?" Edwin just stared at him, occasionally blinking.

Alister shrugged. "Yeah. I decided a long time ago that living on UBI wasn't for me. I wanted something more."

"Whoah. The Green is a tough area."

"Sure. Where were you born?"

"Just down the street in Mayfair."

"So you're parents aren't on UBI?"

Edwin shook his head, the bulge in his neck moving as he swallowed. "None of my family has been."

"Lucky."

"I guess." His gaze shifted to the side and then back. "I knew you were driven. I just didn't realize how much."

"I just don't believe you are stuck with what your born with."

"I can see that."

They sat there in silence for a moment before Edwin's eyes widened.

"Hey. I almost forgot."

"What?"

He waved his hands around his head. "We're all going to

Canary Wharf for some drinks after work. Why don't you join us?"

Alister grinned with his lips together. "Thanks. But I need to get home to Synthia."

Edwin shrugged and turned his chair around. He rolled it across the floor back to his workstation. "Your loss."

Sweat beaded up in the small of his back. He swallowed the dryness in his mouth. He needed to get involved with people or they would start to wonder why they never heard about his life outside the office. They would start to put their noses into his business.

"Fine."

"What?" Edwin turned around, his smile broad across his face. "Really?"

"Sure." Alister shrugged. "One drink after work won't hurt. I'll just ring Synthia and let her know I'll be late getting home."

"Yes. We get to be graced by your presence before you forget about us after your promotion."

"I don't have it yet."

"Don't worry about it." His shoulders lifted, and waved his hand like he was brushing something out of the air. "We'll just treat this as your going away and congratulations party."

"One drink."

"Yep."

Edwin shifted back to his desk. He reached over and activated his earpiece and mic. Alister knew he was letting the others know. Now he needed to break it to Synthia.

Later when he walked into the apartment, he found her sitting at the kitchen table. Tears streaked her cheeks, glistening in the dimmed lights from the living area.

"What's wrong, love?"

She looked up at him, her blue eyes shining and the corners of her mouth drooping. Her shoulders shook as a shiver ran through her, and she breathed in through her nose.

"You left me all alone."

He locked the door behind him and walked across the kitchen. Guilt started to inch its way through him. His stomach wrenched, and his heart started pounding.

"I told you I had to go."

"But did you have to stay out so late?"

He shook his head. "I only had two drinks, sweetie."

"Two?" She whined, her lips puckering and brows arching. "You said you would have only one when you rang."

"You're right." He cupped her cheek in the palm of his right hand. "I shouldn't have lied to you. Will you forgive me?"

She pulled her away and looked at the wall. "I just worry that you felt compelled to do that to me."

A lump came up in his throat. Whenever she acted like this, it became more and more difficult for him to remember that it was her programming. It wasn't real. But that mattered less and less.

"Do you want them to separate us, dear?"

Synthia looked back at him over her shoulder. She blinked and shook her head once to each side.

"Then I have to keep up the charade that we are a normal couple."

She gasped. "Is it all pretend to you?"

Alister screwed his face into a scowl. "No. You know we would lose everything if they found out I had illegal tech in my possession."

"Why am I illegal?"

He exhaled loudly and threw his hands up. "I don't know. It's just been that way for decades. They're afraid of the artificial. Even networks are closed now."

"That's silly."

"I agree."

After taking his jacket off and letting it fall onto the floor, he walked over and fell into his plush chair. He sunk into the cushions, letting it envelope him.

He felt her hands on his shoulders, and for a moment, he tensed. As her fingers started kneading the muscles that ran from the back of his neck to his shoulders, he relaxed.

Her thumbs worked deeper into the crevasses between the fibers. Heat slipped down his back, invigorating him at the same time as it loosened the tension that had started to give him a headache.

He closed his eyes, letting the comfort settle over him. Lowering his chin, he rested it against his chest. Synthia pressed her lips next to his ear just before he slipped into sleep.

"I missed you today."

"And I you."

"Show me how much."

Her hands fell away from his shoulders, but she kept one touching his arm as she walked around. He opened his eyes to see she had already somehow removed her clothes without him realizing it. He knew he could never resist her.

The sun would be coming up in a couple of hours and five kilometers remained before getting out of the Barrens and across two local areas to his home. His pack felt immensely lighter on the return than it had when he set out four hours earlier. Twenty tins of canned meat and vegetables had pinched the muscles in his lower back and made his hips feel like they had moved out of place.

An hour trek through abandoned warehouses and burned out shells of ancient vehicles with the pack empty hadn't improved his discomfort. The dim glow from his datapad did little to light his path. Water soaked his socks after one misplaced step into some brackish water. Images of his foot being lost to gangrene or staph filled his mind and refused to be pushed away.

Rows of naked iron girders marked the edge of the Barrens. He squeezed through the narrows gaps of dilapidated chainlink fences topped by rusted barbed wire.

Alister first had to get across Old Maiden with its moderate homes for middle management and Curfew Patrols every ten minutes to keep out the riffraff. After that he'd need to wind his way through the green spaces and multi-family units of Gardenlock before reaching his own Graystone local area.

Later, he saw yellow swirling lights of a CP cruiser rounding the corner a couple blocks away. He racked his shin against a low stone wall when he threw himself over it. He tore his hands fumbling to get the front compartment of his pack open. A quick glance revealed the circuit board resting undamaged in its velvet-lined case. His breath slipped out in a long sigh before he snapped his mouth shut. Synthia needed a capacity upgrade because her original designers hadn't set a governor on her memory capacity. She never stopped learning.

He waited five minutes after the cruiser passed before staying at the edges of the shadows to reach his building. After he pulled the slender rubber strip from between the door and its contacts, he released the cough he'd been holding the past two minutes. Nothing moved in the foyer, and he crept to the stairwell.

A light flashed on when he reached the landing below the seventh floor. He squinted his eyes and put his arm up to block the light as he peered around the edges.

"What do you want?" His heart hammered in his chest, and sweat ran down his spine between his shoulder blades.

The light moved down and illuminated the steps in front

of him. His eyes still couldn't pierce the gloom at the top of the stairs.

He stopped midway up. "I'm not taking another step until you tell me who you are."

Nothing but silence answered him.

"If you're a Scrounger, I don't have anything for you."

"Sure you do, Alister."

His breath caught in his chest. "Moira? Is that you?"

She chittered a quick laugh. "Who else would it be out at 0400 in the morning?"

He scrunched his shoulders. "I don't know."

"And you're supposed to be the bright one."

"So they say."

"Well, maybe they need to ask me about it."

He started up the stairs. Taking a breath with each step at first, until he scrambled up the last few and tried to squeeze past the ResMan. But she stepped in front of him.

"You don't get off that easy."

"I'm sorry I was out after curfew, Moira. If you need to report me, I understand. But I was just trying to clear my head."

She stepped closer to him, and he backed up until his shoulder blades pressed up against the wall. Her face, just centimeters from his, looked like some old-time horror movie. The yellow light lit up the bottom of her face and nose, but her eyes remained hidden in shadow.

"I know what you're up to, Alister."

He sniffed and nearly darted around her to the door.

"What's that?"

"The wife has you by the balls and you're out trading foodstuffs with subBlock tramps for a little moment of understanding."

"What makes you think that?"

"What's in the bag?"

His fingers gripped the straps over his shoulder. "Nothing."

Moira nodded. "Because you gave it all away."

"Really?" He let the tension leave his shoulders. "Is it that obvious?"

She arched her eyebrows and pressed closer to him. Her full breasts pressed into his chest. He turned his head to the side when she leaned in closer to him. The flashlight beam pointed up and lit up more of the stairwell.

"For me it is." She looked down for a moment before lifting her eyes to his. "Yes, I can make you happy. Instead of you risking everything just for a little peace and quiet."

"You know I'm married, Moira."

"She doesn't have to know." Her tongue slipped between her lips, out and back in. "I know you're up for a transfer to the twelfth floor over at Lonford."

The skin in his forehead crumpled into a deep furrow. "How'd you find out? That's supposed to be confidential information."

She shrugged. "I know some people over there and ask about you from time to time."

"You're spying on me?"

Her eyebrows arched, and she tilted her head to the left. "I'm interested in you, Dear. If that means I'm spying on you, then I guess I am."

He closed his eyes and pinched the bridge of his nose between his forefinger and thumb. Even though he tried not to touch her, he couldn't help but feel where his forearm rested against her breast. She shifted, settling more of it against him.

"This is really too much."

"I think we can go places together." She rested her left hand on top of his shoulder. "As a team."

Pulling his straps tighter against his chest, he squeezed from beneath her and walked toward the door. He reached out and grabbed the handle. But he didn't turn it and looked back over his shoulder.

"I'm sorry, Moira, but I'm married."

"Just think about it." A thin smile spread across her lips. "Remember, I've got my eye on you."

"I know it looks bad, but I'm happily married." He twisted the handle and pulled the door open.

"I'm somebody in Society, Alister. I can help you get where you want to be."

He frowned. "What? You're just a ResMan. I don't mean to sound callous or unappreciative, but I don't think you could impact my department."

"That's still more push than you have."

"I'll think about it." He stepped into the hall.

Before the door closed, he heard Moira call after him. "Not too long. The offer does have an expiration date."

The cursor blinked on his monitor beneath the last line of code he'd written over ten minutes ago. Different trains of thoughts and ideas waged a battle inside his head, and Alister could not find the focus he needed to finish writing the program. This project of simplifying the collating process of physical documents in the sequestered network within Lonford separated him from the other candidates that had interviewed for the spot on the twelfth floor. It was the only differentiation that made him stand out. Everything else, he imagined, looked unremarkable.

If he didn't finish it today, he doubted he'd be getting the message on his datapad he hoped for. But Moira's attention on him last night rattled him. She could ruin everything. Why can't people just mind their own business? His fingers shook so bad from the confrontation he barely secured the processor in Synthia without damaging some of her other circuits. At least she made him forget about Moira pretty quickly after he closed her up and the upgrade integrated.

His clock read 1548. The announcement was scheduled to come out today. By 1700. Would they make the applicants wait until the last minute? Would Moira really have a chance at stopping the promotion? Paranoia. Nothing but. He hated how everyone else thought they knew better than he did himself how to run his life. They tried to tell him what books to read, how to say his words, where to live and eat. And their houses were in no better condition than his own—most often worse.

Sequential pattern recognition algorithms needed to be applied in the right line. But a couple looping chronologies stood in the way. The muscles on the side of his jaw clenched until he heard his teeth grinding. He clenched his hands into tight fists and set them on either side of his embedded keyboard. He needed the promotion. If he got it, he could move out of Graystone. That would easily solve the situation with Moira.

"Did you hear me?"

"What?" He whirled around in his chair.

Edwin stood leaning against the the entry into their cubicle, one arm draped across the partition. He watched as his cube mate looked from side to side before meeting his gaze.

"I guess you didn't hear me? Were you too busy working or too busy worrying?"

Alister chuckled and pushed back in his chair. "That obvious?"

"Only if you have eyes." The young man lowered his head and stepped into the space.

"What is it?" Frowning, Alister glanced past Edwin to the corridor.

"Covington just came off the lift with half his department and Mr. Hedgewick from the twelfth."

His heart pounded in his chest, and Alister felt beads of

sweat form up along his hairline. He suddenly couldn't get enough breath. Coughing twice, he leaned over and put his head in his hands.

"That means they've decided."

"Sure does, mate." Edwin nodded. His grin stretched across his face. "And since they're down here, it means it came down between you and Becca."

He sucked in a deep breath and pushed out though his pursed lips. "She's good. Very good."

Edwin slapped him on the back. "Dogs are going to bark."

"What?"

"Don't worry about it. You're pretty sharp yourself."

Shrugging, Alister lifted his head. "You know me. I worry."

They heard muffled voices coming down the corridor. Edwin rushed over to his desk and tumbled into it. He slapped the top of his desk, waking his monitor. Alister twisted back around to his station and pulled up closer.

The longest ten seconds he had ever experienced ticked by. Everything wrestled for his attention. The air through the ventilation whistled. The back of Edwin's chair creaked every time he shifted. The sounds of the floor mixed together into a dull roar until it all blurred into chaos.

"Mr. Alister Morton?"

He took a calming breath and turned around in his chair. Misters Covington and Hedgewick peered into the cube from the corridor. Alister saw shadows on the floor beyond them, but only two could fit into the entrance.

"Yes, sir." Alister stood and extended his hand. "Good evening, Mr. Covington. How are you doing?"

The director of Human Resources nodded his head and gripped Alister's hand firmly. "Quite well. Thank you."

"Good."

Covington motioned to the man beside him. "Mr.

Hedgewick, who you spoke with earlier this week, would like to tell you something if you have a moment."

"Of course." He looked over at the other man. "Hello, sir. Are you doing well?"

Hedgewick nodded. "Great."

He nodded at monitor at Alister's station. "Is that the program?"

"Yes, sir," Alister said, stepping out of the way.

The man raised an eyebrow. "You've gotten closer in such a short time than we thought you would."

"Sir?"

Hedgewick waved his hand at the desk. "It is this kind of drive that makes us on the twelfth look forward to working with you."

Alister gasped. His chest felt tight, and he forced his throat to swallow. "You mean?"

The director nodded. "Welcome aboard, Mr. Morton. That is if you want the position."

"Absolutely, sir." Alister beamed so wide, he didn't think his cheeks could stretch that far. "I won't let you down."

"I know you won't." He patted Alister on the shoulder.

The two men smiled, nodding briefly at Edwin, and turned. Both of them watched the two managers leave. Neither said a word until they couldn't hear the measured steps and muffled voices.

He looked over at his cube mate, and he felt a broad smile stretch across his face. His fingers spread out and shook until he clenched them into his palms.

"Yes." He wanted to shout, but it came out as a hoarse whisper.

"You bloody did it." Edwin shot up from his chair and jumped into Alister's lap. "Take me with you. Don't leave me all alone with this rabble."

"Get off, you oaf." He pushed him onto the floor but

couldn't help laughing at his friend's antics. "Don't ruin it for me before I even pack up."

Edwin stood up and walked back to his desk where he flopped into his chair. He spun it around and reached for his datapad.

"What are you doing?"

"Telling everyone, obviously."

Alister shook his head. "Let's just keep it between us. I don't want the attention right now."

"Too late."

"What do you mean?"

He jerked his thumb to his right. Ginnie and Maurice from the next cube over were both peering around the side.

"He got it, didn't he?" Ginnie asked as she skipped into their cube.

"Well, I have an offer—"

"Oh, bollocks." Edwin leaned over and punched him in the side of the arm. "Let's all go down to Canary Wharf to celebrate? Call Cynthia and ask her to join us."

Alister leaned back and held his hands up in front of him. "Oh, no. This is too big. I need to go home straight away and let her know."

"You're not going to call her?" Maurice asked, his dark, bushy brows raising. "My wife would have me by the short and curlies if I didn't tell her right away."

He shrugged. "She's probably napping now. I'd hate to disturb her."

Ginnie put her hands on his forearm. "You really should bring your wife down to the Wharf so we can all celebrate."

"I don't know." He pulled his arm back. "I think I just want a quiet evening with my wife tonight."

"Tomorrow?"

"We'll see."

Edwin clapped his palms together. "See. He's already separating himself from us."

"That's not fair."

"No more dealing with us peasants."

"Hey."

"We just want to celebrate with you, mate."

Alister opened his mouth to respond, assuring his friend he wouldn't forget about him. But Lindsey stepped into the space, and he snapped his mouth shut.

"Leave him be, Edwin. If he was smart, he'd forget about all of you dead weight."

"Thanks for that rousing endorsement of our abilities, boss lady."

She ignored him, focusing her attention on Alister. "Never mind him. There's only a little bit remaining in the day. Go ahead and take off. Celebrate with your wife."

"Much obliged, Lindsay. I appreciate it." He turned and closed down his station, securing the programs and saving his progress on the algorithm.

"Don't be a stranger," Edwin called after him as he hurried down the corridor.

Nothing other than telling Synthia the great news and discussing all the myriad ways their lives would be different held his attention. On the tube, he watched station after station go by without even hearing the announcements. His stop came and he felt trapped by the press of people getting off the car or jockeying to get in through the doors.

None of it mattered to him. He couldn't do anything to make the people get out of his way. He couldn't make them move faster. But his hands still shook with excitement. Sweat beaded up on his forehead and rolled down the bridge of his nose. As many cold records as the last summer broke, this year seemed to break the same number of heat records.

And Graystone's air conditioning had long been on forty percent capacity because of the energy shortages. Yet when he made his trips to the Barrens and crossed through Old Maiden, the middle management homes didn't appear to be suffering from the brownouts as completely as Graystone and other residential towers.

Now he would be able to set the climate control where he would be most comfortable. And the cooler temperatures would be better for Synthia and her heat shunts. They were going places. With the privacy afforded to him by having a single-family detached home, the stress of keeping her safe and hidden wouldn't weigh on him as much.

Climbing seven stories would take too much time. He sprinted across the lobby and slid up to the lift doors. They opened immediately, and he jumped in. Seventh floor. The amber lights across the top of the car brightened and then dimmed with each passing level.

It settled to a stop at the fifth story. His shoulders slumped, and he let out a quick sigh. A man holding a cocker spaniel on a leash waited on the landing when the doors opened.

"Sorry," Alister said, holding up his hand. "This car is going up."

He hit the close button and stepped back as the doors shut. The man never said a word, only looking down at the dog.

By the time he reached his apartment door, his heart raced hard enough in his chest the rushing of blood filled his ears. His breath came in ragged gasps as if he had just run up the stairs instead of taking the lift.

He reached out to the security pad and carefully pushed each number in sequence. The last thing he needed was to get locked out and have to get Moira to help him open the door.

The lock clicked, and he pushed into his home—but not for long. He waved his hand over the sensor to turn on the kitchen lights. Synthia must be charging because the drapes were drawn and a deep darkness had swallowed up the details of the room.

"Synthia, love," he called out as the door closed and

latched behind him. "I'm home. Come out here. I've got tremendous news."

He set his satchel down on the table and turned to the bedroom. Standing in the doorway, framed in the light stood Moira. His breath caught in his throat. He struggled to find his voice.

"Good evening, dear." Her husky voice drove into his head, making him wince. "What's your news?"

"Moira." His jaw tensed, and his nails dug into his palm. "Why are you here?"

She shrugged. "I just came by to see if you had called your wife to tell her the news. I told you I had connections at Lonford."

"What have you done?" He pushed past her into the bedroom.

Synthia lay on the bed in pieces. Her extremities and head separated from her torso like puzzle pieces pulled apart. He spun on his heels and raised his clenched fist above his head.

"I told you we're going to go places together." She backed into the living room. "Now, come in here and let's celebrate."

against the side

. . .

JC Crumpton

He didn't mean to hit her that hard. If she had kept her mouth shut, he never would have done it in the first place. His mother never talked to his father with that kind of attitude. Where did she get off thinking she had the right to address him like one of the servants? Good thing he hadn't grabbed the heavy crystal apple sitting on the coffee table.

She whimpered, making little whining sounds like a litter of hungry kittens. The skin on his forearms tingled, and he took deep breaths through his nose, trying to steady his pounding heartbeat. Juliana pulled her knees up to her stomach and tucked her chin against her chest.

"What are you doing, Marco?"

He jerked his head around to the sliding glass door leading to the back patio. His brother Alessandro and sister-in-law Cleta stood in the kitchen. Both their eyebrows furrowed into knots above their noses—things they always shoved into his business.

"Fuck off. It's no concern of yours," Marco said.

His younger brother glared at him, his eyes blinking and lips drawn tight. Cleta stood beside him, her arms crossed in front of her as she stared at Juliana.

"You're a big man aren't you, Marco?" his sister-in-law said. She lifted her chin and curled the corner of her mouth into a snarl.

He clenched his fingers, feeling the bones and joints cracking. "Are you going to let her talk to me like that?"

Alessandro shrugged. "Don't you deserve it?"

"What do mean?"

"Don't be an idiot."

"Watch your fucking mouth." Marco jabbed his index finger in the air.

"Not in my house." They all looked over at Beatrice standing beneath the dining room archway. Her eyes darted back and forth between her sons. "You know I won't have language like that in my house. Even your father knows better and keeps it to his study."

"Yes, Mamma," Alessandro said quietly, bowing his head.

He had a lot of nerve. Then again, his mother always treated Alessandro better. Why she could never see how easily she was manipulated by him, Marco never understood.

"Now, what's going on?"

Cleta unfolded her arms and pointed at the sitting room floor. "Your eldest has done something to Juliana again."

The skin around Marco's mouth tightened. "I told you to mind your own business, you bitch."

"Marco!"

He turned around, staring at his mother and inhaling deeply through his nose. His body didn't relax. His hands clenched. "What?"

"Boy, I better never hear you talk that way to your mother again." His father's voice came from the dining room.

When Enzo stepped past his mother, Marco lowered his chin against his chest. Juliana lay on the floor at his feet. She had tucked her knees up against her chest and wrapped her arms around them.

"Am I understood? Can you get that through that Neanderthal skull of yours?"

"Why do you have to call me names?" Marco turned to his father.

Enzo pointed his thick finger at Juliana and then his mother. "Why am I always having to clean up your messes and teach you how to treat people?"

Heat welled up the back of Marco's neck. "Mother doesn't talk to you like Juliana does to me."

A low laugh began in his father's belly and grew until his whole body shook and jiggled. "Because I'm not stupid enough to talk to your mother the way you do to your wife. I don't want to wake up one night with a knife in my heart."

The others watched them, their eyes glancing back and forth between him and his father. He knew they enjoyed the show. They never wanted anything but his humiliation. Being the eldest came with responsibilities none of them would ever understand. The obligations. The burdens.

"She doesn't respect me as her husband."

Alessandro shook his head side to side slowly. Marco narrowed his eyes, glaring at his brother. Always getting in his business. None of them just left him alone.

"Mind you own affairs, Alex."

His jaw muscles tightened. He pulled in slow deep breaths, feeling his lungs press out against his chest. His pulse surged in his temples. The corners of his brother's lips curled up, and he still waggled his head. What? Did he think he was the eldest admonishing his younger sibling?

"You made it our affair, Marco."

"How'd I do that?" His nose scrunched in a sneer.

"When you married Juliana and brought her into the family?" Alessandro answered.

The family? The little shit *was* trying to push his way into their father's confidence, trying to come between them.

He opened his mouth, but his mother walked over and

pushed her way past him. She knelt beside his wife and started stroking Juliana's forehead. He stepped out of the way and frowned. If he even thought about preventing his mother from doing what she wanted, his father would have his hide flayed from his bones.

"You poor thing," Beatrice murmured.

Images flooded Marco's mind. Long ago, a fever kept him in bed for weeks. His mother held a cool clothe over his forehead and sang soft lullabies to him. He shook his head.

"Is that necessary, Mother?" he asked.

Beatrice lifted her head. "Of course, it is. I've done the same for all my children when they're hurt or bullied."

Marco swallowed. The retort caught in his mouth when he heard his father clear his throat. He swallowed again.

Cleta left his brother's side and crouched beside his mother. He squeezed his hand so hard his fingernails bit into the palm of his hand and started to sting. If he didn't get away from the situation, he would end up saying something that would really piss his father off.

"What's for dinner, Mamma?" he asked.

Everyone popped their heads up to stare at him. Juliana groaned, shifting her shoulder over to hide more of her face.

"Are you serious?" Cleta rolled her eyes and shook her head.

"What?"

"You're worried about food at a time like this?"

He shrugged. "That's why we're all here, isn't it?"

"You're unbelievable."

His father's hand settled on his shoulder, and he looked over. Enzo motioned behind him into the dining room.

"You, too, Alessandro."

Enzo left the kitchen, and the two brothers followed him. Marco and Alessandro waited until their father sat in his chair at the head of the table. When Marco went to sit in the spot to his father's right, Enzo shook his head.

"Move over beside your mother." He motioned toward the second chair on his left.

"Do we have a guest tonight?" Marco asked, pulling out the chair and settling into it.

Shaking his head, Enzo replied, "No. This is for Alessandro."

"What?"

Alessandro stood behind the chair, both of his hands resting on the back. His eyes shifted between Marco and their father.

"I have something important to talk about tonight," Enzo said. "Alessandro will be taking a central part in it."

Marco licked his bottom lip and exhaled. It had already started. His kid brother always wanted to squeeze into his place with their father. Looks like the prick had been working subtly behind the scenes whenever he could. Sweat beaded up on the back of Marco's neck. His vision blurred, forcing him to blink his eyes several times to moisten them.

"What is it?"

He leaned to the side, resting his elbow on the arm of the chair. If he acted casual, maybe he could find out what was going on.

"Is this something I can help with, Pop?"

Enzo swung his head over and stared at Marco. His eyebrows bunched above his nose, but he remained quiet. Finally, his eyes widened, and he shook his head.

"No," he said.

Never a wasted word. Always simple and straight forward. Growing up, Marco always thought his father's favorite thing to say was to explain how he never spoke to hear his own voice.

Sitting up, Marco pushed his back against the chair and tried to relax. But his breathing felt labored, an effort to get enough air. He tugged at the collar of his shirt. *Was the heat on?*

"Sit by me," Beatrice said. "Move down one, please, Marco. Juliana is going to sit by me."

He jerked around in his seat. Beatrice held her arm around his wife's shoulder as the three women came into the dining room.

"Are you serious?"

"Marco."

One word from his father. That's all it ever took. He pushed the chair away from the table and stood, holding it for Juliana. His mother patted him on the shoulder.

"It's okay," she said. "We've got it."

He pulled his hands off the chairback and dropped them to his sides. Every single one of them wanted to push him out. None of them knew how to treat him. He had the talent and ability to more than double the profits of the family business. He had contacts his father never dreamed of cultivating. The fruit was ripe for the picking. When Juliana told him they had been invited to the house for a family dinner, Marco had wanted to use the opportunity to tell his father his plans. The man was getting older. It was time to let his sons—especially him—take over the day-to-day minutia of the business.

Juliana sat in the chair. She kept her eyes down at the plates in front of her. Beatrice took the seat to the left of her husband. Always at his side. Enzo reached over and held her hands, his palm swallowing his mother's slender hands folded in front of her.

Cleta walked around the end of the table. She leaned over and kissed Enzo on the top of his balding head. None of them even glanced at Marco. The *bitch* took the chair beside Alessandro. Marco finally pulled the chair out, sitting on the edge. The other four spots remained empty. The placings hadn't even been set.

"What's going on, Pop?" Marco unfolded his napkin and set it across his lap.

Enzo set his hands palm down on either side of his plate

and drummed his fingers one after another a few times. Air whistled through tight lips like he blew through a straw. After blinking a few times, he inhaled slowly and glanced over at Marco.

"After dinner." His fingers relaxed.

"But I have something I need to go over with you."

His mother leaned forward. "It can wait, dear."

"No." He scrubbed the ends of his fingers over his scalp back and forth a few quick times. "I don't think it can. It's important."

"Your mother said it can wait," Enzo said.

Marco sniffed and gritted his teeth. Alessandro watched him and slowly shook his head. Fuck it.

"This is for the good of the company, Pop."

The words tumbled out of Marco in a rush. He needed to tell them. If they followed his advice, they could build an empire the Avella family would sit on for many generations.

"I've been working on this for over a year," he continued. "The plans have been laid. All the right people are in place. I just need your blessing."

Enzo kept his gaze toward the other end of the table. The vein on the side of his neck bulged and pulsed. Muscles in his jaw stretched taut.

"You mother and Mary have worked hard all day to prepare this meal for us," he said.

"But you need to hear me out, Pop."

"It can wait."

"No, it can't."

"Marco," Alessandro said.

"Stow it." Marco jabbed a finger at his brother. "If I need anything from you, I'll send the request in a memo."

"Enough."

Enzo slammed the sides of both fists against the top of the table. The dishes rattled, and the wine in the decanter sloshed, threatening to topple. Marco's brows shot up, and he whirled around to face his father. He felt droplets of sweat pop up across his forehead.

"Not one more word about it." Enzo said slowly, articulating each word separately. "Understood?"

Marco wanted to shout back at the old man, but he closed his mouth and nodded. "Sure thing, Pop."

"Good." Enzo placed his napkin in his lap and motioned for Alessandro to hand him the wine. "And after dinner, after my announcement, we will listen to your proposal."

"Fuck," Marco mouthed under his breath.

"What was that?" his father asked.

Marco shook his head. "Nothing. It can wait."

"Thank you." Enzo nodded. "You can begin the service, Mary."

They ate dinner in silence. The roast leg of lamb with spinach and Greek yogurt and pine nuts tasted incredible. The asparagus was crisp and flavorful, baked with a parmesan cheese crust. Olive oil bread rolls and the hints of dark cherries and cinnamon in the Tuscan red capped the meal off perfectly. Everything tasted so good, Marco relaxed and quit obsessing about telling his father his plans.

Juliana didn't speak to him once, but she laughed at Cleta's idiotic jokes and smiled at Alessandro's stories of their childhood in this very house. His father ate in silence, watching everyone and nodding occasionally. Beatrice mothered over everyone, filling plates and topping off wine glasses.

"Who's ready for dessert?" Mary said, coming out of the kitchen.

Everyone looked at Enzo. He smiled and waved at Mary. "I think we all are. How are you two going to top this perfect dinner?"

"Oh, no," Beatrice said. "The dessert is all Mary. She shooed me out of the kitchen when she was making it."

Mary set a silver tray ladened with small buns in the center of the table. They all gasped.

"Maritozzo," Alessandro cried out. He even clapped like a little kid getting a sweet after celebrating Mass.

The buns were split down the middle and stuffed with a simple filling made from butter, eggs, flour, honey, and a touch of salt. Everyone loved Mary's maritozzo. The combination of creamy filling in the sweet bread did something to the inside of a person's mouth. In the summer heat, they cooled from the inside. And in the cold winters, they warmed anyone from the tips of his toes to the top of his head.

His mother passed around the pastry plates. Two tongs waited next to the tray. Marco grabbed one up and pulled a filled bun over onto his plate.

Enzo cleared his throat. "You don't serve your mother anymore?"

Marco sighed. "Sorry, Mamma." He grabbed the best looking bun and set it on his mother's plate.

"Here you go, honey," Alessandro said.

Marco looked up. His brother gave his *bitch* a bun before getting his own. He looked over at Juliana. He better give her one or he'd get all hell from his parents.

A leader serves. One of his father's endless wise sayings. He hated to bear bad news to his father, but one day he wouldn't be able to avoid it. Leaders didn't serve. They led. If they didn't, they got run over by the hired staff.

When he set the maritozzo on his wife's plate, she just looked at it. Not at him. No thank you. No show of gratitude. She eventually glanced up at Enzo. When his father dug his fork into his bun and popped the bite into his mouth, she finally grabbed her own fork and started eating. Ungrateful whore.

Mary served a tawny port with the dessert. The rich wine with its blend of spices and fruit went well with the maritozzo. If Marco didn't have such important news to share with his father, he would be content. But they had things to discuss.

"Pop?" he asked.

Enzo stopped chasing a lone crumb around his plate and set his fork down. He lifted his gaze and stared at Marco. He blinked a few times.

"Not yet," he said. "I have something I have to tell the whole family. Then if you think it's still important, we can talk in my study."

Marco sniffed a quick gasp of air through his nose. Important? He never felt so belittled in his life. His fingers dug into the arms of his chair, and he bit the inside of his cheek until he tasted the iron tang of blood.

"Is that good with you?"

He shrugged. "I guess it'll have to be. It's your house. Your rules."

Enzo stared at him, slowly tapping his right forefinger against the table. His eyes never left Marco. His chest expanded and relaxed. Nothing to give away his impatience. Other than the irritating finger. How many times did that same finger tap against Marco's sternum whenever he fucked up?

"You're right."

His father pushed his chair back and lifted his wine glass, the golden-brown liquid sloshing against the side. The others all reached out and grabbed hold of their own glasses.

"I will be retiring from the daily duties of running the company in the next few months."

Beatrice sucked in a gasp of air. Her free hand shot to her chest, and she grasped the broach pinned to her dress.

"Are you sure, Enzo?" she asked.

Enzo nodded. "It's time I passed on the responsibilities and took advantage of what we've built, my love."

"What are you going to do, Pop?" Alessandro asked.

"Is this why you invited us to dinner tonight?" Marco asked.

Their father nodded. "It is. I will remain chairman of the company, but I will be splitting up ownership between you and your brother. You two will have control of day-to-day operations."

"What does that mean for us?" Beatrice asked.

"Simple." Enzo smiled, looking down at her. "You say you've always wanted to travel. Now, we can do it in style."

"Are you serious?"

His head bobbed up and down while a wide grin spread across his face. "I couldn't be more serious, love. You deserve it. We deserve it."

"You're right," Cleta added. "You both deserve everything. You have given each other and all of us so much."

"A toast then," Enzo said. Everyone lifted their glasses and watched the head of the table. "To many adventures and a strong future for the family."

"To you," said Alessandro.

They lifted their glasses to their lips and drained the contest. Except for Juliana. She sipped at her port but kept her eyes down.

"Where are you going to go first?" Cleta asked Beatrice.

His mother shrugged. "I've always wanted to see the old country."

"You've never been?"

Beatrice pursed her lips and shook her head. "We always intended to but never had the chance."

Enzo reached over and put his hand on her shoulder. "Well, we do now. Should we see Rome?"

"No," Beatrice laughed. "I want to see the real Italy. Florence, Milan, Naples, and Venice. Too many pilgrims, politicians, and quick trip tourists stay in Rome."

Laughing, Enzo squeezed his wife's shoulder and sat back down. "A weight has been lifted from my shoulders."

Marco set his empty glass on the table and pushed his plate away. He covered his mouth, coughing into the side of his fist.

"Can we go to your study, now, Pop?" he asked.

Enzo glanced at him and clicked his tongue against the roof of his mouth. "Not yet. There's something else we need to go over."

"What now?"

Sighing, Marco leaned back in his chair. The night started out crappy, but if the old man was retiring, then Marco could use his inheritance to take the company in the direction it needed to go. Maybe things were turning out how they should.

"With the reduction of my involvement, we need to set up the officers of the company," Enzo said. He put his palms together and touched his fingers to his lips.

Marco nodded. "I will do you proud, Pop. With Alex following my lead, we will grow this company even more. Neither you nor Mamma will ever have to worry about anything."

"Yeah." Enzo lowered his hands. "I'm giving 51% of the company to Alessandro."

"What?"

"You will retain 49% control. You will both be nearly equal partners. But Alessandro will have final authority as far as the managerial decisions."

Marco threw his napkin on the table. "You have to be kidding me. This is a fucking joke, right? I'm the eldest. It is my inheritance."

Enzo spread his hands apart. "You're too hotheaded to be an effective manager, son."

"What are you talking about?"

"You let your emotions rule you," his father said. "There is a place for passion, but it must be measured and controlled. Not displayed as front and center in your decisions. What if you're negotiating with another company and they talk to you like one of the servants?"

Marco's lip quivered. The corners of his eyes clenched. Everything he had worked for was slipping through his fingers. He looked across the table at his brother. The little prick wore a smug little smile on his face as his wife held his hands.

"You're behind this, aren't you?" Marco lurched to his feet. He pointed his finger at Alessandro. "You talked him into this. You were always jealous I was first."

Shaking his head, Alessandro looked at him. "I had no clue, Marco. It surprised me as much as I'm sure it did you."

"How'd you do it?"

His brother snorted once. "I told. I didn't know about it."

"Bull shit."

Marco had to get away. He was losing everything. Everyone always attacked him. It wasn't anger. It was passion. And that was needed. Otherwise, nothing got done. He flipped the chair onto its back and stormed into the kitchen. Mary almost had everything cleaned up and stepped out with the garbage as soon as he came in.

"Don't worry about it, Pop," he heard his brother in the other room. "I'll go talk to him."

Perfect. The great manipulator was going to calm the beast. That's how they all treated him. But they were all too docile to take the company to the next step. If he didn't manage it, everything would fall apart, and it would collapse around their ears.

He stood by the couch and looked up when Alessandro entered the room. "What the fuck do you want?"

"Man, this surprised the hell out of me, too," Alessandro said, walking over and squeezing in behind the coffee table to stand next to him. "But Pop knows best. I'm not going to leave you out of anything, Marco. You'll own almost as much as me. I will listen to you."

"Sure," he snapped. "You say that now."

Alessandro reached out and held Marco's arms. "You're my brother. I may not agree with how you treat your wife, but that has nothing to do with the company. You have a good business head on your shoulders. And we'll use that."

"Oh," Marco raised his eyebrows. "Already making leadership decisions, are we?"

"What are you talking about?" His brother scrunched his eyebrows. "Let's go have some more wine."

"Telling me what to do now?"

"Whoa," Alessandro squeezed tighter. "That's not it at all. Let's finish celebrating with Pop and Mamma. We can hash this out tomorrow."

"Really?"

"Sure."

"Going to have your people call my people?"

"Come on, Marco."

"Fuck off."

"Hey," Alessandro said. "There's no call for that. Pop made his decision. We have to abide by it."

Did they? Why did they? Marco knew enough politicians he could have his father declared incompetent and take over the company. He just had to get Alex to agree. But his little brother never would. He was too much of a *Mamma's Boy*.

Marco stepped to the side and hooked his right leg behind his brother's. He brought his hands in and gathered Alessandro's shirt in his grip. He pushed, forcing Alessandro back. With all his strength, he forced his brother's head down on the crystal apple.

Alessandro twitched twice, his eyes going wide. His mouth opened and closed. Then, he let out a long exhale and remained still.

Marco stood and looked down at his little brother. It was an accident. They were arguing and wrestling. It happened all the time. Thoughts raced through his mind, trying to grab his attention, but all he focused on was the blank stare his brother had.

A scream pierced the air, driving a spike into his head. "What have you done?"

He jerked his head up. Cleta barreled across the room and dropped down beside her husband. She held his face in her hands. Tears streamed from her eyes and fell onto Alessandro.

"Baby, no," she cried. "Wake up, baby. Don't go. No. No. No."

Powerful arms grabbed him by the front of his shirt and yanked him from his feet. He felt his father's hot breath against his face. He smelled the wine they'd just had.

"What did you do to my son?"

Marco blinked his eyes. *I'm your son.*

"I'm the eldest. I deserve the respect."

"You are not my son. I disown you. I cast you out."

Where did it go wrong? If Juliana hadn't mouthed him with attitude, none of this would have happened. Everyone always hated him. They were jealous of his superiority.

"If you send me out, who will take over the family business when you are old and feeble?"

Enzo gritted his teeth. His eyes narrowed into slits. "Corso will do well."

"Ha," Marco snorted. "Your whore's whelp? You can't be serious?"

Pain flared behind his eyes. His face hurt where his father's fist struck him. His cheekbone shattered. The cracking echoed in his head. His father hit him again and again. His body was in agony. Enzo hit him in the ribs, breaking them. Marco fell to the floor and curled up, trying to protect his head with his arms.

He wanted it to end. He wanted to die. Anything to stop the pain. He whimpered, lying on the floor of his parent's family room and bleeding onto the carpet.

"If you want him," Marco heard his father say, "take him from my sight for I have lost two sons today."

Who was he talking to? His mother. Surely, she would sit with him and put cold compresses over his cuts and broken bones.

"I don't need him," Juliana said.

Marco started to cry.

"Call the police," Enzo said. "It's over."

Cleta screamed.

JC Crumpton is the award-winning author of the poetry collection Newspaper Reading *and will be re-releasing his novel* Branches through the Window *and his story collection* All the Water Held in One Hand*. Born in southern California, he grew up all over the world and currently resides in Northwest Arkansas with his wife. JC earned a degree in English with a Creative Writing Emphasis from the University of Arkansas.*

uncovering the ozarks' secret

. . .

Gary Rodgers

R umors filled the crisp fall morning air in Eureka Springs, like fog covers the valley where White River meanders through the Ozark Mountains. All folks knew was somebody found a dead body at the Crescent Hotel, but they did not know what happened. It's not every day something like this happened in the place folks called Little Switzerland.

I met my brother, Darrell, mid-morning at Myrtle Mae's restaurant for lunch, to get the scoop from him. Since he was a Carroll County Deputy, he could tell me who they found and what the circumstances were. My part-time journalist career with the Madison County Record wasn't paying many bills. If I was going to make my way to a larger paper, I needed a career making story.

"Come on in and have a seat, Danny. I'll buy your lunch today, and you can get the beer for the cookout this weekend." Darrell joked as I entered the restaurant.

"Unless you have a story that will make me rich by this weekend, I don't know anybody who could afford to buy beer for one of your cookouts." I shot back.

I enjoyed hearing his laugh, which he did as I took a seat at his table. A waitress I knew as Carol came from the kitchen with two glasses of sweet tea. We had ordered nothing yet, but she knew what we would want to drink from our frequent meals together.

"Morning, Deputy. Good to see you boys today. You over here investigating that body at the Crescent?" she asked.

"I am over here on business, Carol. But I can't say what that business is. You know we have to avoid the rumor train that runs non-stop through Eureka." He smiled and winked.

She gave him a wink back and asked, "You boys want the lunch special today? It's meatloaf and mashed potatoes with green beans and a roll."

We both said we would like that and watched until she was back in the kitchen. I knew she was close to Darrell's age, and this wasn't the first time I had a feeling the two of them knew each other away from Myrtle Mae's. I was about to mention it when Darrell interrupted.

"Okay, little brother, do you have a recorder with you or something to write on? We need to get this conversation over with before the lunch crowd gets in here."

I pulled a notepad from my pocket and said, "Give it to me."

"Housekeeping at the Crescent found a body in room 204 this morning after getting an early check-out request. It's female, late twenties, or early thirties. We don't know because there was no identification on her or in the room. There was an empty vodka bottle and a bottle of sleeping pills on the nightstand. We're still trying to locate her vehicle and identify her. But it looks like suicide, and Sheriff Wade wants it to stay that way."

"Doesn't sound like suicide to me. No identification sounds strange."

I looked into my brother's eyes for what he wasn't saying, hoping he would open up, but he wasn't sharing. He waited a few moments, then continued.

"If I was a reporter, I would ask around town. Maybe she

bought some souvenirs with a credit card. The sooner we know who she is, the sooner we can close the investigation. But don't go nosing around the city police headquarters or the coroner's office. And definitely don't call the sheriff's office."

Carol interrupted, "I hope it's not the lady I served breakfast to yesterday. She seemed awfully nice. She was doing research for a book she's writing about that sheriff that drowned a few years back, the one over in Madison County. I told her I remembered it happening, but everyone around here kept quiet about it."

"Did she mention her name?" I asked.

"It was Sharon or Samantha, or something like that. Her last name was Reed. I remember that because I used to have a fellow by the same name come in here all the time," Carol offered.

"Carol, I need to do an official interview with you after Danny and I finish lunch. You shouldn't be eavesdropping like that. But there weren't any names like that on the hotel registry." Darrell spoke dryly.

"Ain't eavesdropping. Your voice carries like a bullfrog on a pond bank, Darrell. Maybe it wasn't her then." She smiled and turned to leave.

"Yeah, and you just happened to be on the pond, huh?" Darrell quipped after her with a smile.

I finished writing my notes as Darrell watched. I could tell he had something to say, but wanted to wait till I finished.

"What else is there, Darrell? I know something is eating at you."

"You tell me, little brother. Something struck you about what Carol said. Did you recognize that name?"

I thought for a moment before speaking. "No, I didn't recognize her name. I won't put it in my story for tomorrow's paper either. I'm sure a search of the internet will give me information on this Sharon or Samantha Reed, and if she's an author. It surprised me to hear her mention the Madison County sheriff drowning a few years back. What was the name on the registry?"

"I can't tell you that yet." He scowled. "What if someone wants to know your sources?"

"Haven't you been paying attention, Darrell? As long as you or Carol don't change your names to anonymous, there's nothing to worry about." I laughed.

"You can do your internet search, but you're right, you need to hold off on using any names in your story. Just because Carol met someone staying at the Crescent Hotel doesn't mean it's our dead woman. We need to wait until the fingerprints tell us who she is. Sheriff Wade is already worried about the publicity of someone dying in a room that's supposed to be haunted."

I had forgotten the room number she died in was supposed to be haunted. I never put a lot of credibility in those stories. But the public would. The Crescent wouldn't mind the increase in visitors, but my brother and the sheriff's department wouldn't like it.

"I'll hold off on names. But I need to know who is running the toxicity screening on the girl. Carroll County doesn't have a medical examiner right now."

"Her body is being taken to the state crime lab in Little Rock. It'll be a week before we know the results. Hopefully we can know who she is before then. I'll send you a photo of her. You can do that thing you do with computers and find out quicker than we can."

I agreed, and we changed the subject as more locals made their way in for lunch. Several wanted to question Darrell about the incident, but he waved them off like a professional.

We finished our lunch and, as we were about to leave, I waved Carol over to the table. I had noticed a couple of other reporters from the bigger newspapers coming in for lunch and setting up their laptops. Chances were, they had spoken to the sheriff's office and were preparing their stories for the next day. I had considered doing the same, along with some research, but I didn't want anyone getting a scoop on my story.

"Carol, can you do me a favor? Don't mention the name you gave me earlier to anyone else. We don't want to drag an innocent person in on something like this." She nodded her head in agreement.

Darrell told Carol he would come back after the lunch rush to interview her. Once outside, he asked what my next stop would be. Worried he would steer me away from my plans, I hesitated before answering.

"Find some place more private than here to do some research." I answered. "Then I might go over to the Crescent Hotel and take a couple of pictures to put with my story and then head home." I noticed his grimace and continued before he could speak. "Of the hotel, not the room. I know that's off limits."

"Don't be nosing around there, Danny. I don't need Sheriff Wade asking me why you are there."

I left and drove to the hotel. The room and hotel weren't my interest at the moment. An old classmate of mine, Mandy Bennett, was head of housekeeping. I was hoping she could give me more information about the dead woman. I needed something to scoop the other reporters in town.

When I noticed a deputy at the front entrance, I drove to the lower side of the hotel where maintenance was located. Ben, Mandy's husband, was outside working when I parked. Before I could get out of my car, he walked over, holding his finger to his lips.

"Danny, you need to stay in your car and go to the Basin. Mandy works there today, and she needs to talk to you." Then he walked away before I could ask what about. I had an idea.

I parked a block away from the Basin. The Basin Park

Hotel is a sister hotel to the Crescent, but is in the old downtown part of Eureka Springs. I drove by a few times before parking, to make sure deputies hadn't been posted there.

At the front desk, I was told Mandy had gotten a phone call and said she was going down the street for coffee. I knew the shop she was going to, and I hoped Ben had called her and she knew I was coming. There wasn't a reason for her to avoid me.

Mandy sat at a back table when I entered the coffee shop. She waved me over, and as I approached, I could see she had been crying.

"Mandy, what's wrong? Are you okay?"

"I'm fine, Danny, other than being scared to death and trying to avoid the police. I knew the girl that died at the Crescent. Her name is Laurie Barker. And they can't make me believe she killed herself. She wouldn't. Not with everything she had going for her." Her eyes darted around the room to make certain nobody had heard her.

"Maybe we should go somewhere more private to talk. You seem pretty shook up."

"No, my friend runs this shop and is watching for anybody that doesn't belong. I'm staying in the public eye till I know I won't be next."

"What are you talking about, next? Do you know something the police should know?" I asked softly.

Mandy reached into her purse and placed a flash drive in my hand. "Laurie said if anything happened to her, to get this to someone I trusted, as long as it wasn't anyone associated with the local police. That's you, Danny."

"What is this, Mandy?"

"It's the research Laurie did on Sheriff Barker's drowning. He was her uncle. I met her when we were in high school. She would stay with her uncle in the summer. When she saw me at the hotel two months ago, we struck up a friendship. She was doing research for a book, but she found some things that scared both of us. His drowning wasn't an accident."

I looked at the flash drive and thought about calling Darrell. But if local law enforcement was involved, I didn't want to put him in danger. Besides, if this drive had evidence of a murder, and if Laurie was murdered, this could be the story I had been waiting for.

I thanked Mandy and told her to stay in public locations and keep what she knew to herself. If there's a connection to Laurie's research and her death, I would do everything I could to find it. Darrell hadn't mentioned having suspicions about her death not being suicide. But I remembered his look when we spoke earlier, and I was thinking he might have had his doubts.

I headed for home, but changed my mind when I noticed a car that appeared to be following me. I would have to take my chances with Darrell, so I called him and he told me to meet him at his house. If somebody was following me, he could warn them off. When I pulled into his driveway, the car passed, then it sped away.

"Hey little brother," I jumped at his voice, "I think you were right about being followed. But I didn't recognize the car. What have you gone and stirred up?" His voice filled with worry.

"I found something I hope doesn't get me or you killed, but I haven't seen it yet. I wanted to look at it with you and get your take. Now, can we get inside?"

When I opened the files from the flash drive, a video file was first on the list. It contained an interview with Bobby Turner. Darrell and I looked at each other, surprised to see someone we thought had died when we were in high school. He looked much older than us now, and he was sharing details neither of us had ever heard about the sheriff drowning. From his statement, we gathered he knew the people responsible, but didn't name them.

Two hours later, Darrell was on the phone with an FBI agent he knew in Kansas City. I was busy typing up my story for the Madison County Record and searching for places to disappear. The names on the file involved several county officials from both Madison and Carroll counties, as well as state officials.

"If you can get security for Mandy and Ben that doesn't involve your office. I would appreciate it, Darrell." My voice shook. "I'm sending my story to the Kansas City Star, as well as to my boss. Then I'm going to find someplace away from here until the FBI shows up. Will you be okay?"

"I'll be fine, Danny. And so will you. We're meeting agents in Springfield tonight, and they are sending more agents to put Mandy and Ben in protection. Then we're headed to the Lake of the Ozarks till all of this gets settled. If I lose my job, so be it. The two guys Laurie videoed following her are bad news. Sheriff Wade uses them for undercover work, or so I thought. Now I know he's part of the drug trade being run through here." I could hear his disappointment.

"At least we have a plan to stay alive. I'll call Mandy and let her know to stay at the hotel till the FBI agents arrive."

I read my first story, without names mentioned, in the Kansas City Star three days later from the comfort of a houseboat on the lake. Two months later, I read my detailed feature story from the comfort of my living room couch. The Star held onto it until the investigation wrapped up. Darrell was being asked to come back and run for Carroll County Sheriff, and I was being offered a position with the Kansas City paper. They had arrested the two men in the video for Laurie's murder, thanks to a hidden camera she had placed in her room.

As for the drowning of Sheriff Baker that she was researching, an official state autopsy revealed he didn't have water in his lungs. The complete story is still unfolding, but everyone knows dead men don't drown.

Gary Rodgers grew up in rural Arkansas in an age when children were expected to be seen and not heard. As a result, he learned the art of tall tales and lively storytelling at the feet of his grandparents and many uncles, aunts, and cousins.

After a tour in the Army, then a job which took him to all fifty states, all provinces of Canada, and Jamaica, he retired to his rural Arkansas roots. Gary lives with his wife, writer Kimberly Vernon, and an assortment of rescue pets.

Gary has won numerous awards for his stories, some of which have been published in anthologies and magazines.

missing maggie

. . .

Kimberly Vernon

J im Bryce stared into space, puzzled that Maggie still wasn't answering her phone. She was the most responsible person he knew. Between her work for him and her freelance work as a writer, she was usually quick to respond to a call or text. She was rarely ever sick. Concerned, he decided to run over and check on her.

The cross-town drive was brief. In less than fifteen minutes, he pulled into the driveway of Maggie Wallace's neat brick home.

Maggie had worked for him for over ten years, and he'd been to the house a few times. He knocked on the door and heard yapping from inside. He couldn't remember the dog's name, Bitsy, Bugsy, something fitting for a twenty-pound furball.

Getting no answer, he wandered over and looked in the window of the garage door. Inside the dark interior, he could see Maggie's mid-sized SUV. He walked around the side of the garage and through a gate into the backyard. Bitsy/Bugsy shot through the small pet door on the porch and danced around his feet, barking incessantly.

He stooped and patted the small dog on the head, then

climbed the steps onto the deck that doubled as a back porch. The curtains were closed, and he pounded on the back door.

"Maggie, you here?"

He lifted several flowerpots, sliding his fingers along the bottoms, before finding what he was looking for. He pried up tape to remove a small key hidden there. Using the key, he let himself in, shouting as he entered, "Maggie!"

The dog barked and jumped around his feet, making it difficult to walk. Noticing the empty bowls on the floor, he opened a couple of cabinets until he found the dog's food. He scooped out some kibble and filled the water bowl at the sink. With the dog occupied, he hurried through the rooms, looking for Maggie.

A quick search revealed the house was empty. Maggie's purse and keys hung on a hook near the garage door. Worried now, he searched again more slowly, looking in closets and under beds. He found no obvious signs of an illness or injury, no sign of a struggle.

In Maggie's home office, her glasses and cellphone lay on the mostly empty desktop. A laptop or computer was noticeably absent.

Maggie's laptop had all of his business records on it. Records he didn't trust anyone but Maggie with. Now he was really concerned. What was going on here?

He returned to the kitchen and sat on a barstool. Frowning, he found the number and dialed Maggie's daughter.

"Hello? Mr. Bryce?"

"Kenzie, I'm at your mom's house. She's not here, but her car's here, her phone, her purse, her glasses. She's been gone long enough the dog's out of food and water."

"Mom wouldn't leave Bugsy for long. Did you call the police?" Kenzie asked.

"I don't know if we need to do that. Surely there's a reasonable explanation."

Kenzie's voice was shrill. "Like what? Give me one

reasonable explanation. Something's wrong, and the sooner the police get started, the quicker they can find her. You call, and I'll head your way. I'm six hours away."

"You're right. I'll call right now. Drive safely, and try not to worry. We'll find her. Let me know when you get to town."

Jim placed the call and made a final search for the laptop while waiting for Joplin Police to arrive. He didn't really want that laptop to fall into their hands.

After explaining to the officer why he was there, and how he got in, he headed home, an uneasy feeling following him.

After a search of the Wallace house, Officer Paul Layman stood on the small porch across the street, shuffling his feet. "Mrs. Davis, when was the last time you saw Maggie Wallace?"

"I guess Thursday was the last time. I saw her come home in the afternoon. Then I saw the big truck over there later that evening. I do hope she's not getting involved with that man again. He is nothing but trouble."

"What man is that, ma'am?"

"I don't know his name, but he drives a big, loud truck. They were an item for a while last year, but then he got in some kind of trouble with the law. Drugs, I think. She sent him packing, but then Thursday night he was over there again."

"Do you know what time this was?" the officer asked.

"Well, I was watching *Grey's Anatomy* when I heard the loud thing pull up. I said to myself, 'Oh no. Not that no-account scoundrel again.' I got up and looked out the front there, and sure enough, it was him. Strutting up the walk like he owned the place."

"Mrs. Davis, did you see when he left?"

"No. The truck was still there when I went to bed right

after Grey's went off. But when I got up to use the bathroom at midnight, I looked out, and it was gone. I must've been sleeping hard, 'cause the loud rumbling thing didn't even rouse me when he left."

"Did you see or hear anything else unusual in the last few days?"

"Not that I can think of."

He handed her a card. "If you think of anything, please call us. Thanks for your time."

Officer Layman knocked on several other doors nearby, but got nothing helpful. Returning to the Wallace house, he relayed the scant information about a man in a loud truck to Detective Stricklin, who was taking photographs. "Apparently a former boyfriend. Any idea who it would be?"

Stricklin replied, "Nothing here to indicate a boyfriend. Daughter's driving in from college. Maybe she can shed some light."

"You think there's any chance this woman took off with a friend for a while?"

"Without her purse, her phone, or arranging for someone to at least feed her dog? Not likely."

"Yeah, the dog's the kicker." Layman walked over to the bar, where several pieces of paper were sealed in clear plastic sleeves. "What's this?"

"They were in a desk drawer. Someone was leaving Ms. Wallace threatening notes. No idea when or how they arrived, but we'll process them for prints. Might be something."

"What do you make of the boss? He just happens to know where a spare key is and comes in? Sounds fishy to me."

"Yeah, I've got the tech team doing a deep-dive on him and his business. He seemed twitchy to me. Other than the computer, there's no way to know what else is missing until the daughter gets here, which will be nine or ten tonight. After the techs leave, I'm going to seal the house and have the daughter stay at a hotel. We'll bring her over first thing in the morning to look around. By then, we should have access to Ms. Wallace's phone and email records."

The following morning, Detective Stricklin drove Kenzie Wallace from the police station to the house. Going inside, he asked her to look around and see if she noticed anything missing.

Kenzie cuddled the excited dog and wandered through the rooms. Entering her mother's office, she said, "All her computers. A desktop and a two laptops are gone."

"Three computers?" Detective Stricklin asked.

"Yes, she had one strictly for Bryce Holdings' business. She didn't even have her personal email on it. The other one was everything else. Her personal accounts, and the interviews she did for her features, even her novel she was working on. The desktop was for tax records, family pictures, and personal stuff."

"Do you have any idea what she might have been working on recently?"

"No, but there may be a way to find out." She searched through the desk drawer, then pulled out a small device that looked like a miniature remote control, holding it up triumphantly.

"What's that?"

"It's a voice recorder. Mom uses it to record all her interviews. The files on here should tell us what she's working on. Maybe she stumbled onto something someone didn't want her to know. We have to listen to this," Kenzie said, excitement rising in her voice.

Detective Stricklin took the device from her hand. "This could be evidence, so I need to listen to it at the station. Thanks for finding it for us. Please keep looking around." He gestured around the room.

After looking through the rest of the house, she shook her head. "I can't see anything else. But I know Mom wouldn't have left without making arrangements for Bugsy."

"The forensics team went over the house last night and didn't find anything to indicate foul play, so we have no reason to believe your mother's been harmed. You're free to stay there while the investigation proceeds. Let me know immediately if you hear from her."

"I think I'll feel better taking Bugsy and staying with a friend until I know something, but thanks."

"I understand," he said with a smile.

She fastened the dog's harness and gathered food and supplies as they prepared to leave.

"One neighbor mentioned a former boyfriend with a loud truck. Do you have any idea who that is?"

Kenzie chuckled. "I'm sure that was Mrs. Davis across the street, talking about Mike Hawkins. They dated for a while, but he got into trouble. He was arrested and charged with selling cocaine, and Mom broke it off with him."

"Mrs. Davis said he was here Thursday evening."

"Oh, wow. That's surprising. Mom was shocked when he got arrested, and she wanted nothing to do with him. Drugs cross the line as far as she's concerned."

"I'll go talk to him," Stricklin said.

On the way back to the station, Stricklin asked, "Was your mother having trouble with anyone? Anyone mad at her or threatening her?"

"The crazy guy at the end of the road. Claude Dale, Claude's Salvage. She wrote a piece about cleaning up the neighborhoods, and he accused her of trying to shut down his business."

"So what did he do?"

"He left her a couple of ugly notes. If it went beyond that, she never told me."

"Okay, I'll go have a chat with him, too."

After Kenzie left the station, Stricklin met with Officer Layman for an update. He repeated much of what he'd learned from Kenzie. "I've asked tech for everything they can find on Mike Hawkins and Claude Dale, and to transcribe recent files on the audio recorder. What did they find on Jim Bryce?"

"A lot," Layman replied. "Bryce has multiple rental properties in a wide range of neighborhoods. He also has a long-haul trucking company, half a dozen coin-operated laundry mats, two strip clubs, and a beer joint. The businesses seem legitimate, but the combination looks pretty shady. You can't ignore the possibility of moving contraband through the trucking company and laundering the money through the cash-heavy business establishments. No evidence yet, but we're still digging."

"Reckon she found something wonky, and he had to shut her up?" Stricklin asked. He enjoyed working with the sharp young officer. They bounced ideas off each other in a way that worked well. He suspected Paul would earn a promotion to detective soon.

"If Maggie Wallace has worked for him for ten years, she didn't suddenly discover something fishy. She'd have to know something was off. She's doing his books. And if he did something to her, why even report her missing?"

"Well, according to the daughter, she wasn't the type to go along with anything illegal. Of course, that's coming from the daughter, for what it's worth. Let's go see what they've pulled on the boyfriend and the neighbor. You want to interview one of them?"

Officer Layman jumped at the chance. "Absolutely! Just tell me where you need me."

Stricklin thought for a minute. "See what tech dug up on the salvage yard, then go talk to him. The daughter said he wrote a few ugly notes, but I found seventeen notes in the drawer. That's a lot of angry messages. I'll take the ex-boyfriend. Check in with me later."

It took only a few minutes for Detective Stricklin to read the report on Mike Hawkins. The man owned and operated a garage specializing in auto restorations and modifications. A year earlier, a traffic stop had revealed cocaine inside a truck leaving his shop, leading to his arrest.

The investigation had dragged out until two weeks ago, when a shop employee admitted to stashing the drugs. As a result, they dropped the charges against Hawkins.

Stricklin drove to the garage on the outskirts of town and entered the building.

A muscular, dark-haired man with a sleeve tattoo approached. "Hi, can I help you?"

"I'm looking for Mike Hawkins."

"I'm Mike Hawkins," he said. "How can I help you?"

Stricklin showed his badge. "I'd like to talk to you about your relationship with Maggie Wallace."

Mike frowned and said, "We don't have a relationship. Why?"

"Why were you at her house three nights ago?"

"What's this all about?"

"Please answer the question."

"Look, Maggie and I used to date. I was, still am, crazy about her. I got accused of some things, and she broke it off. It took me a long time, but I was finally able to clear my name. I wanted her to hear it from me, and see if there was a chance for us."

"And how did it go?"

"Not as well as I'd hoped. She was glad to hear I'd been cleared, but said she'd have to think about whether we had a future. What's going on?"

"Ms. Wallace is missing."

"What? No!" Mike deflated and dropped into a chair, rubbing his forehead and trying to calm his breathing.

"Do you know anyone who had a problem with her or would want to harm her?"

"She had a crazy neighbor who was harassing her last year. Runs a salvage place. I wanted to go have a chat with him, but she wouldn't let me. He's one of those Nazi wannabes. I can't think of anyone else."

"I'll look into that. Thank you for your time."

Climbing into his car, Detective Stricklin received a call from the precinct.

"Maggie Wallace's last interviews centered on some militia group that's been recruiting and training in the area. The leader is an explosives expert. She's talked with some former members who dropped out when this guy started talking about targeting power grids and water supplies."

"Great. Sounds like she was kicking a hornet's nest."

"Yep. And guess where they've been meeting? Claude's Salvage."

Detective Stricklin hung up and called Officer Layman. "Are you out at the salvage yard yet?"

"Pulling in now. There's a padlock on the gate, and no one answers the phone."

"Wait there. I'll join you. This guy's part of some crazy Nazi-want-to-be group. That tracks with the content of some of those notes. Let's proceed with caution."

Nearing Claude's Salvage, he took a side street to see the layout of the business. It sat at the end of Mountain Street at the edge of the city limits, with Pecan Street running along the side of the property. Piles of metal, old appliances, and wrecked cars stretched into the woods that surrounded the other two sides. Layman sat parked at the Mountain Street gate, near the office. Stricklin spotted a familiar person approaching a gate on Pecan Street. Jim Bryce.

He called Layman. "Meet me at the gate over here on Pecan. Our buddy Bryce is here."

Stricklin parked and approached Bryce, who looked like he wanted to run. "Mr. Bryce, what are you doing here?"

"Maggie's in there."

"What makes you think that?"

"The tracker on her laptop shows her in that house back there."

"You have a tracker on her laptop, and you didn't think to tell us?"

Bryce lowered his head. "It activates at unauthorized log-in attempts. It alerted twenty minutes ago."

Layman got out of his car and approached.

Stricklin said, "Maggie's laptop is inside. This driveway runs straight to the house in the back. I don't see a chain and lock. Let's go in." He turned to Bryce. "You stay right here. We have more to talk about."

Stricklin and Layman squeezed through the rusty gate and followed the dirt driveway to the house. Stricklin stepped onto the shaky porch and beat on the door. "Police! Open up."

Layman stood back, trying to watch in all directions.

A man yelled from behind the door, "What do you want?"

"We want to ask you some questions."

"I'm busy. Come back tomorrow."

"It won't take but a minute," Stricklin replied.

A woman's faint voice came from inside. "Help! Help!"

Both men drew their weapons and stepped forward.

"Open up. Now," Stricklin ordered.

They heard a crash and sounds of a scuffle inside the house. Layman radioed their location and requested backup.

Stricklin drew back and kicked open the door, but it struck a cabinet the man had overturned, partially blocking the entry. Shoving hard against it, he gained an opening wide enough to squeeze through.

As they hurried through the house, they heard a door slam in the back.

Stricklin yelled, "I'll follow him. You find Maggie," as he dashed toward the back door.

"Maggie Wallace, it's the police." Layman shouted.

"In the basement," the reply came.

He found the door to the basement in the kitchen. A shiny new padlock secured the door.

"Stand back," Layman shouted, then slammed his heavy boot against the door. It splintered like kindling, leaving the padlock and a strip of door dangling from the frame.

She rushed up the steps to meet him.

"Are you hurt?"

"No."

"Let's get out of here."

They stepped out the front door as Stricklin walked up, leading a large, grizzled man in handcuffs. The prisoner glared at Maggie. "I knew you were going to get the cops in here and ruin everything."

Wailing sirens grew louder.

"He wanted me to write their hate-filled lies and spread their propaganda," Maggie said. "When I refused, he tried to get into my computer and do it himself."

Stricklin nodded at her. "Thankfully, you're safe now. Let's get you out of here."

murder at turpentine creek

. . .

Kimberly Vernon

A leg protruded from the tiger's den. A human leg. It was obviously female. And likely dead.

Janie's shouts brought her staff, the curators and interns of Turpentine Creek Big Cat Sanctuary. They maneuvered close enough to get a clear view inside the eight-foot square cement den. Spike, the adult male tiger, lounged inside, one giant paw resting across a torso attached to the leg in question. Long curly hair obscured the face, while the head lolled at an unnatural angle.

Several of the staff sobbed, while others muttered and whispered among themselves as they waited for police and rescue workers. *Who was the woman? How did she get inside the tiger cage? Had the tiger killed her? And if so, what did that mean for the sanctuary?*

Janie called the office. "Put a sign on the gate. We're closed until further notice. Send the emergency workers to the main compound as soon as they arrive."

She turned to the maintenance supervisor. "Ray, this is urgent. Check all the gates, locks, and fences. We've got to figure out how she got in there. Plus, we've got to make sure no one got out. Do a full count."

By the time police and rescue arrived, Ray was back with his report. "Someone tampered with the lower gate into the feed alley. I've made sure all the animals are secured and all cages locked."

"Thanks, Ray. Will you show the officers through? I'll help the rescue squad figure out how to get Spike to give up his new prize."

"Don't you have tranqs?"

Janie turned toward the voice behind her. "Excuse me, but who are you?"

The short, stocky, ginger-haired man wore mirrored sunglasses. "I'm Detective Klein. Can't you tranq the cat?"

"He's a tiger, Mr. Klein. We don't 'tranq' them unless it's absolutely necessary. It's very hard on them."

"We have a dead woman in there. I'd say it's pretty hard on her, too."

"Well, our tiger didn't kill her."

"You can't possibly know that. We can't even get close enough to see her yet."

"Mr. Klein, if Spike had killed her, someone would have heard her screaming. Plus, everything you see inside there would be covered in blood."

Using food, they lured the other tigers into adjacent pens and secured them, but Spike wasn't leaving his den. He growled when they probed through the bars with the long hooks frequently used to reach inside the cages.

"We'll have to use the fire hose," Janie stated.

"What? Wait a minute! You'll compromise my entire crime scene."

"Mr. Klein, this is not your crime scene. This is that animal's home, and it's my workplace."

"We have to retrieve the body and look for clues. You can't turn a firehose in there. You'll destroy evidence."

"If you want to retrieve the body, you have two choices. You can march in there and take her away from Spike. I'll hold the gate for you. Or you can let me distract Spike with the hose, so we can get her out of there. Choose quickly, because your precious evidence is being destroyed by the minute."

She pointed toward the tiger, which was licking the body meticulously as if giving her a bath. Janie couldn't help but smile when she heard Klein's curse.

The fire hose sent a long stream of water crashing against the wall outside the den. Spike pressed his ears against his head and hissed. When the stream of water entered the doorway and struck the wall behind him, he rose. Grasping the body, he attempted to drag it through the doorway. As the water continued to splash around him, he gave up and slunk from the den. He crept toward the gate that opened into the next pen. As soon as he was safely inside, interns closed the gate. They turned the water off. It was safe to enter the cage.

Detective Klein rushed through the gate and to the body. He photographed from every angle, before turning it over.

When the hair fell away, Janie gasped. She recognized Trisha Colby, a young woman who worked at the general store down the road. She'd volunteered at the sanctuary a few times and was well liked by the staff. Janie could see a half dozen shallow bite marks on Trisha's arms and legs. But more startling were the purple bruises staining Trisha's face.

Sunglasses in hand, Klein shifted his weight, shuffling his feet on the wooden porch. "Mr. and Mrs. Colby, I'm sorry for your loss. Can you think of anyone who would want to harm your daughter?" In the doorway, a tiny woman wearing a faded apron peeked from behind the hulking figure in overalls.

"She was askin' for trouble. Flirting and carrying on down at the store. Goin' out to bars. Forgettin' her raisin'. I told her nothing good was gonna come of it. I warned her! The wages of sin is DEATH!" Jeb Colby slammed the door to punctuate his pronouncement.

Klein shrugged at the uniformed deputy beside him and descended the steps.

"Hardly the grief-stricken father," Deputy Smith mumbled, following him to the car.

"Yeah," Klein admitted. "We need to look a little closer at Mr. Jeb Colby. But first, let's visit the store where our victim worked. Her best friend, co-worker Amy Staggs, should be there now."

Amy Staggs wiped her eyes. "I just can't believe this!"

"Ms. Staggs, how well did you know Miss Colby?" Klein asked.

"We've been friends since grade school."

"Can you think of anyone who'd want to hurt her?"

"No. Everybody liked her. She was really sweet."

"Ms. Staggs, I'm sorry to say it like this, but someone beat her pretty badly. Those kinds of injuries are usually personal. You know anyone who might have a reason to be angry with her?"

The color drained from Amy's face. Her voice was barely a whisper. "She was pregnant, you know. She said her daddy would kill her when he found out. You reckon he did?"

Klein stepped closer. "Pregnant? Who was the father?"

"She never would tell me. Said she couldn't say until she told him, and they figured out what to do."

"What did she mean by that?" Klein pressed. "Who'd she been dating?"

"I don't know. I never knew her to date anybody, really. She used to have a terrible crush on one of the guys who worked down at the tiger place. But I don't think he ever paid her any attention. Besides, he hasn't been in lately."

"Who was this guy? What's his name?"

"I don't know his name. The guys just called him Hoss. Big guy. He seemed kind of unfriendly to me. But Trisha was crazy about him."

"Thank you, Ms. Staggs. If you think of anything else, please call us." Klein handed her a business card.

"Y'all catch who did this to her. Please?"

"We'll do our best," he assured her as he strode out the door.

Deputy Smith rushed after him. "Looks like we need to talk to Mr. Colby again."

"Yep. But first, let's go by the sanctuary and find this Hoss."

Janie met them as soon as they parked in front of the sanctuary office. "What have you found out?"

"I'll ask the questions, if you don't mind," Klein snapped.

"Then start asking. I want answers as much as you do, Klein. The press is having a field day. Our phone is ringing off the hook."

"We need to talk to an employee they call Hoss."

"Hoss? We don't have… wait a minute. Hostetler, maybe? Come to my office. Let me check."

The men hurried to keep up as Janie's boots crunched through the gravel and into the low brick building. She yanked open a file cabinet and thumbed through thick folders.

"Ah, here. Mike Hostetler. Worked as a handyman; built fences, fixed tractors, whatever needed doing. We let him go about six weeks ago."

"Why?"

"We caught him on the grounds after hours. He wouldn't say what he was doing. We figured he was planning to steal tools or equipment. But what we actually caught him doing was teasing the animals, and that's enough for termination. I won't tolerate that."

"You have an address for him?" the deputy asked.

"Here." She handed him a sheet of paper. "And here's his parole officer's card. That guy practically begged me not to fire him, since he didn't actually steal anything. But a grown man who will mistreat an animal, especially a caged animal that can't defend itself, is not much of a man in my book. We take that seriously."

"Thank you." Klein turned to go.

"Detective Klein, do you think he's the one who killed Trisha?"

"I don't know. But whoever did it managed to hurt your sanctuary, too. And it sounds like Mike Hostetler might have had a reason to want to do that. I plan to talk to him, for sure." He closed the door behind them.

"When have you been over to Turpentine Creek?" Klein asked casually.

Mike Hostetler dragged on his cigarette and sneered. "I ain't been back there since they fired me. That crazy woman said I was teasing her tigers! What does that even mean? They're tigers. They'll eat you if they get a chance."

"How well did you know Trisha Colby?"

"Who?"

"Cute little girl. Dark, curly hair. Worked at the general store down the road from the sanctuary. Ring any bells?"

"Yeah, I might remember someone like that. Why?"

"Was it your baby she was pregnant with?"

"What? That's crazy! I barely knew her."

"So, you'll be happy to give me a DNA sample, right?" Klein smiled at him.

"I'm through talking now."

"That's fine for now. But we'll talk again soon, Hoss."

Klein walked away, leaving Mike Hostetler glaring at his boots.

Back at police headquarters, Detective Klein entered the interview room where Jeb Colby sat waiting. "Thank you for coming in, Mr. Colby. I have a few more questions about your daughter."

Colby grunted.

"When did you learn about Trisha's pregnancy?"

"Don't know what you're talkin' about."

"Mr. Colby, your daughter was pregnant. The autopsy will prove it. Who was the father?"

"I don't know what you're talking about," Colby said through gritted teeth.

"Who's the father of Trisha's baby?"

"Nobody."

"Who was it?" Klein shouted.

"I don't know!" Colby shouted back.

"Mr. Colby, someone defiled your daughter. Didn't you want to know who?"

"She wouldn't tell me!" Colby growled, his words coming hot and fast. "I couldn't make her tell! I hit her. Again and again. She was screaming and crying, 'No, Daddy. Stop.' But she still wouldn't tell me! I whipped her good, but she just cussed me and said she'd never tell." He buried his face in his calloused hands.

"So you killed her."

"No!" Colby jerked his head up. "No! I worked her over some. I had to. She was so dang headstrong! But I left her in the yard, cryin' and cussin' me. I told her to get gone before I got home from work. Told her she had no place in this family.

That's the last I seen of her. I swear." Sobs ripped through the big man.

Klein slipped quietly from the room.

"Let's take a ride," he said to Deputy Smith.

"Where to?"

"We need to pay a visit to Mrs. Colby while he's still here. If Daddy beat up Trisha and left her crying in the yard, Momma knows something."

The house was dark when they parked in front.

The meek little woman opened the door a crack. "Jeb ain't here."

"Yes, Ma'am. We'd like to talk to you," Detective Klein stated.

"What for?"

"Tell us what happened Tuesday night."

"I don't know what you mean."

"Mrs. Colby, we know Trisha was pregnant. We know your husband beat her up trying to make her name the father. We just want to know what happened after your husband left for work."

"You may as well come in." She led them into a tidy living room that appeared rarely used. She sat and folded her hands in her lap before speaking.

"Trisha was sitting in the yard, cussing a blue streak, hollering about how mean her daddy was. Well, I knew she had to be gone before he came home from work, or there'd be more of the same. I found Trisha's phone. She didn't think I even knew she had one. I found his number in it."

"Whose number?"

"Mike Hostetler."

Klein and the deputy exchanged glances.

"Oh, I knew who he was. The no-good bum. Well, I called him up and told him to come get her. He laughed and said no thanks. So, I told him Jeb had already beaten her half to death, and threw her out because she was pregnant. I told him if he didn't come get her, I'd tell Jeb who the baby belonged to."

"Mrs. Colby, what happened then?"

"Well, a while later, a truck pulled in and stopped. After a few minutes, it backed out, and they were gone. The next thing I know, you're here telling us they'd found Trisha dead in the tiger cage. I guess Mike killed her."

"So, don't you feel guilty that you got your daughter killed?" Deputy Smith clenched his jaw.

"No, sir. The way I see it, her sin got her killed. The wages of sin is death. Says so in Romans 6:23."

Klein replaced his sunglasses and shook his head as they headed to the car. "I'll never understand some folks. Doesn't even seem upset her daughter and unborn grandchild are dead."

Deputy Smith slammed the car door. "Some days I hate this job. Let's go get a warrant for Hostetler's truck."

Klein pounded on the door until Hostetler opened it.

"We know you picked Tricia up at her home Tuesday night. Want to tell us what happened next?"

"That's a lie! I ain't seen her."

Klein lifted a folded paper. "This is a warrant to search your truck. What do you bet we find blood and trace evidence inside?"

The big man seemed to shrink before their eyes. "Stupid girl!" He snarled. "She thought I was gonna marry her and raise her brat. She said her daddy'd kill me if I didn't."

"What happened?" Klein prompted.

Hoss stared at him, then sighed. "I just wanted her to shut up a minute, so I could think. But she kept on screaming and crying. I grabbed her around the neck to get her to shut up. I didn't mean to kill her."

"How'd she get in the tiger cage?" Deputy Smith asked.

"I panicked. Then I remembered the feed trolley at the tiger place. I drove over there, through the lower gate, into the alley. I loaded her onto the trolley and used the pulleys to lower her into the cage. I figured the cats would eat enough of her to cover up what had happened."

Klein brandished handcuffs. "Well, Hoss, looks like you're going to get your own cage now."

Kimberly Vernon Rodgers is an award-winning writer of short stories, essays, and poetry. Her stories and poems have appeared in anthologies and magazines, as well as winning many state and regional writing awards. Her children's book, Toolshed Surprise, was published in 2022 by Young Dragons Press, a division of Roan & Weatherford Publishing Associates. She writes a monthly non-fiction feature for a regional magazine.

Kim lives in central Arkansas with her husband, writer Gary Rodgers, and their rescued pets. The two enjoy traveling, reading, and competing in writing contests. See kimberlyvernon.net for more information.

careful what you wish for

. . .

R. H. Burkett

"She did it, didn't she?"

"Bet my badge on it."

"Think we'll ever prove it?"

Detective Johnson spit out his toothpick with a soft poof. "Doubt it. You know what they say—"No body. No crime."

"Yeah. Unfortunately. Nevertheless, I bet she did it."

Well, of course, I did it.

After all, the rich bitch had it coming. Was I remorseful? Ha! Only if caught. But that will never happen.

The victim? Tammy Bedford. Tammy hated and tormented me all through high school. For what reason? Who knows? I suspected it was because of my intelligence of which she had little. Plus she was just a snotty bitch. I loathed her Barbie Doll beauty. Detested her prom dress of satin and lace. Envied her star quarterback boyfriend who escorted her to the ball while I cried alone in the dark, dreaming of a non-existent Prince Charming. Unlike her, however, I never voiced my feelings or was mean to her in any way. To this day, her taunts haunt my dreams:

"Dottie? What kind of frumpy, old maid name is that?"

She flipped her blonde ponytail and wrinkled her turned-up nose. "Where in God's name did you get that dress? The Cow Barn?

Her gang of clueless marionettes, who tagged after her like hungry pups, laughed and chanted. "Dottie is a heifer. Dottie is a heifer. Moo cow, moo."

Determined not to let them know how hurtful their words were, I shrugged it off. "Stick and stones." Spurred on by her clique's idolization, Tammy, however, continued with her jeers and stepped over the line.

"That purple birthmark on your face is hideous."

Gut-punched! All the air left my lungs. I could withstand the insults about my weight and oversized clothes, but the birthmark was my Achilles heel. That's when it happened—a strange voice whispered in my ear and turned my heart to ice and froze my soul black.

"Make her pay, Dottie. Make them all pay."

I killed Tammy during our freshman year in college with a machete. Timid, shy, little ol' me! Butchered her like a cow. The irony wasn't wasted on me. "Who's mooing now, Tammy?"

The brutality of the act scared the hell out of me yet was exhilarating and oddly titillating at the same time. Cool as a cucumber, I stuffed her parts in garbage bags and drove two hours to a hog farm in a nearby county. Under the cover of dark night, I tossed her limbs to the hogs. That's one body that will never be found. "Sooie Pig!"

After college, I combined my business degree with my hobby and opened a little photography shop. Still, the jeers continued from debutantes who married neckless football players who, courtesy of their fathers-in-law, became CEO's and bank presidents.

"I guess it's true what they say, 'those who'll never have a wedding of their own, photograph pictures of those who do.'"

The old resentment and hate that had laid dormant for so long began to churn. Oh, how I hated them! I wished to cut their hearts out.

The man who strolled into my shop a few days later made the hair on the back of my neck stand straight up. It was a hot, sultry day outside, but a spooky chill ushered him in.

"Good morning. May I assume I'm speaking to the proprietor of this lovely shop?"

That voice. I knew that voice, but from where?

"Yes. I'm Dorothy Cantrell. Dottie for short."

He reached out a hand. "Most excellent. Pleased to meet you."

Hesitant, I shook with him and tried not to grimace. His fingers were long, cold, and reminded me of Daddy Long Legs spiders. Creepy looking. I focused on his face instead. Not much better, unfortunately. Paper-thin, almost translucent skin stretched too tight over his cheekbones. *If he smiles, his face will split.*

"What can I do for you today?"

"Oh, how amusing. It's not what you can do for me, my dear Dottie, but rather what I can do for you."

How arrogant. He probably thought himself quite handsome wearing that black suit that fit him like a glove and the sharp trim of his dark hair and matching Van Dyke beard.

"I assure you. I do not."

Taken aback, I stammered, "I . . . I don't understand."

Hooded, dark eyes crinkled at the corners. "Oh, don't play coy, Dottie. We both know why I'm here. After all, your wish summoned me."

"What wish?"

He ignored me. Instead, he reached out his gaunt hand and touched the birthmark on the side of my face. I flinched and itched to run but was held captive by his charm and hypnotizing smile.

"Society girls. You hate their arrogance. Envy their beauty. Covet their wealth and prestige. Not that I blame you. They ridicule your plainness. Shame your body. Look down their noses at your off-the-rack clothing and lackluster life."

Tears inched down my cheek. How did he know? He wiped them away with his thumb. "It isn't fair, is it?"

I tried hard not to react but felt myself being pulled in by his demeanor. I sniffed. "They make me feel like dirt. Always have, since I was a kid. I feel invisible, like my life doesn't matter. The therapist said I take beautiful pictures to compensate for my lack of beauty and self-worth. Some help that was. That made me feel *twice* as bad."

"Yes, yes. I understand. But. I can fix all of that. You once wished for a way to cut their hearts out."

"Yes, but I didn't really mean . . . wait. How do you know that?"

"I know all things. And, yes, you did mean it. In fact, you were quite serious."

Shit! My heart jumped into my mouth. Who was this guy?

"Who . . .who are you?"

"Oh, what's in a name? I've been called many." He gave a wicked chuckle. "None are important."

A blast of fear washed over me, and I pressed a hand to my chest. This wasn't real. Wasn't happening. Just my imagination playing tricks on me. Must be the heat.

"Dottie?"

"Go away! You're not real. I'm . . . sick to my stomach, that's all. Maybe a tinge of food poisoning, and I'm so very hot. I need to lie down."

"Oh, bravo!" He clapped. "How amusing. You think I'm just a piece of undigested beef. The Ghost of Christmas Past, perhaps? How very Dickens. Well, I suppose if you must have a name, you may call me Dante."

Knees weak, I sank onto a chair. Thoughts swirled like a whirlwind in my head. "I'm so confused. Am I dreaming?"

"No, my dear. I assure you, I'm quite real. Now. Back to the point. What I need to hear from you is, if there were a way to . . . let's say rid yourself of those holier-than-thou ladies, would you do it?"

His cold hand on my wrist grounded me. The cobwebs cluttering my mind vanished and blessed coolness washed over me. The bitter bile of resentment and hate simmered, boiled over, and spewed forth with a vengeance. An evil laugh escaped from me.

"You bet I would. But. I don't know how."

"I will show you."

Intrigued, I scooted closer. "Why? What's in it for you? What do you really want, *Dante*?

"Well, their hearts, of course. You see, I'm a collector of sorts. However, I'm very selective."

"What's in it for me?"

"Payback, my dear. In addition, for every heart you bring me, I will grant you a wish."

"Promise I won't get caught?"

"I give you my word." He offered his hand. "Do we have a deal?"

Without a minute's hesitation, I shook hands with him. "Deal. How will I know whose heart you want?"

"Oh, it's rather simple. Just continue taking your pictures. Be assured, I'll make my choice known."

Deep in the bowels of my darkroom, I examined the proof closely. There it was—a slight blur right over the bride's shoulder. With a magnifying glass, I studied the anomaly closer.

I must be sure. No room for mistakes. Sure enough, there

was a man's face. A man with a neatly trimmed Van Dyke, black eyes, and a mesmerizing smile.

With care, I sharpened my knives.

With the first heart, my purple birthmark disappeared. My skin was radiant and beautiful.

With the second, I grew a mane of silky blonde hair.

The third brought me a slim waist and toned body.

Four gifted me fame and fortune.

What would the others bring? Perhaps a snappy, cherry-red Corvette convertible? Maybe a condo by the oceanfront. Or a yacht. Perhaps I'd try my hand at politics. The first woman president had a nice ring to it.

So what if I'd sold my soul? No big deal. It was worth it. *Dot's Shots* was known nationally as *the* best wedding photography shop around. My pictures were "simply to die for." Too much emphasis is put on salvation anyway. I wish people would just get over the whole "saving of the soul" bunkum.

Dante clapped his hands in glee. "Oh, how amusing these mortals be. Be careful what you wish for, my dear, Dottie. After all, as you well know, paybacks are hell."

R. H. Burkett, aka Ruth Weeks, is an international tarot card reader who draws from her deep Cherokee and Cajun roots to write riveting tales of the paranormal. From her travels to ancient stone circles in rural Ireland to her explorations in the French Quarters on New Orleans, she tells stories that encompass her love of all things mystical.

Her latest release <u>Broom Flyers Tales and Spells</u> is a compilation of her short stories, one of which was nominated for a 2023 Spur Award (Western Writes of America). Her first novel, <u>Soldiers In the</u>

<u>Mist</u>, was voted Ozark Writers League (OWL) 2012 Best Book of the year. Her second novel, <u>Daughter of the Howling Moon</u>, was the Oklahoma Writers Federation (OWFI) 2015 Book of the Year.

As a child, Ruth was fascinated by stories about her Grandmother Ely, who was part Cherokee and part Cajun. That was the inspiration for her adopting the handle Witchy Woman. She currently lives in Springdale, Arkansas, with her familiar, Fred. Check out her website rhburkett.com and follow her author page, where you can watch videos of the author talking about her travels, her heritage, and the people she meets both from this world and the next.

death by faulkner

. . .

Cly Boehs

[We catch two elderly, fadingly well-to-do, women, in the middle of a conversation at the beginning of all three scenes; and in all, they are in Audrey's diminishingly well-dressed living room--soft, sagging sofa chairs--having 4 o'clock tea. All this can be suggested by a bit of off-center finery here and there. Nothing hard to manage. One thing though: a lot of books are piled around. Audrey is usually breathlessly charged with barely subdued energy, dressed much younger than she is, and as disjointedly as she speaks; Mildred is quietly on guard, almost bashfully submissive to her sister until the end; she's always conventionally, respectfully dressed.]

scene 1

AUDREY

....the one that's locked is hers, of course; though I don't know how I can use the possessive with it; it's not hers, strictly speaking, because she's not there anymore...well, she's not *seen* anymore, how do they put it, the expression in novels?

Ah, 'indisposed.' She's indisposed. Though that implies she's ill, which he says she's not.

MILDRED

[Not a question] He told you she wasn't sick.

AUDREY

Well, by indirection. He said, to those who've cared enough to inquire, that she's on holiday, his continental way of putting her on vacation. I don't like it. It's positively unacceptable whatever it is, and I've said as much, not to him, of course, because he doesn't know that I know he's got her room locked up there near the attic, but I've told a few in the neighborhood, after the butcher told me. They don't seem to think much about it. And those that might, aren't accepting what they see--or not see, in this case, at least not to me. [falsetto on quotes] "Maybe she locked it herself, you think of that, Audrey? before she went abroad," or this one, Rasmussen up the block has this to say, "Upstairs room? It's probably part of the attic. Give the man his own house, woman!" The old codger never liked me. "Do people separate at their ages?" a young couple up on Parkview wanted to know. "You say he says she's gone? I thought I saw her yesterday," is what Myrtle Cambridge has to say. This is the watchdog neighborhood I live in. "If he wants to keep her things to himself, that's all right by me. Poor thing, her running away and all." That's Mrs. Coldrich's view. She thinks she up and left him, like her husband up and left her thirty years ago. Everyone else believes him--she's visiting relatives in Italy. No real suspicions. No real questions. No unsettling inquiries. Properties aren't threatened then, is what I say.

MILDRED

Audrey, you have yourself tied up in knots over something that's probably got the simplest explanation. I'm sure she *is* off visiting.

AUDREY

[Sharply] Not the maid's idea. She thinks it's odd but not odd enough, of course, to get herself involved outside the house. She talked to the butcher the week she started and now's sorry she did--at least that's his point of view, because now she comes and goes to market in silence, buying her pork loin for the week and her roast for Sundays, not looking left nor right. Nobody will get anything more out of her. Or the butcher now either. Pamsy-wamsies! The whole lot of them.

MILDRED

[Subdued curiosity] What the maid's idea?

AUDREY

It's the wife's bedroom that's locked. She thinks, thought, it's odd it's the wife's room that's locked. Especially since he got himself so worked up when she inquired about how she was to clean it.

MILDRED

How did she know it was the wife's bedroom. People their age have separate bedrooms? Now that's what's odd!

AUDREY

Harry and I did, always did. Don't try to be covert,

Mildred, it doesn't fit with your self-righteousness. Having your own bedroom is a way to gain privacy when you need it, is what Harry and I both felt. And it makes sex intentional. [Mildred looks down, fluttering around] None of this pulling the shades, turning off the light, lying down in bed like each of you are going to sleep and then one of you just happens to roll over on top of the other one.

MILDRED

Since you so obviously are preoccupied with this...situation, I suppose you could call the police...*anonymously*, of course. If nothing comes of it, fine. But then you would have done your duty. That's what I'd do.

AUDREY

[Excited] Will you?

MILDRED

Me? Call? Oh my, heavens, no. It doesn't concern me. [looks at Audrey's crushed face] Audrey, come on now, you can't expect me to....He's *your* neighbor. You're the one who's...into this. And in my judgment, you ought not to be. The police wouldn't understand my calling them....I live on the other side of town, for heaven's sakes, well, I suppose anybody could call of course...especially if you don't identify yourself...and if it continues--her not being seen; well, perhaps the neighbors ought to...but I really don't feel I should intrude...anyway, with you and me and the police, there's already been somewhat of a history....

AUDREY

[Pleading] Any concerned citizen can call. They know my voice, you know they do. They will be suspicious of me, since he's next door!

MILDRED

[Getting up, acting as though she's about to leave] Oh no you don't. You know I can't do this. Edward would divorce me! "Not another time," he says. So don't throw yourself into one of your snits in an attempt to place me where you want. [slowing down] Audrey, it was a mistake to suggest you call. I was thinking you just might make a simple report, get it out of your system and then drop further proceedings on this idea. Silly me! [sighs, starts to leave, sternly] This time, you are on your own. I won't, can't, come get you out of it. [sympathetically, softening] You know I can't support your ....unsupportable escapades any longer...I absolutely cannot end up at the police station, or in the courthouse, bailing you out, not another time! Audrey, Audrey, please keep to the simple life. It's enough for you, for me, to handle.

AUDREY

...and that's exactly why I can't be the one to notify them, don't you see? Even if I disguise my voice, they will know me from the other....investigations. It's true that there were only two, well, three, if you count------

MILDRED

Investigations is not the word...reckless acts to satisfy your insatiable curiosity is what they were...are! You're right, the police will recognize you and well they should. I wish you would consider joining our church and getting involved in some programs there. You're bored and have been since

Harry died. Edward and I have talked about this often. He's urging me to talk you into joining, becoming involved in Seniors For Global Peace or with the children's Sunday School...

AUDREY

You act like this is the first time you've introduced churchy ideas to me! You know I hate kids...they remind me of little birds chirping, chattering, running around at random. [shutters] And seniors are old birds awking, gawking, squawking...[in a blast] No! Stop before you start, Milly.

MILDRED

Well, you need something to preoccupy your time. Figuring out how you're going to intrude yourself into the life of that old man next door isn't....

AUDREY

Obtrude, Milly. It's 'intrude' with some umph!

MILDRED

[Exasperated] Someone else will have to tell you what I just have, Audrey. You're not listening to me. I really must be going....

AUDREY

It's how I put things that they'll recognize! [sighs] Besides, it's too early for either one of us to go to them, isn't it? We don't know enough.

MILDRED

Audrey, [very cautious] I must admit, you are very good at this. I'm being especially stubborn right now for a reason. You can make anything, everything sound so...*plausible,* no matter how outlandish these librettos are that you orchestrate. I don't know where that talent comes from... [realizes she's into it now] It's your great...great...imagination, which is a gift, really. But you must try, no, you must control yourself and keep out of these...situations.

AUDREY

[Increasingly worked up] Don't patronize me, Mildred! Our mother was a victim of dementia toward the last, but I don't need to hear the echo, as though I'm standing on edge, the cliff beneath my feet. Our mother is not ourselves. But if you are going to hint at genetic tendencies, remember, you are her daughter as well. The genes can be carried far and wide...prayer will not protect you against biodetermination...so be careful what you say to me. There *is* karma, a spiritual condition that's not affected by what science or religion chooses to call it--evolution, inheritance, the Lord's Will or whatever you like.

[some silence, Mildred again almost going, Audrey suddenly mollified]

[Sighs] I'm sorry I brought this up. Of course, you're right. This doesn't concern you.

MILDRED

[Pleasant but stern] Or you either.

AUDREY

[Good little girl, rote] Or me.

[Mildred readjusts her gathering and going; resumes tea;
some quiet]

It's just that I'm in his house sometimes.
[Mildred looks up, extremely attentive, close to alarm]
...to visit, looking in on him. I feel it's only neighborly. He
and his wife have been here forever, well, as long as any of us
can remember, and these folks, around here...on *this* side of
town are, you know, [reluctantly] mostly my age. It's true
nobody knows them well, as I say, but they are a part of the
neighborhood, we *see* them, together, rarely alone, if ever, and
now he's...without her. I feel compelled to…to inquire…to
look in on him. [no response, just a stare] At any rate, I do
look in from time to time. [justifying] They were charitable, if
not friendly. They stood for something, something solid,
something....old...what am I trying to say? They were
foreigners in one way, but in another, they felt like founders,
the immigrants that made America [trails]...what this country
has become...at least this part of it...

[goes over and sits next to Milly, solicitous]

They always gave to the funds, the church needs. I
suggested a maid to him--when I took over some banana
bread some weeks ago--someone to clean up, I mean, heavens, the place was abandoned when she...left. She's been gone
now over three months. I know the Italians have extended
stays...extended families...and all that, but this seems
extremely excessive. [haltingly, slow] He just sits and watches
TV. I see him from my dining room window. He doesn't
bother to pull his shades.

MILDRED

Well, why should he? [Mildly pleading] Audrey, you simply must not snoop.

AUDREY

He did finally get some woman in. I don't know if she's from an agency or his church--guessing he has one, who would know for sure? It's said that he's Episcopalian, for heaven's sakes--wherefrom she comes, I'm not sure, though she goes with him, to Collinsville on Sundays. Being Italian, one doesn't have to guess, really. [pause, shifts topics] But it looks ever so much better in there. And smells better too, of course. My first visit, the smell was overpowering, it took me back, I didn't think I could stay. I assumed it was the dishes, food left out, the trash, not cleaning up behind himself in the bathroom...men are so unmercifully clumsy about their aims.

MILDRED

Audrey, spare the details!

AUDREY

Thank goodness, the maid didn't come just once like I thought she might, to do the deep cleaning, as they say. She's stayed on. Came weekly for a while, then it was daily, now I don't know that she leaves! I never see her except when she comes out the back door with her basket on the way to the grocery. And that's how I know for sure, you see.

MILDRED

[Hopelessly falling into the magic] That the wife's not coming back, you mean?

AUDREY

About the *room.* The maid, said something to Mr. Ammons...the butcher....you know Ammons [Milly nods] at the IGA. The butcher at the IGA. Well, when I mentioned Radner not going out much, how does he eat? Whether he comes to market. This is when I learned the cleaning woman, the maid, had started for sure, and that's when Ammons told me that the room's upstairs, near the attic, was definitely locked, that the old man wouldn't under any circumstances let the cleaning woman go in there. Now, after all this being told to him, you'd think Ammons'd be, at the very least, *curious,* wouldn't you? But no, it doesn't work that way in this town. He's curious, all right, but he talks to me about this like he'd tell me that the old man's not mowing his lawn...which he's not, by the way! Though he was never very good about it even when she was there, gardening too, imagine! Why don't they hire somebody?

MILDRED

Audrey, can't you see how you heighten situations? Under all the rhetoric, you're telling me that the butcher's not curious enough, to your way of thinking, because he's simply not talking to you in conspiratorial tones at the moment. Look how much he's told you already. Audrey, I'm fearful of these escalations. I'm pleading with you to just let this run its course without you.

AUDREY

But you know what I mean. This community has no *real*

curiosity. She drops off the face of the earth. So what do they do? They call on the old man, the ladies of the church, then the minister, and Radner puts them at ease, nicely, saying she's visiting relatives in Italy, and that's that. Then they listen to what comes around by chance, they talk among themselves, but that's where the story ends. I'm not sure the maid even let them into the living room. I saw everybody sitting stiffly in a huddle near the window in the entry parlor. When certain people call on him--the mayor, aldermen and such, the maid opens the drapes, lifts the shades! [sighs] It is true they were both very reserved. They never really *participated*, and that's what's got the neighborhood talking. They attend church in Collinsville, where they have an Episcopalian service--if that's where they go all dressed up Sunday mornings in her car. I call it her car because he never drives that I've seen. The minister's wife had plenty to say to the women at church about their religious attitudes, which means she offered, once again, for them to join the Baptist church here, and they respectfully declined. She didn't find out anything of substance or she's not saying. I didn't know there were *German* Episcopalians, if that's what he is. I thought Episcopalians were mostly English. The state church and all that. It's the Lutherans in Germany, isn't it? She's got to be Catholic, being of Italian extraction. It wouldn't go well in this town for her to go to one church, him another. Collinsville is safer from everybody's eyes and ears by a long shot.

MILDRED

[Snorts] "Radner" *is* English, isn't it? And haven't I seen her out and around in town? Didn't you say that she gets around in her car? Now you're implying they're almost reclusive. I've seen them while I'm visiting. She's been out in the yard. He, as well.

AUDREY

Of course. In their *yard*. And she got around in town, for the necessities, is all. Nobody talked to either one of them much, as their signals were that they wanted to keep to themselves, but there's always been plenty to say _about_ them. She was excessively quiet, I thought. Maybe under his thumb. He's a Sieg Heil German, I'm almost certain of it--you sure "Radner"'s English? She's Italian, a *quiet* Italian, have you ever heard of such a thing? Anyway, all this is beside the point. She was there and now she's not. She was alive and well and in and out of the house, to the market and back, still driving the car. And then one day, gone. *Gone*. *Without* the car. It sits in the garage. I looked.

MILDRED

You cannot drive to Italy from here, Audrey. [raises her hand to stop Audrey's commenting] And I don't want to know how you looked.

AUDREY

He's pulled the shades this past week. I went to call and he's...*they* are not answering the door. A maid should answer the door. I thought I'd try just once more.

MILDRED

Oh, Audrey, can't you see, he wants to be left alone, that's obvious. Maybe she went to Italy and decided not to return. Maybe she went to Italy and *died*. Traveling is hard on old people. [laughs in light exuberance] Listen to me. What am I? Thirty-nine? I don't go anywhere anymore. I feel like I'm going to die when I go up in an airplane...and the bus--who can travel by bus at our age? We don't have the stamina. [anticipates Audrey's approaching impatience] I do hear you, Audrey, and admit there are some irregularities in all this. But we older ones have our...oddities. Our small claims to our diminishing lives. I heard about this old man who just walked out of his house when his wife died and left the place to fall down on itself. Left her clothes, his clothes, their two cups half filled with coffee right on the breakfast table. He went out to get the paper and when he came back into the kitchen, she had slumped down into her eggs. He walked out the door and left everything there, including her. They found him wandering the streets. When they finally got the story out of him, he said he wanted to mandate a will of non-intervention with anything that was theirs while they lived together. Of course, the civic councils, administrators and politicians had their legal say about such a thing happening in the choicest part of their town; and his wishes were never granted! I read this in the paper, I think. It happened somewhere in the Midwest. Oklahoma maybe. These things are hard on men and women who have spent their lives together. I'm just saying that what appears to be untowards usually isn't when all the facts are out...in. Maybe Radner's lost her in Italy and the family is keeping the remains there, that would be proper, and he feels too old to travel, has instructed the maid not to say anything. He doesn't want solicitors, the excessive sympathy from people he doesn't feel close to, to say nothing of the excessive number of chocolate cakes people bring to wakes these days. He doesn't want to gain weight on top of his other problems. You say he's reserved, so you should understand this, surely. He's keeping her room as a memorial.

AUDREY

Even if all you say is true, you think it's perfectly fine for him to be living in their house with the maid, with the door to her bedroom locked, while he sits staring day and night at the TV? Nose to tube? No lights, just the flickering blue haze, a beam in the settling dust? It's morbid. [almost shrieking] It's *unnatural*.

MILDRED

[Impatience] Settling dust? The maid is dusting! It's what maids do. And, anyway, you aren't certain what the arrangements are with the maid...you said so yourself. I have to admit that what you're suggesting is out of the ordinary, to be sure...but since when have you been an advocate for conventionality? You've too much of a descriptive bent, Audrey. You are always talking a novella!

AUDREY

[Miffed] I'm describing honestly what I've seen with my own eyes. [Sudden connection] It reminds me of that story about the woman, the one about this old man's long ago lover [pause] was it an old man? I can't remember. [pause] Yes, when the story was told, he was old, but he was young when it happened... but a love....he kept her upstairs in a bedroom after she died, not reporting her passing. He just put her up in the bedroom and left her....I can't remember whether he killed her or not. Yes, he *did*, that's why he [excited] kept the door locked to the room where she was....he....didn't want to let anyone know his mischief and [remembering] yes, it was more to keep the love, you see, *forever*. To preserve her....always. He put her in some kind of an....intimate....position and from the pillow, [quotes] "the yellowed and moldy pillow"--I remember that phrase distinctly--they knew he had been sleeping with, beside, her, even when she had turned to dust, because... oh, what was it. [Eureka!] They found his rose, he gave her a rose each morning. On the indented pillow where he slept next to her. Yes. That was the part that I remember most. Anyway, the story became the prototype for *Psycho*. I'm sure I read that somewhere. [no response] You know, the film by Alfred Hitch....

MILDRED

Of course, I know the film, Audrey. Goodness, everybody knows *Psycho*! But ....you are making too big a leap from the silver screen to your neighbor's upstairs bedroom! Where on earth do you find concepts like "prototype"?

AUDREY

Well, if you ask me, the whole thing next door is getting more and more curious. I'm wanting like everything to unlock that door, get into that house and pick the lock when Radner's sleeping. It would have to be then because he never leaves the house anymore, the maid is bringing in his groceries, tending trash, watering outdoors plants, sweeping the porch and walk, I have the lock picks, I found where Harry left them. [giggles lightly] I haven't the foggiest notion what he ever needed them for!

MILDRED

[Greatly alarmed] Audrey. No!

AUDREY

Oh, don't get your nose out of joint, Milly, I don't know how to use the things. [Mildred barely has time to show relief] But I could practice. On my doors! [grins sympathetically] Poor Milly. [pause] Poor Mrs. Radner.

MILDRED

Audrey, I forbid it. You are so exasperating. You live...you live in your head too much. You think up places to go others wouldn't dream of going and it's....causing...a great deal of..... [drifting] d i s m a y...

AUDREY

[Overlapping] Exhilaration. Tantalization. [hissing] Promissssse! Admit it, the potential for finding out...is....*e* n o r m o u s.

MILDRED

It's a tomb, a self-sanctified tomb. Sealed. We can't possibly... without violating ...What am I saying? [close to hysteria, trembling] This is simple. This is very simple, Audrey. It's breaking and entering. What you are thinking of doing is *unlawful*! Do you hear me? You, me, my God, we will go *to jail*.

AUDREY

[Chuckling] Yes. It is on the margin, I admit. Isn't it simply delicious. [Mildred's definitely leaving] So you aren't going to do anymore than anybody else? Pamsy Wamsy!

MILDRED

I am extricating myself from this scene that is about to ensue...I am walking out of this door and heading home where there is a loving atmosphere of peace and contentment....

I WILL NOT ANSWER THE TELEPHONE, AUDREY!
[Milly stands mesmerized during the next speech]

AUDREY

I tell you I've read about this in stories. And I do read, Milly. Not like you, of course, but I'm not literally deficient! Oh, what was his name, the writer of the story I've been telling you about....he's so well-known....damnation....Oh, I just don't remember like I used to! [drops her arms] Awk. Not anything recent. Stephen King maybe, though I never read his popular grime. But this, this Radner thing is positively Poe-ish, don't you think? I'd give my eye tooth to see what he's up to.

MILDRED

[As calm as she can muster] Radner's *story*, as you put it, Audrey, is your imagination getting ahead of you...from the reading you don't even remember well. I've said that to Edward. I have to tell you that I have. "She reads too much," I tell him. [thinking] I say, "She reads too much into what she reads." This story, this one you are into at the moment, is about this very old man, who happens to live next door--to his misfortune!--who wants to preserve his loved one, maybe even protect her by locking up her things, [panting] this is providing she isn't going to return. I don't want to offend you, Audrey, but I need to say that I think you are improperly [snide] *obtruding* yourself, at this point, into his state of affairs. You need to honor his desire to protect her memory. [near exhaustion, hand on door knob]

AUDREY

HA! [Mildred jumps] He never protected her in life. He got at her every chance he could.

MILDRED

Audrey! You are inventing as you go...living off your own momentum...where has this come from all of a sudden?

AUDREY

From their backyard. In the summer with the windows open. He went at her plenty. Trust me on this one, Milly.

MILDRED

You said they were reserved, stand-offish, you said she especially never talked to anyone, that he had her under his thumb. You said he is turning people away at his door. Now you are saying he was going at her in their backyard! I'm hopelessly lost.

AUDREY

Those are not mutually exclusive, Mildred! It's the duality of the private and public persona! You ever see *Rear Window*?

MILDRED

[Shakes head; whispers anxiously] Murder! [Frantic] This is an idea you must not play with, Audrey!

AUDREY

I keep thinking, what if she's in there decaying with the flowers? Remember, I smelled a kind of odor, a *loud* odor.

Nobody has been to see him in at least a month. I haven't *seen* him now for weeks. The house is dark, absolutely motionless, except for the coming-and-goings of the maid.

MILDRED

[Exaggerated delight] Maybe the maid did it, yes, that's it. It's the maid!

AUDREY

[Ignoring her] There *is* some talk of that, her being there, not answering the door anymore. But nobody is *doing* anything about it.

MILDRED

Exactly what is it that you think they should be doing, Audrey?

AUDREY

Investigating!
[Mildred opens the door to leave, turns back to say...]

MILDRED

You must promise me you will not do anything without me. Promise me, Audrey, or I'll tell Edward about this latest venture and he *will* do something. Trust me. He'll call somebody and it won't be the police about Radner.
[Audrey only nods stiffly, reluctantly]
[Softening] I'll be back tomorrow afternoon. Tea time.
[Mildred turns to walk out the door and stops dead in her tracks]

[Trembling] She's back, Audrey. Mrs. Radner's come back...from Italy. The maid is letting her in the back door! See! See, all this's for naught.

AUDREY

[Rushing to the door, peers around Mildred out the door, turns back looking at Mildred full-face in astonishment]
Faulkner! It's by Faulkner!

LIGHTS OUT

scene 2

[Both women are in Audrey's living room; tea is done, cups, saucers scattered on the table. Audrey has binoculars looking through the window, squatting low on her sofa chair, as though not to be seen; Mildred is seated in her chair reading a book, turning pages back and forth, totally consumed]

AUDREY

It isn't her, Milly. It's not her, I tell you. This woman is younger and there's something...too straight about her...I'd know Radner's wife any day of the week and this just...is not her under any circumstances.

MILDRED

[In reading voice] No, it's *him*.

AUDREY

[Whirling around] Him? Come see for yourself. This's not his wife, I want you to be my witness. This is not Radner's wife. It's somebody passing for...Him? what do you mean, him?

MILDRED

Faulkner, like you said. I found the story. You have it back-wards, not to mention the details all out of sequence, and accuracy, you've no accuracy in the details at all. She kills *him* with poison, arsenic, not the other way around, and leaves him in the upstairs bedroom. Audrey, you didn't make this up, it's here....it's positively gruesome, it's all here, but, you've botched the storyline plenty. I think you need to see for yourself.

AUDREY

[Continues looking through the binoculars] I have? But I remember it so vividly. The story...the one about Radner?

MILDRED

It's not about Radner! It's somewhat like the goings on next door but it's as though... [looks up at Audrey, announces] You've imprinted reality with fiction.

AUDREY

[Continues binocular-ing] Isn't that what reality is? [turns around, a little amused] I remember reading somewhere, where was it? Ah, *Harper's Monthly*, I think, or was it *The New Yorker*?, it was a few years ago, about this storytelling gene.

MILDRED

[Still into the book] Now what are you talking about?...a story gene?

AUDREY

[Still into the binoculars] They called it a "scripting" gene, I think. No, it's not a gene, it's something about how the mind works. [as though a quote] We tend to describe reality to ourselves in the form of stories, but more than that, we organize what we experience *as* a story. [end of quoting] Everybody does it...without realizing. Isn't that interesting?

MILDRED

Where in heaven's name do you find these things...[back to presumed reading] Heaven knows, I can't spend my time checking your sources...though in this case, I may have hit pay dirt.

AUDREY

[Uninterested, continues to watch out the window] Fiction is where the truth slips through the cracks into real life. Haven't you heard that?

MILDRED

Not exactly. I have heard that truth is stranger than fiction. I think Mark Twain, it was. [flipping pages] There are elements here that I can....I can see how you thought of this. There's no rose though...on the pillow like you said. There was a hair left on the pillow. That's what makes it work...She had this particularly....remarkably memorable grey hair.

AUDREY

[Conspiratorially] Come here....quick. *Now*! [Milly goes to her window; takes the binoculars]

MILDRED

What am I looking for? I haven't the slightest idea what I'm seeing!

AUDREY

There [points through window] See *there*. Under the hat... [grabs the binoculars back] Who the devil wears hats nowadays?

MILDRED

...maybe in Italy.

AUDREY

Fah! Look! Under the hat....*Red* hair!

MILDRED

What am I looking for? I don't see what...[sees] *red hair*. Audrey, I don't remember what Radner's wife looked like. I don't think I've seen her half a dozen times over... how many years? [searching, flatly confirming] Yes, there *is* red hair under the hat on this one.

AUDREY

[Grabs the binoculars, Milly moves back to her chair and the book] They were here when I moved in. 1959, it was. Over forty years. Goodness, how times evaporates when you...

MILDRED

Read.....

AUDREY

Oh, I don't read like I used to; can't because of my eyes, even with glasses. Prescriptions don't work anymore, they just make everything bigger, including the blurs.

MILDRED

[Exasperated] I mean, come here and *read* this. You've made a mess of this story. It's a disservice to Faulkner. This is a well-constructed story and you've turned it into a farce. What's more, I have to tell you, Audrey...after reading this, I think you are fusing the reality you are viewing next door with this one [She flops book overhead; Audrey is half listening] at least, as you've put it in your head and memory has distorted it!

AUDREY

[Searching with the binoculars] Mrs. Radner had, has, grey hair, as grey as porch paint. Not a streak of any other color in it....Awk! Her hat blew off! She's essentially a redhead, auburn at the very least, red auburn, come see for yourself, a red-haired old lady! Can you believe it? [binocular-searching, simply humming] And not so old....

MILDRED

[Straining to see through her own glasses she has hung on a neck strap; finally into it] Oh, my...heavens, she truly is... [looking at Audrey, lecturing, teaching] Do you know how many redheads there are in the world? Only about 2% at the most! I looked at the library once when I was reading a novel in which I just couldn't picture the main character as a redhead...

AUDREY

a ginger...

MILDRED

C'mon, Audrey, don't be cute! It doesn't become you!!
[Audrey is chastened, but grins a little]

MILDRED

In the U.S. it's only about 4%, as it is in England. Scotland has the most redheads at 13%. I'm talking about naturally red hair, of course. [pause] But Audrey, remember Mrs. Radner's been to Italy. You know how the Italians are. Sanguine. Operatic. Mischievous....maybe she's had her hair done to please him [looking at Audrey's questioning face] or to make homecoming a surprise. It could be many reasons unknown to us. Maybe she's straining to get him to fancy her again. Ha! [looks away, starts to return to chair] I'm as silly as the town folks.

AUDREY

Movie stars do that, Milly...Shirley MacLaine dyed her hair redder when she tumbled over the hill; the Irish do it, perhaps, in advancing years, to brighten what they already have, but little old Italian ladies do not do this, at all. When they reach our age, they put on black and frequent the cemeteries. The travel calendars show you that, along with the ruins. Anyway, it's not her, don't you see? It's not her features and Mrs. Radner was stooped, this woman's posture is positively vertical. Ramrod.

MILDRED

[Retreating from the window, pouring tea, falling into her sofa chair] Maybe it's one of her cousins. Visiting. The wife's coming later, she's not home yet. Or more likely the cousin came to make arrangements for a memorial here...considering the wife's probably been buried in the family plot in Italy. [almost flippant] Or maybe she's just checking in on him for the wife, that's if she's alive...though that's doubtful, the checking, I mean.

AUDREY

Her cousins? You know she has cousins? How do you know about cousins?

MILDRED

[Sliding book under the sofa cushion] I've done a little snooping of my own. She has two female cousins. Though on whose side I'm not sure, but her father was upset enough over the grandmother's will, being cut out, I think it was, that he didn't attend her funeral.

AUDREY

[Thinking] Radner's wife's grandmother? Is that right? How do you know this? Who told you this, Ammons? You marketed there yesterday! You sly fox! [excited] Radner was cut out of her will, via the grandmother, huh?...wait, why would he be included in the first place?

MILDRED

Yes, well, he could be included only by marriage. They cut him out because they cut *her* out, you following me?

AUDREY

Why would they do that? She's visiting them. If the family was that upset, she wouldn't be visiting, would she? [light coming on] Oh, my goodness, she's *not* visiting, is she? That's it, isn't it? That's what you're telling me, no, that's what I've been telling you! There's the justification. [slyly] See, I'm right. [looking through the binoculars] They've gone inside. Shades drawn. [slumps down in her chair] So she *is* upstairs drifting to dust! Oh, Milly, I do this so much better with you along, so why do you think they cut her out of the will?

MILDRED

[Enjoying the lead] Nobody has said. It was some dispute with...Radner though. Perhaps because she married him. She's got social status. He's a commoner or perhaps because she was the black sheep of the family. Who knows? It could be any number of reasons. Anyway, I'm *guessing* about which side of the family they're from. If it was the old man's aunt, the cousins could be Radner's family. (somewhat addled, dismissive) It's a point not very clear.

AUDREY

But it *is* a cousin...come to stay? But you say two...there are two cousins?...why only one showing up? The redhead is younger, no doubt about that. So they can't be Radner's wife's cousins, unless they are second generation.

MILDRED

[Flatly] The cousins are Emily's....[covering, fast] first cousins, that was understood, so they would be the same age. [pause] Well, I'm assuming that, really. But perhaps she's one of these women who....can't accept her grey.

AUDREY

Emily? Mrs. Radner's name is Emily? I never knew that. Where did you get this information? No one has ever referred to her by her first name. Emily? But I thought she was Italian....

MILDRED

[Rushing] It may have been the great aunt that was Emily. I'm not clear on details. [fluster] Oh, I'm messing this up, I fear. I was so eager to get the gist of it all. Actually, Audrey, I will fess up. I *overheard* all this in a way. I happened upon the telling, so to speak. I do hate gossip so. But I claimed the information, nonetheless, so I'm party to it. The cousin's come to look in on him, no doubt, the more I think about it. Perhaps he notified her family of his wife's leaving. I've heard of criminals doing this. Playing both ends...[Audrey is rivetted] you know, telling one party one state of affairs and telling the other party the other side of the state of affairs and if the two parties never meet, it can work out to your advantage...the criminal's advantage.

AUDREY

[Very into it] So...if he told just enough to the town folks to lead them to believe she's vacationing in Italy....and then he turns tables and told the cousin...cousins, that she had flown the coop and he had no idea where...nobody would be suspicious of him. The family was sure to inquire by coming, as it looks like they have, sending a representative in the cousin, even if they weren't on close familial terms, they could hardly ignore a member of the family, gone, to who knows where, they have a duty to help, I mean, after all, the runaway is hardly a teenager. Perhaps they think she has wandered off and he's disinclined to look for her, they don't trust him this way, and Alzheimer's patients can do remarkably ingenious things. She could have hopped a sixteen-wheeler and be on the coast by now, if not dead in the bushes. [shutters] Anyway, with the cousins out of the way by coming and seeing for themselves, as hard as that might be, and the town folks satisfied thusly, he'd be....

MILDRED

...off the hook. [foxy] Now, here's the catch...in my books, [grins mischievously; Audrey is hanging on her every word] both cousins will eventually visit him. One cousin comes to give everything a cursory going over. If she thinks she's going to stay on a while, she will send for her sister. It's a way of trying to catch him off guard. The family is coming to look, to see what's going on for themselves but they're telling him they are coming for support. Remember he is suspect because he never liked their grandmother [pauses] or the great aunt... and there's bad blood because of the will. Nothing like money to get...

AUDREY

[Shakes her head, thoughtfully] No....nnno.

MILDRED

What do you mean, no!

AUDREY

It's too convoluted. Plots, especially those in life, are simpler than this. [grabbing the binoculars and into the window]

MILDRED

Not in Faulkner.

AUDREY

Ah ha! Milly, you are a marvel! There *are* two! There are two of them! The two cousins are look-alikes, [ecstatic] they are *twins*!

MILDRED

[Rushing to her, grabbing the binoculars, in a faint] Oh my stars, there *are* two...[falls into Audrey's chair] and they look exactly alike, down to the buttons on the shoes! This is myste-rious beyond words!

AUDREY

Hats on their heads, buttons on their shoes! Who wears hats anymore or buttoned-up shoes. They're positively archaic!

MILDRED

I think you mean anachronistic, Audrey.

AUDREY

Okay, but his wife isn't cold in her grave...correction, in her bed upstairs, and he's two dollies in the house?

MILDRED

Keep to the storyline, Audrey. Cousins. [pauses] Well, I guess they still could be "dollies" in a sense, as they were *her* cousins.

AUDREY

You're sure about the cousins...she had cousins. You over-heard this?

MILDRED

Cousins, yes. We have to think. Take my word for it, she had two cousins, who, by the way, are very solicitous. I don't see how you could have missed it, because they have visited here once before.

AUDREY

Before? Never. I couldn't have missed them for anything. They've never been here...how do you know they've been here? You couldn't have seen them, if I haven't. And believe me, these two I've never seen before.

MILDRED

I've been here without you, my dear, remember? when you took your trip with the Women's Auxiliary to Washington, D.C. I watered the plants...I even slept here one night.

Edward and I had a little argument then. He knew I was here but... I got my privacy this way.

AUDREY

Wait a minute, we've been staring at this redheaded cousin next door all afternoon and you haven't said a word about any of this. You saw them when I was away? Both of them? Good heavens, Milly, are you sure? That was....several years ago.

MILDRED

It just occurred to me, when I saw the second one. They look so different. I mean, back then. I'm telling you that they fit...Mrs. Radner's image to a tea those years ago. I'm sure now. It's her side of the family. Who knows, Audrey, these two could be those two cousins' girls.

AUDREY

[Finding all this strangely hard to follow] The ones that you saw visiting when I was away are *mothers* of these?

MILDRED

[Milly nods, reflecting] It's possible.

AUDREY

Their girls, well, one of their girls...or [narrowing her eyes] I suppose it could be that the older cousins had one apiece...no, [stamps her foot] simplify, simplify! They look too much alike, they're twins, and they're younger than first cousins.

MILDRED

It is a distance to see much of what they are!

AUDREY

I need stronger binoculars.

MILDRED

You need a shorter nose!

AUDREY

All right. But you're into this as much as I am now.

MILDRED

[Looks are her watch] Oh my goodness, look at the time! Edward's supper hasn't been started and I've marketing to do.

AUDREY

[Winks at her knowingly, walking her to the door, chant-ing] To market, to market, buy Ammons's fat pig! home again, home again, jiggity-jigg-jigg! [kisses her cheek] See you tomorrow afternoon. I can't wait!
[After Audrey shows Mildred out, she slumps down into the nearest chair to the door--Mildred's sofa chair; she feels a lump on the side of the cushion, runs her hand under it and comes up with the Portable Faulkner, investigates it a bit, opens it....and begins reading.]

LIGHTS FADE OUT

. . .

LIGHTS UP

scene 3

[Audrey is setting tea when Mildred walks in, stamping and shaking her umbrella; she hangs both her coat and umbrella on the coat tree and after some preening, joins Audrey who's pouring the tea by now.]

AUDREY

Two sugars, today?

MILDRED

Yes, please. Well, how goes it next door. I wouldn't guess you've seen much since it's been raining all night and today. They couldn't have gone out in this.

AUDREY

He did. Alone. Close to midnight.

MILDRED

[Settling into the sofa, tea and the story] Midnight? You were up at midnight, watching? Oh Audrey, this has gone too far....

AUDREY

There is no doubt about the time. He came over here.

MILDRED

[Clattering her cup onto the table] Over here...oh my Lord! did you call the police?

AUDREY

Of course not. He didn't stay long and he...

MILDRED

You let him *in*?! Oh, Audrey [hand on chest] this is way beyond "too far."

AUDREY

I didn't say I let him *in*, Milly. Just listen, please. I don't want to repeat myself, I'm too exhausted.

MILDRED

[Taking her hand] Oh, my dear, what an awful fright! I'm listening...do go on. You didn't let him in....

AUDREY

No, because he came into my backyard....

MILDRED

[Almost screaming] ...your backyard, at midnight? What...summoned you...to...to catch him?

AUDREY

I heard footsteps, you know the kind of cautious crunching sound footsteps can make around the outside of the house--in the night sound carries in a way it doesn't during the day, so I found my torch…

[no response from Mildred, just a blank stare]
AUDREY

Flashlight, Milly....

MILDRED

I *know!* Have you been reading P.D. James again?

AUDREY

[Ignoring] I tried to see from the upstairs window, at first I didn't see anything, though I heard scraping noises and then I saw his arm, swinging in a back and forth manner, in the customary way they used to do, long ago, when they were sowing, you know planting something, well, I couldn't make out what in the devil he was doing, not for certain, and I didn't know it was Radner at that time, I just knew it was some…figure…waving its arms around, like so [she sort of waves in a sowing fashion out over "the hole" in front of her] and then I realized that it, the figure, was digging, anyway, that's what I thought, what I didn't know is that he had already dug…a sizable hole…he was just finishing up.

MILDRED

Oh, Audrey…why in God's grace, didn't you call the police… or *me*? Why did you put yourself in such a compromising position? Oh, my dear [Audrey pulls her hand away, gets up, begins pacing]

AUDREY

You told me not to call you, remember?....Where was I?

MILDRED

A sizable hole...Radner had already dug a sizable hole he was just finishing up...

AUDREY

A hole, Milly, a hole no bigger than [shows with her hands] medium-sized...Remember, I didn't know it was Radner at this point. I thought of calling the police, of course, but what would I say, after they questioned me and found out...well, you know the rest of *that* [points toward the ceiling, then over next door], anyway, I decided to go downstairs so that I could see better or perhaps down into the basement...

MILDRED

Oh my stars! Tell me you didn't do this!

AUDREY

Just listen please. Just let me tell it all. I did finally go into the basement and looked out of the rear window, after stacking some milk crates up so that I could see, well, I opened the back door first and couldn't see a thing that way because the door is lower than the yard, one has to go down steps into the basement from the outside, so I stacked the crates and looked through the back window. I could see immediately at that level that it was Radner, without the trees in the way and the rain letting up just then, and he was placing something in the hole wrapped in a blanket or sheet or canvas bag or…whatever. I have to tell you, Milly, I know what it is now, but I didn't then.

MILDRED

Oh, what is it…you really must tell me, I cannot wait, not another minute, Oh, I will collapse. I see that you are all right, it's the only way I can bear to listen… to think you were so close to…such danger…I'm horrified!

AUDREY

You will hear it all in good time, but I really must tell you how it happened, as it happened…as it came upon me, minute by minute, so to speak. It was strange and frightening…straight out of an Edgar Allen fiction, to be sure…but there was an odd contentment in the scene as it played itself out there in the moonlight, with all the *grave* suspense--I felt utterly in control. Something mysterious was happening and I was directly in the middle of it, centrally placed on the scene and this made me feel oddly at peace, though I knew the danger, oh, I knew something very unnatural was going on, but I suppose what it was that drove me to it, was that thing that one doesn't know.

MILDRED

[Shrieking] Which is! which is!

AUDREY

I opened the window to see better and I heard him scattering dirt. That's what I thought at first, it's dirt he's scattering. He's covering up what he's buried, but there was something about it…him. And then I *knew*. He has gone over the edge, like mother, he really is daft, you see. I knew beyond doubt that I was dealing with a very maniacal situation. And then, it hit me! I smelled it!

MILDRED

Oh, Audrey! What?! Her? Was it her? It was a body, wasn't it? You were right. Why did I ever doubt you? In your back-yard, imagine!

AUDREY

Yes, well, it wasn't her. It was an acrid, penetrating odor...not at all like decay, just the opposite...it smelled like a mixture of dirt and chemicals, and I knew this odor, I knew whatever he put in the hole was being covered with lye...

MILDRED

[Weakly] l y e ? [something slowly moving in the lizard mind] You say, lye?

AUDREY

[Seductive, intimately] Yes. I let him finish because I figured I could go to the police in the morning, though I hadn't the foggiest notion how long it takes lye to do its work...but I couldn't see calling...dealing with all the ramifica-tions after midnight, they would never come out in the rain, you know they wouldn't, especially if it was *me*, in *my* yard, and it seems it was the best decision, because I went upstairs and promptly fell asleep.

MILDRED

You went to bed!? How could you go to bed!?

AUDREY

I told you. I felt strangely at peace. It was comfortable to me after I had it figured out.

MILDRED

Figured out...what?! [demanding] What did you figure out? What's the...a n s w e r?! [Audrey is very still] Oh, you are brave....you are very brave.

AUDREY

[Matter-of-fact] You think so? Well, I thought that too. I do feel brave. After the initial terror, everything just fell into place.

MILDRED

What?! What fell into place?

AUDREY

The story, silly girl.

MILDRED

What story, what are you talking about? [light coming on, cautious] You mean, Faulkner's story.

AUDREY

Faulkner, yes, oh, but it was so very much more. Faulkner's story was just the *beginning*. Remember I told you that his story was the prototype for *Psycho*, well, I got this right, but I'm ahead of myself. The grave Radner was digging in the back was for his dog.

MILDRED

His *dog*?

AUDREY

Hmmm, well, *the* dog. And this is pure Faulkner, too, because in an early story, one of his first, he kills a puppy by giving it a pinch of something that looks like salt; well, Faulkner doesn't kill the puppy, his character does, oh, what was his name?

MILDRED

Who? Who...what are you talking about now...a...p u p p y k i l l e r?

AUDREY

Doom, his name was Doom...

MILDRED

[Confused] Doom?

AUDREY

Yes, Doom, who went by David Callicoat but whose real name was Ikkemotubbe, he finally becomes The Man, but before he does, well, how he does, really, he demonstrates his ability to control life and death in front of the men he is soon to dominate, so he kills off this...

MILDRED

Audrey, this is frightening me, what does this...story have to do with the other one? Just tell the better parts, please. I'm becoming a little sick, to say nothing of how confused...I'm not following...not separating the fiction from what you say really happened in all of this...

AUDREY

Ah, hmmm...just get the gist of it, Milly, we can fill in the details later. So Radner has put the dog to rest in my backyard, smothered it in lye, and...

MILDRED

He had a dog?

AUDREY

He got one, don't you see? That's what the Doom story was to reveal...he needed to try out the poison.

MILDRED

Oh, how dreadful! [weaker still, taking time to follow] This is a very, very sick individual, Audrey. You must not stay here, not another night!

AUDREY

After this, he came... *Rear-Window*-style, you remember

this movie, don't you? Hitchcock, pure Hitchcock, James Stewart...

MILDRED

[Still behind, the brain won't seize it] Radner came as in...a movie? Hitchcock?

AUDREY

All right then, you know how Stewart sees the man next door through his window...he watches him chop up his wife and ship her out in a trunk, well, he doesn't actually *see* him chop up his wife, but she is there and then she is gone and then the trunk appears ready for shipping; anyhow, Radner comes walking steadily to my outside basement door, very much like he did after he saw Jimmy Stewart's binoculars in the window...oh who played the killer? Burr, Raymond..or was it Massey, anyway, let me tell you, I put two and two together fast! I abandoned my place on the milk crates, almost breaking my neck in the process, when I see Radner approaching my back door. Remember, I'd left it unlocked when I first looked out to try and see him!

MILDRED

Wait! He came into your basement? Last night at midnight, in the rain? Is this...t r u e?

AUDREY

[Furious] Of course, it's true; it happened to me, last night, right in this house! Just let me get it all out, will you, please. So I know I can't make it up the stairs...no amount of teenage energy could have made it up those stairs before he came through the door, so I slipped into the utility closet, to the left of the stairs, keeping the door ajar so that I could watch him. He comes in, galoshes sloshing mud across the floor and then he pulls out of his back pocket, a small torch...

MILDRED

[Flatly] Flashlight.

AUDREY

[Ignoring, going full steam] ...out of his back pocket, and scans it around, then the strangest thing happened that's ever happened to me, he cut off the light, just like that and starts ascending the stairs, then just as suddenly he stops dead in his tracks, looks around--remember, without the torch this time--and starts backing *down* the stairs, I mean, stepping down backwards, [faster] then he turned on his heels and went out the door from whence he'd come. I ran to the milk crates, hopped up on them just in time to see him disappear inside the mudroom leading to his kitchen in the back. He had left the mudroom light on so I was able to make out how he was dressed. It was the complete suit of a man meaning not to be seen at midnight, even in the rain, black from head to toe; he had blackened his face...and his hands too.

MILDRED

[Any suspicions gone, trance-like] He had accidentally come into the wrong house; he realized that on the stairs! Perhaps he even buried the dog in the wrong yard. [shrugs] Too late! How very strange.

AUDREY

My thoughts exactly. So when I got up and around, I went out there this morning to see...

MILDRED

He could've seen you, Audrey!

AUDREY

...and the grave for the dog is right on the property line. Lye is all over the ground, partly soaked in, of course, but I was worried about other animals finding it, perhaps smelling it, before it became completely decomposed, getting it on their paws, licking it, and dying as well, so I covered the area with some top soil I'd put back for repotting the succulents this fall.

MILDRED

But how can you be so sure it's a dog buried there? With all the carryings on next door, the missing wife, two new women in the house, his whole disguise, if *Rear Window* is the guide, she could be chopped up, in a body bag, and he's burying *her*, in shortened form, of course, back there! You say the hole's medium-sized? That would do for a frail, old woman!

AUDREY

Well, that is certainly what I thought at first. But I've investigated further and discovered...

MILDRED

You didn't go *into* his house!

AUDREY

No, I've not had time for that.

MILDRED

Not had time! Oh my word! You will *not* consider something so absolutely stupid, Audrey. Not now, not after we
know what we now know!

AUDREY

Of course not. Now, reason this out with me, this old man
has killed a dog with poison he *plans* to use on his wife...if he
had already used it...on her...there would be no cause to try it
out on the dog...you see where I'm going with this?

MILDRED

[Beside herself] No, no, I can't say that I do! I thought she
was dead already...upstairs, settling into dust? [Thinking,
trying to put it all together; finally decides on asking...] How
do you know it's a dog, I mean, for sure?!

AUDREY

By the fur.

MILDRED

You saw fur? Where? [stubbornly] You have said that it
was covered with dirt and lye, you said that you made sure of
that yourself!

AUDREY

Covered yes, but before I put on the top soil, I saw fur...well, hair, maybe.

MILDRED

[Exasperated, near screaming] Hair, fur! That's a big difference!

AUDREY

It's not like a tail or leg was hanging out of the grave, for easy identification, Mildred. I did see something, in that moment, before the brain covers things up, I saw a tuft of hair.... or fur...well, in some characterizations, it's not, actually, too much different. [thinking] It was that French novel, yes, the little Parisian monster, what was his name, he was so hairy...the serial killer with the keen sense of smell...

MILDRED

Dispense with the details! Get on with it! You told me you know what's buried in Radner's hole...do you or don't you?

AUDREY

[Thinking]...nnno....

MILDRED

No?

AUDREY

...it's not the Parisian monster because he was slick as a pig, not a hair on his body. Ah ha! Peter Suskind's Jean-

Baptiste Grenouille in *Parfum*...no, noooo, it's recent, very recent [in a flash] Cornwell's French monster, Chandonne, long hairs all over his body, in her last two novels. A contemporary Jack the Ripper whose family connections were as powerfully useful as those of Queen Victoria's nephew...very disturbing, maniacal quintessences both of them, all of them, every one! [lecture tone, upping Mildred] These storylines are mythologies going back hundreds, sometimes thousands, of years...archetypes of good and evil, if you follow the Jungian bend in the psychological road...

MILDRED

Audrey, Audrey, Audrey! [desperate] You really must keep to a more veritable path. You simply must stop these digressions. You cannot lead me down the main road and take all these detours. Just tell me pure and simply: *who is buried in your backyard?*

AUDREY

I think it's a dog. But I couldn't swear to it in a court of law!

LIGHTS OUT

scene 4

LIGHTS UP

AMMONS

[He stands behind a butcher block table in a butcher's apron, slightly smeared with stains, and a meat cleaver in his hand]

I don't know why people tell the local butcher their stories but they do. Like bartending, it comes with the profession. I suppose with bartending, storytelling is the free flow of liquor in the blood that loosens the tongue and allows the telling without limits. But with the butcher, well, all I can surmise is that it's *this* [brings the cleaver down, sticking it to the table] —the acute awareness of mortality. Perhaps the storytellers feel that their stories need to come to surface and be told or be forever lost.

Mostly I attempt to let go of what's told to me, not just because of the sheer amount I hear, but because of the significance to others beyond the teller. People talk about their neighbors without discretion. Now, in the case of the Gaines sisters, Audrey and Mildred, I literally mean neighbors. They have escaped slander charges in the courts because old Judge Mayfield didn't want to insult the ladies' reputations and because the folks around them were provoked by hearsay to complain about them as much as anything else—just town people's speculations and what they gathered in tidbits about the sisters here and there. There simply wasn't enough justification to hold them on charges, Mayfield told the town board.

I speak to both the ladies, listen to their stories—their outlandish claims about others, if you will, gossip, that's what it is, but from their own observations and peculiar perspectives. I say sisters as though they are equally involved; but Audrey, seems to me, to be the instigator—the storyteller— and Mildred, her, oh how can I characterize her? She's Audrey's support, no, that's not exactly right. She attempts to lessen her sister's deliberate claims on her targets, the crimes she's accusing them of. And I have to say, I've played my part in their stories.

Like Mildred I get suckered in to Audrey's storyline whether it has any known references to reality or not.

Unwittingly I told Audrey Gaines Barker what Radner's maid had told me—that Mrs. Radner's bedroom upstairs by the attic was locked. This is after the Missus had been gone for a noticeably long while. It wasn't just the sisters whose assertions about this spread. The whole town was abuzz. I was to find out that the police knew the story well and its possible conclusions before I called them after Mildred's last visit with me to pick up her husband's dinner of beef round for Swiss steak and tomatoes.

A grave in the backyard can't be ignored. I felt it was my civic duty to call, and the follow-up was fairly benign, if you want to call it that.

It was a dog that Radner claimed he found dead on the line between his property and Audrey's. It had been poisoned but since no proof of foul play could be established, it was considered an accidental event. The lye had done its job but enough of the dog could be confiscated to get results from the lab. It was arsenic, not the lye, in Radner's possession that prompted the attention of the authorities. But they discovered several dead rats in his garden and concluded the dog had ingested the poison from a rat through its mouth, nose or paws. The dog was greatly decomposed through the rain on the lye so that by the time the police obtained the lab results, their conclusions were already based on a string of connected observations. The dog was feral, belonging to no one in the neighborhood so things stood as they were rendered.

[starts to gather his equipment, takes off his apron; stops and turns back to say...]

Oh, when the police opened the door to Mrs. Radner's locked bedroom, they found all her things as she had evidently left them the last time she was in the room. And after a search, "her cousins," as the Gaines sisters surmised, turned out to be Radner's nieces who had come, taken a look around and at him and left for home in Boston within a week, never to be seen or heard from again. They had come because their mother, the old man's sister, had felt guilty for not checking on him in several months and was too frail to travel.

So Mrs. Radner was, and still is, gone. She evidently up

and left her husband as Mrs. Coldrich's endlessly-told story about her husband leaving her thirty years earlier. As to Radner, he admits he made up the story of his wife visiting relatives in Italy to save face—she had left him without so much as a fare thee well, an embarrassment so great, he sold the house within a month, with her room as is, and was gone too, forever.

[Quite a long pause; picks up the cleaver]
The truth is: fiction is a puzzle; it's life that's the mystery.
[Brings the cleaver down hard, sticking it in the table]
Or is it the other way around? Go figure.

LIGHTS OUT

Cly Boehs (pronounced Klī Bāz) was born and raised in Oklahoma. She received her MFA in Design and MA in Art from the University of Oklahoma in the '70s. Now retired, she has taught art on Long Island and in upstate New York, where she has lived in the Finger Lakes area for over forty years. She taught art education as lecturer at Elmira College for eighteen years. She has been a member of writing circles in Ithaca, New York, and various regional writing and art groups including The Georges and The 3pm Club and was a playwright, stage and costume designer, and participating member of the original theater group, 3rd Floor Productions, in Ithaca for nine years. She has exhibited her art and has created art ritual-performance in Oklahoma, Pennsylvania, and New York. She has read her stories publicly, including on television and radio.

She believes that we can be saved by deep conversations, books, and art, while our imagination and wonderment are what really keep us alive.

about bumbershoots writers society

"Wouldn't it be great if we could pool our talents and resources under one umbrella?"

I nodded in agreement as I read those words in a message from one of my Pen Pals, or at least that's how I always think of Cyndy Prasse Miller. Over the last five years, she and I have been in constant communication, sharing ideas, giving support, and we have become friends, a term I don't use lightly. The "we" she was referring to was the core members of our circle of confidantes, and I leaned back to let her idea fully bloom in my mind. I knew the possibilities such a thing could bring.

My name is Marlon S. Hayes, and I'm a writer, poet, author, and publisher. Back in 2018, I received a contract for a novel, and the acceptance email was sent by a guy named Gordon Bonnet, who wore many hats at this particular publisher. He was an editor, acquisitions manager, as well as being a prolific author. I still have the email. I don't want to name the publisher, neither to promote them, defame them, or lay their business practices bare. Let's just call it 'Them.' Lol. Anyhow, over the next two years, I signed contracts with 'Them' for nine books, and I was in constant communication with Cyndy, Gordon, and Venessa McDaniel Cerasale, relationships which blossomed into more than just business via emails and messages.

As the relationship with 'Them' soured, I began thinking about how to extricate myself from those contracts, not knowing that I was not alone in my desire to move away from 'Them.' I started my own publishing company *Voices from the Bleachers*, as well as creating an erotic one *Delicious Escape Publications* with Venessa and two other partners. My questioning of tactics and strategies of 'Them' led to me being freed from all contractual obligations. It was a breath of relief.

"Way leads on to way"- Robert Frost

We started a messenger group where we could vent, share our ideas, inspire each other with our progress, because all of us were in the process of severing our ties with 'Them.' Gordon, Cyndy, Venessa, Gil Miller (editor and author), JC Crumpton (author), and myself. Sometimes I'd have an idea or need guidance on a solo level, so I'd reach out on an individual level. That's where I read Cyndy's idea. I knew that if we could bring her idea to fruition, the possibilities were endless. See, the people I've mentioned are all multi-faceted creatives, whose skills, knowledge, and talents encompass photography, painting, sculpture, free-hand drawing, poetry, editing, publishing, music, fiction in many genres, non-fiction, and there's a spark within each of us that can create something wonderful out of nothing much.

We brought the idea to the group and a buzz began as we each thought of how amazing it could be if we formed a collective for business purposes, creative endeavors, and a more structured support system. I like face-to-face meetings way more than Zoom or messenger, and we began planning for a weekend where we could express our ideas and put them into motion. It was decided that we would rent a large home with accommodations for everyone, and we would discuss our possible collective. Gordon was bringing his wife, Carol Bloomgarden, who, unbeknownst to all of us, would be the final piece needed.

I was beyond excited as we exchanged handshakes and hugs, especially since it was my first time meeting Gordon in person. He'd been editing for me, beta reading, and I was grateful we had this chance. Within thirty minutes of everyone being settled in, the laptops and notebooks were out and ideas were zinging back and forth. It was like being in a creative beehive.

Gathered in the large living room there were seven people, six writers, five publishers, four editors, three artists, two couples, and no, not a partridge in a pear tree. Just one new shiny thing called *The Bumbershoots Writers Society.* We discussed marketing, books, ideas, wants and needs, and we relaxed in the company of like-minded individuals. It felt like coming home, because I was finally in an atmosphere where I was not an anomaly.

Over the course of the weekend, we decided how we wanted to move forward and the ever-changing roles we would play. There was even a field trip to a book store, where I bought *The Collected Western Stories* of Elmore Leonard. The conversations held on the deck and in the living room were amazing and inspiring as we discussed art, our favorite writers, movies, food, and anything else under the sun, with the exception of 'Them.' That's in the rearview mirror now, and there's no point in looking back. Especially when the view ahead looks so amazing. We're here.

"What should we call ourselves, this collective?" someone asked. "We'll be under one umbrella."

And that's what a bumbershoot is, an umbrella.

Peace.

- Marlon S. Hayes, May 2023

www.bumbershootswriterssociety.com